GARBAGE

TOWN

GARBAGE TOWN

A NOVEL

RAVI GUPTA

GREENLEAF
BOOK GROUP PRESS

Published by Greenleaf Book Group Press
Austin, Texas
www.gbgpress.com

Distributed by Greenleaf Book Group

For ordering information or special discounts for bulk purchases, please contact Greenleaf Book Group at PO Box 91869, Austin, TX 78709, 512.891.6100.

Design and composition by Greenleaf Book Group
Cover design by Greenleaf Book Group
Cover images used under license from ©Adobestock.com

Publisher's Cataloging-in-Publication data is available.

Print ISBN: 979-8-88645-313-3

eBook ISBN: 979-8-88645-314-0

To offset the number of trees consumed in the printing of our books, Greenleaf donates a portion of the proceeds from each printing to the Arbor Day Foundation. Greenleaf Book Group has replaced over 50,000 trees since 2007.

Printed in the United States of America on acid-free paper

25 26 27 28 29 30 31 32   10 9 8 7 6 5 4 3 2 1

First Edition

For the Victory Boys

"All I care is what the boys at the forks of the creek think of me."

—Huey Long

CONTENTS

PROLOGUE

Thursday, October 18, 2001
Fresh Kills Landfill

ireworks shook the air, painting the sky in vibrant hues. The
pyrotechnics had their intended effect, sending turkey vultures
scattering like crabs fleeing a rising tide, their wings beating fran-
tically as they sought shelter in the cracks of the rubble.

Detective Barbara Bucciero tried to enjoy the obscene beauty of it all.
But the type A in her, ever on patrol, quickly reasserted itself. Her focus
drifted from the sky to the terrestrial crime scene before her.

By instinct, she inventoried her team. All accounted for, all on task.
Under the harsh floodlights, they worked in white protective suits, duti-
fully carting debris across the barren landscape like astronauts on the
surface of the moon.

Booch's office was a repurposed trailer, once home to a classroom of
eager kindergartners in the early '90s when the city scrambled to remove
asbestos from nearly every public-school building. The green chalkboard
still clung to the wall; its surface haunted by the etchings of past lessons.
A laminated alphabet, missing a few letters, adorned the top. Within
these four walls, Booch made a home for herself, organizing schedules
and dividing her team into shifts to grant them a sliver of rest. For over
a month, she had lived and breathed this trailer.

The first load had arrived sixteen hours after the South Tower collapsed, and she'd been there to greet it. In the weeks that followed, barges and truck caravans brought millions of tons of wreckage mixed with human remains.

Her job was to sort through it all.

Nothing about this investigation was routine. She wasn't there to solve a mystery. The perpetrators and their motives were well-known to everyone on the planet. Her mission was to give closure to the families of the lost. That meant locating the remains and personal effects of 2,606 victims. A melted cell phone, a deformed credit card, a scorched wedding band—anything tangible to help the families grieve.

Booch was grieving too, and her job was the only thing keeping her from being consumed by it. She stared out the window and thought of every colleague she'd lost in those towers. Every friend. Whenever they found a fallen officer's firearm or badge, she would play bagpipes into the walkie-talkies. They'd played bagpipes six times that week.

Unable to rest, she woke her ancient Compaq. It groaned to life like an old dog with arthritic joints, each day's start-up a little more labored than the last. As MS-DOS commands crawled across the screen, Booch caught her reflection in the dusty glass. The years had etched deep ravines into her face, each line a case closed, a victim avenged, a secret buried. Geological artifacts of life as an NYPD detective.

Little about Booch fit the cop stereotype. She had a confounding balance of soft and sharp features. Her dainty nose and cascading brown hair woven with silver threads made her appear almost fragile. Yet, her dark eyes and bold brows carried an intensity that warned you to tread carefully.

The day's big news was a severed hand they'd found and sent to the lab for prints. While she plodded through the report, she was interrupted by a knock at the door.

"Come in."

Detective Andrew Sweeney waddled in, his NYPD windbreaker flapping behind him as he held his mask and helmet by his side. His usually chubby red face was now a ghostly white, covered in a fine layer of dust that settled everywhere except for the ruddy orbit around his mouth where the mask had been. He looked like a man who was rotting from the outside in, his eyes sunken and tired, staring down at his mud-caked shoes. With a sigh, he got straight to the point, the pleasantries long behind them.

"You're gonna wanna see this, Booch."

Without a word, she slipped on a jacket before following Sweeney out of the trailer. Instinctively, she pulled her collar up over her mouth and nose in an attempt to shield herself from the stench of rot. The ground was uneven beneath her feet, her boots sinking slightly into the soft earth, a muddled mix of trash and dirt. She hopped on an ATV and trailed behind him through a maze of twisted metal and concrete. They parked in front of a teetering mound of crushed cars with a flattened NYPD van at its base. Sweeney led her around the pile into a narrow, rectangular plastic tent.

Inside, officers toiled alongside a belt that endlessly conveyed a steady stream of debris. It was late into the evening, but everyone was still grinding. They wore uniforms haphazardly assembled from supplies purchased at Home Depot: Tyvek protective suits, carpenter's goggles, gardening gloves, and paper dust masks. The city had long since run out of proper gear, so Booch had taken matters into her own hands and directed her team to scour every hardware store in the tristate area.

"Show her what you found, Singh," Detective Sweeney said to a man crouched in the corner of the tent.

Booch held back a smile as she took in the forensic scientist's outfit: a plastic shower cap covering his orange turban and a rubber band reining in his usually flowing gray beard. He held a pair of steel calipers and a round, mud-covered object.

"What is it?" Booch asked.

Dr. Singh lifted the object to the light, and Booch realized why she'd been summoned.

It was a human skull.

"That doesn't look fresh." Booch strained to get a clear view of it from behind her goggles. "Gloves?"

Sweeney produced a box of surgical gloves from a plastic case beside the conveyor belt.

"What do we know?" Booch fiddled with the gloves, struggling to squeeze them onto her prematurely arthritic hands.

Dr. Singh pulled off his mask. "There's no way this came from the towers. It's been decomposing for years."

Normally, Booch would scold him for violating protocol, but she followed his lead and ripped off her mask as well. She wanted a closer look. "What pile did it come in with?"

"Pile thirty-two," Sweeney said. "We must have accidentally unearthed it when we moved this shit in here."

Booch examined the skull in her hands. "Any other bones?"

"Not yet."

"We're looking for teeth," Dr. Singh said. "That would help with identification."

"Sweeney, shut down all sorting on Pile thirty-two and bring in a new forensics team," Booch ordered. "I'll call One Police now," she added, referring to One Police Plaza, the NYPD's citywide headquarters.

Concern creased Dr. Singh's forehead. "Booch, there's one more thing."

"Yes?"

"This skull belonged to a kid."

—

Booch stepped out of the elevator onto the polished marble floor of One Police Plaza. A sign directed her to the Commissioner's Conference Room, where the city's top brass awaited.

The hallways brimmed with hushed tension. Uniformed officers hurried by with a sense of purpose, their faces marked with the strain of long, pressure-filled days. Conversations were clipped, and the air was charged with a new weight of responsibility.

Booch flashed her badge to a desk clerk, who waved her through with a tight smile. The meeting room itself was a juxtaposition of opulence and functional austerity. Heavy mahogany furniture dominated the space, and the large conference table was scarred and worn. Each nick and stain served as a memorial to the countless CompStat meetings of the past decade, heated gatherings where the NYPD leaders waged a war on the city's record crime, with tremendous human cost.

This was now a different kind of war room. Around the table, a dozen high-backed leather chairs were filled not with the usual NYPD middle management but with the leaders of the city's key agencies: fire, sanitation, emergency management, and, yes, police. She recognized two city council members around the perimeter, as well as a few FBI agents.

The windows, which once offered a glimpse of the Brooklyn Bridge, were now covered with blinds, obscuring a city forever altered. Bureaucratic beige walls, normally adorned with framed black-and-white photographs of former commissioners, were now plastered with maps pinpointing areas of concern, marked with red circles and annotated with intelligence tips. The fluorescent lights even seemed to buzz with more urgency.

Booch settled into a folding chair at the foot of the table behind a placard bearing her name and her new title, Fresh Kills Site Manager.

A square-jawed man in a black suit commanded the head, someone Booch didn't recognize but whom she assumed was from the FBI.

"Captain Bucciero, thank you for making the trip."

"No problem."

"Can we get you some coffee?"

"No, thank you." Booch glanced at her watch. "Let's just get to it."

"Fair enough." The G-man chuckled and exchanged a smirk with the NYPD commissioner to his right. "We understand that you intend to keep the burial and sorting paused through the weekend and into next week?"

"That's correct."

The commissioner cut in. "How can we speed this up?"

"It's an active crime scene," Booch said. "It's hard to say. We've got a lot of ground to cover."

"It's one body."

"One that we know of."

The commissioner crossed his arms. "We've got our own active crime scene up here. Thousands dead. Maybe you've heard about it."

The G-man cut in. "Let's not get emotional here. Captain Bucciero, is there anything we can do to help make this go faster?"

"We can use more equipment. Ground-penetrating radar would help."

The G-man exchanged nods with another suit standing to the side of the room. "That shouldn't be a problem. Anything else?"

"Just a bit of time. This is a complicated situation. We can't rush it."

"Can't rush it?" The police commissioner sneered, a vein on his bald head swelling like the Hudson after a storm. "Are you kidding me? I've got thousands of city workers down the street waiting around."

Booch forced a smile. "Give them the weekend off. I bet your guys have been working nonstop for over a month. I'm sure they'd appreciate the time with their families. I know my men would."

The police commissioner's jaw flexed. "Your men are my men."

"I'm just following routine procedure." Booch bored into him. "We can't be sure it's just one body. This could be the last time we can search the area. Once we finish depositing the rubble, we'll lose any chance of—"

The G-man cut her off. "What's your theory? What makes you think there could be other bodies?"

"For one, the history of Fresh Kills. We've pulled bodies out from there before. I've personally overseen those investigations."

"We are well aware. Though that's not new information. What's your theory about *this* body? Are we even close to an ID?"

"We've sent samples for DNA analysis, but that will take weeks. Our best chance for a quick ID is the dental records, but we haven't been able to locate the jaw or teeth yet."

Booch didn't need any sophisticated science to tell her who that skull belonged to, who that kid was. Some of those faces around the table also knew more than they let on, but no one wanted to broach the subject, to air their dirty laundry in front of their visitors from Washington.

The sanitation commissioner chimed in. "Why not cordon off the area around the body and recommence the disposal of the World Trade Center rubble?"

"I need *my* men to do a proper excavation." Booch emphasized *my* in a way that wasn't subtle or accidental. "Besides, we are doing an exhaustive search that's covering most of the disposal area and more."

Booch couldn't shake the feeling that the very decision to deposit the World Trade Center rubble at Fresh Kills had an ulterior motive. There were mysteries concealed up there that would soon stay buried under millions of tons of concrete, odd objects, and human remains.

Unfortunately for whoever was behind that cover-up, someone screwed up and assigned Booch to the site, an error only possible in the post-9/11 confusion. Now, she had the resources at her disposal to unearth secrets she'd spent years obsessing over—truths that threatened many of the people around that table.

"We need a timeline," the police commissioner pleaded to the G-man. "This can't go on forever."

"Find another place to bury the rubble," Booch said. "I'm sure there are plenty of spots upstate and in Jersey that have room."

"We can't," the sanitation commissioner said. "We can't split the rubble now. No one else will take it."

Booch knew that was bullshit. This was the height of rally-round-the-flag patriotism. No politician would refuse a request to play their part in the 9/11 response.

"I'd be happy to call the governor myself." Booch scanned the functionaries stationed around the perimeter. "Which of you works for him? Should we get him on the line? "

The G-man waved them off. "That won't be necessary. How much time do you need, Captain?"

Booch thought hard for a few awkward beats. Too little time and she wouldn't be able to get the job done. Too much time and her request would be denied. "One week should be enough. But two would be preferable."

The room let out a collective gasp, and all eyes went to the G-man.

"You have until Monday end of day. Unless you find another body up there, we must resume the sorting and sifting operation."

"Sir, that's not enough time."

"Captain, that's the best I can do."

This wasn't a compromise; it was a defeat. The police commissioner flashed a smug grin as he surveyed the room and absorbed the nods of agreement and quiet approval from his colleagues. The air of triumph sent a tingle up Booch's spine. The top brass got exactly what they wanted: to stop her investigation.

—

Now on borrowed time, Booch had to make a bold, perhaps drastic move. She hopped into her car and headed uptown to track down the one person who could crack the case in a matter of a few days.

She pulled up outside of Cooper Union, a stately relic of a building where a young Abraham Lincoln once introduced himself to the country. It was now a tuition-free college for math and science prodigies. Parking her car in front of a bus stop—one of the less celebrated perks of the job—she made her way inside.

After a brief exchange with the receptionist, Booch was directed to the library. "You'll find him there—third row of carrels, second to the right. Always in the same spot."

The library's vaulted ceilings enveloped her, stretching skyward as ornate lamps shed a cozy amber hue over the rows of timeworn wooden bookcases. Each nook was filled with students, their postures curved in scholarly absorption. She noted with a detective's amusement the cleverly hidden coffee thermoses—tucked under desks, nestled in the folds of backpacks—a small, silent challenge to the library's posted rules.

Booch found her man right where the receptionist had said, nestled among a fortress of books stacked like a game of Jenga. His head, crowned with unruly curls, bowed in sleep, emitting a soft snore.

She stepped closer, scanning the array of biology and chemistry texts. The selection didn't surprise her. With the number of people cancer had taken from him, he made no secret of his dream to become a doctor, a dream she was about to ask him to put in jeopardy. She nudged him gently awake, watching as his face morphed from confusion to recognition. "Booch?"

Placing a reassuring hand on his shoulder, she cut to the chase. "Raj, we need to talk."

"I saw the news." He wore a look that carried the weight of things unsaid, balancing on the edge of resignation and relief. "I figured you'd come sooner or later."

She was torn between empathy and duty. She put her hands at her hips to keep them from implying anything unintentional. "Well, here I am."

Without missing a beat, Raj rummaged through the drawer of his carrel. He pulled out a CD and held it in front of his face like a skeleton key.

"This," he declared, "will tell you everything you need to know."

Booch went to snatch the disc, but Raj pulled it away.

"I'm not in the mood for games," she warned.

"I'll give it to you on two conditions."

She smiled. Raj could always be counted on to negotiate, no matter the circumstance.

Booch's hands again found her hips. "And those are?"

"First, you read it here, on these computers in *this* library."

She gave a puzzled frown. "Why does it matter where I read it?"

"I want you to know everything before you decide to download it to NYPD servers."

Booch weighed her options. Time was a luxury she couldn't afford, but the promise of the disc's contents was too crucial to ignore. "Fine. And the second condition?"

"You don't hold against me how I describe you."

"Why would you have to describe me at all?"

With a flick of his wrist, Raj tossed the disc toward her. "See for yourself."

She caught the disc with one hand, her eyes instantly drawn to the inscription on its surface. In bold marking, it read "Garbage Town."

PART 1

1998

CHAPTER 1

RENDEZVOUS

Midnight closed in as my heart pumped a drumbeat in my ears. With each gasp, the thud pounded faster but my legs moved slower. Yet, every step was a victory in the face of my exhaustion.

When the solitude of the service road gave way to rows of familiar houses, I pulled my T-shirt over my head. There I was, hiding like a common thief in the streets where I'd spent my entire life. I was a wanted man now. I'd become one as soon as I stepped foot in Fresh Kills.

Fresh Kills. The name alone had been enough to keep me away for fourteen years. Kids whispered of luminescent rivers, dog-sized rats, and rabid turkey vultures. The adults were worse, with their knowing looks and vague references to a mob presence. The local rag even floated the idea that Jimmy Hoffa's bones were nestled somewhere in its bowels. But myths have a way of crumbling in the face of reality.

On June 19, 1998, Fresh Kills gave up its secrets to me. Just an hour after I scaled that fence, I found myself in a valley of refuse, staring down a choice that would redefine everything I thought I knew about my town. I could turn back, pretend I'd seen nothing, slip back into the comfortable anonymity of my unremarkable life. Or I could step up, be the hero I'd always dreamed of being, and maybe—just maybe—save a life.

I chose the path of valor, not knowing it would lead me on this frantic sprint for survival. Schmul Park materialized ahead, our predetermined rendezvous spot. I slipped through the gap by the handball courts, my feet carrying me instinctively to the baseball diamond hidden in the park's heart. It was a place that had always felt safe, but tonight, even the familiar shadows seemed to hold their breath, waiting to see if I'd make it out alive.

My lungs burning, I stumbled onto home plate, barely catching myself before collapsing onto the chalk-dusted earth. The moon hung low and heavy, transforming the field into a ghostly tableau where she materialized—the woman from the dump. Her voice sliced through the dark. No whimpers, no pleas for mercy, just that primal scream demanding my flight.

Had I twisted her words to suit my cowardice? In that moment of terror, did I hear what I needed to hear—a convenient absolution for my retreat?

Her face dissolved into the shadows, replaced by a lumbering silhouette that cut across the outfield. Adrenaline surged through me, electric and primal, launching me at the fence with the frantic energy of prey. Halfway up, the monstrous shape coalesced into something refreshingly familiar.

"Date and year!" The voice boomed across the diamond.

"Not now, Sam," I called back as I dropped to solid ground.

The voice belonged to the neighborhood wanderer. He had the build of an Olympic shot putter, well over six feet tall and north of 250 pounds. Kids in the neighborhood called him Rain Man and picked on him relentlessly.

Tucked under his arm was a plastic Pathmark bag filled with his few life possessions. "Date and year," he repeated as he pulled out a cigarette and coaxed it to life.

"Only if you promise to go if I give it to you."

Now towering over me, he returned a military salute. "Roger!"

I gave him my birthday. "April 20, 1983."

His eyes rolled to the back of his head while he crunched the numbers. "That was a Wednesday."

"Thanks, Sam. Great work. Good night, buddy."

"Good night, buddy," he repeated, mimicking my tone and cadence. He walked out to right field and disappeared through a hole in the fence like Shoeless Joe Jackson in *Field of Dreams*.

In the quiet that followed, a voice broke the stillness from behind.

"Rajiv!"

It was Georgia, seated in one of the dugouts. She couldn't have been there long because I would have noticed her. She scaled the fence in one motion and stepped into the moonlight. Blood was splattered across her freckled face like war paint.

"Holy shit." I walked over to get a closer look. "Are you hurt?"

"It ain't mine," she said in a way that could only be described as a twang.

That comment sent my mind into a tailspin. I'd never seen anyone covered in someone else's blood.

"Are you okay?" I moved closer to inspect her.

"I think so." She wrinkled her nose. "You stink."

I'd sprinted across a mile of garbage. I hadn't noticed how bad I smelled until then. Suddenly, I wanted to gag.

"We both stink." I gazed down at my mud-caked shoes in embarrassment. "Where's everyone else?"

"I don't know. We all took off in different directions. You good?"

"Still standing," I managed to say. "How did you know to come here?"

"I wasn't too far behind. I followed you."

So much for avoiding detection. "Do you think the others got away? Should we check Val's house?"

"We oughta wait here for a bit," she said.

I checked my beeper but hadn't received any pages for the past few hours. "I'll run to the phone and beep them."

While I went for the pay phone at the park's far end, Georgia climbed the metal backstop behind home plate. Was she scouting for unwelcome visitors or just fidgety? After paging Val, I momentarily considered calling the police but abandoned the idea. Even if I made an anonymous tip, the cops would trace the call to that phone and be at Schmul in no time.

When I returned, Georgia had descended and was seated cross-legged between pitcher's mound and home plate, picking at grass.

I sat on the ground across from her. "Should we go to the police?"

"And say what?" She seemed to ask the patch of grass.

I had no words, only a paralyzing silence that wrapped around me like a heavy blanket. Eventually, my emotions broke loose, crashing out in a raw, wheezing sob. Tears spilled uncontrollably, refusing to stop. I pressed my face into my shirt in a desperate attempt to hide. Finally, I forced myself to look up at her.

Georgia looked at me with a mix of pity and curiosity. "Come on now," she said with a forced smile.

I wiped away tears and snot with the back of my hand. "I'm okay, really."

I was not okay. I took a few deep breaths and attempted to regain my composure, except that every breath seemed to cut through my lungs like shrapnel. Earlier that day, all I wanted was to impress her; now, I wanted to curl into the fetal position.

My pocket vibrated with the buzz of my pager. It said "911"

repeatedly, interspersed with a code I didn't recognize: 173. It didn't have a return number.

I tossed her the pager. "Do you know this one?"

"How would I know?" She tossed it back.

"It's gotta be them. Why didn't they come here?"

"Maybe they found a phone up there," she said.

"I guess that's possible, but then what would this one-seven-three mean?" I asked. When I clipped the beeper to the inside of my pocket, I realized I was missing something.

"Dammit."

"What?"

"My Discman. I must have dropped it when we were running."

"You can have my extra one tomorrow."

"No, my business's name is stamped on the CD." I paused, expecting a reaction from her, but she didn't seem to understand the problem. So, I hammered home the point: "What if those guys find it?"

"What are the chances? That dump is huge and dark."

"It won't be dark in the morning."

She stood up. "Let's go back for it. We have to find your friends anyway."

"Risky," I said. "As much as I'm worried about those goons finding that Discman, we'll be making their job a lot easier if we bring ourselves to them."

"What's your plan?" she asked with her hands at her hips.

Good question. I didn't have one. "We wait, like you said before," I stated, unconvinced of my words.

She began striding toward first base. "I'm done waiting."

"Hold up," I said, trying to block her path.

"I'm of a mind to find Renzo's friends," she stepped around me. "Maybe they have Val and that woman."

"Who's Renzo?"

She tossed the wallet over her shoulder. "This guy."

I snatched it out of the air, and as soon as I opened it, my gut lurched. I recognized the face.

"How did you get this?" I asked. But I already knew the answer.

Georgia had robbed a dead man.

CHAPTER 2

WORLD-CLASS TRASH

Earlier that day

I awoke to my voice echoing through my room. "Watch out," I heard myself say, which was weird because I hadn't opened my mouth. Intrigued, I navigated the attic, pushing aside a bedsheet that separated my space from Uncle Stosh's. He commanded a spaceship of blinking lights from synthesizers and modules, his chaotic long black hair swaying with his precise movements.

"Hey, bud," he greeted me, his focus never leaving his vintage Fairlight CMI. He pressed a key and tweaked a dial, amplifying the echo of my voice.

"You secretly taping me?"

"Home movies." He spun around in his chair. "I needed something for the first track on my new album."

"I'm pretty sure no one wants to hear that."

"I want the refrain to sound mysterious. That *Melt* sound."

The reference was to Peter Gabriel's groundbreaking self-titled album, nicknamed *Melt* after the unsettling cover image of his partially melted face. Its futuristic vibe had inspired countless musicians in the '80s, and Uncle Stosh had spent nearly two decades chasing its ghost.

Curious, I asked, "Which movie did you use?"

"Christmas a few years ago." He pointed to a thirteen-inch Panasonic TV-VCR combo wedged into the corner. The screen displayed eight-year-old me tearing through Christmas presents. Beside me sat my mom, vibrant and beaming—nearly unrecognizable from the woman she'd become. She called my dad over from the couch, where he was sprawled out and shirtless with a Burt Reynolds mustache and a TV controller in his hand . . . exactly how I remembered him. He would pull night shifts managing a gas station in New Jersey, which made him functionally brain-dead during the day. In the video, I unwrapped a Steve Urkel doll I'd found under the tree and tugged at a chord in its back, producing the character's trademark saying: "Did I do that?" My mom and I laughed while my dad stared at the television screen, barely moving.

As much as I wanted to watch the rest, I didn't have time. It was the final day of school, which meant it might be my last chance to make serious cash until September.

Over the past year, I'd built a music empire. On an island where teenagers were lucky to earn five bucks an hour, the standard price of fifteen to twenty dollars per CD was exorbitant for many. Spotting an opportunity, I'd invested in a CD burner from Circuit City, soon amassing a fleet dedicated to churning out bootleg copies at half the retail price. Master copies were acquired and then replicated for a dollar a disc in bulk. Orders piled up quickly. When I walked down the halls of my high school, it was like I was on the New York Stock Exchange floor, swamped with orders from crowds of eager customers. It was the first time in my life that anyone outside my neighborhood seemed to notice me.

Today, I had a mountain of orders to fill before everyone scattered for the summer. Delaying meant losing customers until September. All five burners ran nonstop through the night, demanding my attention every few hours to replenish the hungry machines.

After encasing the final batch of CDs, I tossed them into my bag with a triumphant flourish.

"Remember to have fun on your last day of freshman year," Uncle Stosh yelled across the room. "Don't get too caught up in the business stuff."

"The business stuff is the fun part," I shouted back as I threw my bag over my shoulder and descended the attic steps.

In the kitchen, my mother was perched at the table in her hospital scrubs, as she was nearly every morning. She balanced a portable makeup mirror in one hand, methodically applying a fake eyelash with the other, while somehow managing to sneak glances at the latest edition of the *National Enquirer*. I never understood what she saw in those magazines. She always complained about how they were full of gossip and lies but still read every issue.

"I've got another double shift," she called out without looking up. "There's a ten on the counter for dinner."

I went to grab the money but stopped myself, shoving my empty hands in my pockets. "Thanks, Ma. But why don't you use it to take a cab to work?"

Since my dad disappeared, she'd worked as a nurse's aide at two elder-care homes. She loved and was very good at her job, but it was backbreaking, emotionally exhausting work. She treated patients like family and even occasionally brought them home for the holidays. Though she played the part of the happy warrior, the double shifts took a toll. One pack of Marlboros a day turned into two, three screwdrivers a night became four, and with each passing day, she had a little less spring in her step and a little less life in her eyes. Of course, she would never admit she was having a hard time. She was, like almost everyone else in Travis, a stubborn Polack.

"I can ride the bus," she said, her fingers adroitly navigating a giant lash into position.

"That's forty minutes each way. Just use the money." To get to work, my mom endured the sardine-can squeeze of the 62 bus down Victory, then hustled to catch another bus along Forest Avenue, one of Staten Island's other major avenues. A delay in the first leg often meant a missed connection and an arduous, hour-long journey. I hated the thought of her, already exhausted from long hours on her feet, enduring two more in the claustrophobic embrace of buses overcrowded with ferry commuters and sweaty teenagers.

"Okay, whatever you say," she said. "Just make sure you eat."

That's weird. She usually didn't give in so easily.

"I will. By the way, what's the latest with the van?"

Her car, a 1990 Chevy Lumina APV minivan, spent more time in the shop than on the road. It was shaped like a Dustbuster, which was inexplicably popular in the early '90s.

"Gone." She placed the mirror down and blinked her long, fake lashes. "The boys at Melfi's Garage already sent it to the scrapyard."

Bile rose in my throat. No car meant more bus rides, which meant earlier mornings and later nights. She was already reaching her limit and needed a win.

"Damn. Well, I should have enough money by the end of the summer to get us something workable," I offered.

In truth, I was behind on my savings goals, hemorrhaging cash with each CD burner that broke. I'd also recently been forced to issue dozens of refunds because I tried to cut costs and used low-quality CDs that quickly became unusable after a few listens. That was income I would somehow have to replace over the summer when I couldn't sell CDs at school.

"Don't worry about it. It's summer. You should be having fun like other kids. Spend your money on stuff that makes you happy."

"Getting you a car would make me happy."

This was a common theme in my life: adults requesting that I act more like a kid. Though we both knew I'd worry no matter what she said. Low-level anxiety was my default state.

I pecked my mother's cheek and made for the exit, where I noticed a stack of letters piled up in front of the mail flap. I sifted through a few past-due notices and solicitations, stopping at an envelope from AK Patel, my father, addressed to my mom. The return label was from Pensacola, Florida. He'd been gone for two years this time. Each time he left, he stayed away longer, and this latest absence seemed like it might be permanent.

Initially, my mom suspected he had a girlfriend. She tracked him down with the help of a private investigator, who found him solo, managing a Wendy's in the Carolinas—a revelation more baffling than a clandestine affair. She pressed my dad to explain himself during one emotional phone conversation and didn't get much out of him. They'd stopped communicating after that, but she couldn't muster the courage to serve him with divorce papers. She'd been in marriage purgatory ever since.

Now, it seems, he'd moved on to Florida—in the opposite direction of us. I didn't have the time or the stomach to read whatever he had to say—and I didn't want to put my mom in a bad mood—so I stuffed it in my pocket and headed out.

When I stepped out my front door, I was smacked in the face by a wall of humidity. The "real feel" was like one hundred degrees—and it was still morning—the kind of scorching NYC summer day Spike Lee made movies about. A wafting stench from the dump accompanied the heat. For us in Travis, the ambient aroma of Fresh Kills usually blended into the background, only demanding notice on oppressively muggy days like this.

The grass in our front yard was nearly up to my shins, so I made a mental note to cut it that weekend. We'd long ago given up on appearances—the paint was chipped and peeling off in various sections of our low-slung yellow house—but neighbors would gossip about my mom if we let the grass get out of control. You could be forgiven any number of sins in Travis, but you had to mow your lawn.

As the door clanged behind me, a woman's voice floated down. "Morning," she said.

I peered over the fence in the direction of the comment but saw no one.

"You better hustle," came the directive, now clearly from overhead.

"Jesus," I said. "You scared me."

My neighbor was staring down at me from her roof with a hose in hand. She managed to look dignified in everything she did, even cleaning the gutters. "Hey, kid," she said. "Doesn't school start in twenty minutes?"

I was still "kid" to her even though we'd lived next door to each other for almost a decade. Her name was Barbara Bucciero. Everyone called her Booch. She was an NYPD detective who'd been living alone next door since she was assigned to the island's 120th police precinct in the late '80s. She was a constant subject of fascination from Travis's many resident gossips, who couldn't fathom any woman her age—never mind a good-looking one—without a husband or the apparent desire for one. She'd rejected Uncle Stosh so often that we'd all lost count.

"More like thirty minutes," I corrected, eyeing the beeper on my waistband.

"You don't seem to be in a rush. I would hate to pick you up on truancy charges."

"It's the last day of school, Booch. And isn't that kind of thing below your pay grade?"

"No job too small. By the way, feel free to tell your delinquent friends at the graveyard that I'm sending an officer over there, too—so they better be in school."

"Ma'am, I try to stay away from the 'yard. Mom says I should stay away from the bad crowd."

"You are the bad crowd," Booch said as she aimed a stream of water at my feet, which pushed me along through my front gate and toward the bus stop. Of all the people I could live next to, I was blessed with an ace cop who had my number.

I turned the corner from my relatively quiet street onto the busier Victory Boulevard, one of Staten Island's four major avenues. Victory was our community's pulsing vein, a strange theater where the island's varied tribes collided. Reverend Al Sharpton once likened it to the borough's Mason-Dixon Line. It's where a Black and White islander could be spotted lining up at the bank, or a Mexican and Italian sitting alongside each other in a pizzeria.

Victory started in the dense and diverse neighborhood of St. George by the Staten Island Ferry and blazed a trail westward for thirteen miles; its mighty current gradually eased into a gentle trickle as it culminated at the remote edges of my dead-end town of Travis. "Garbage Town," they called us—not to our faces, of course.

Though we were more isolated than the rest of the boulevard, we, too, served as a meeting ground of sorts. On weekends, the UA Theater at the end of town lured teenagers from every corner of the island. Weekdays brought a different pilgrimage: an army of sanitation workers and Con Ed employees, their heavy boots and weathered faces as much a part of our landscape as the distant mounds of trash that defined our skyline.

Between shifts, the workers would flock to Phene's Deli, a dusty sandwich shop at the corner of my street and Victory. As I passed Phene's that morning, I ran into its proprietor, Stanley Chiechenow—Chickie to us—carrying boxes with a cigarette hanging from his mouth. He wore a greasy apron over an undershirt a size too small that flaunted war tattoos on both arms.

"Good morning, Chickie," I said. "Need help?"

"You can help by getting the fuck out of my way." Chickie had a particular brand of hospitality best exemplified by his decision to remove the Phene's Deli sign from his shop's awning because he believed it attracted too many customers.

"Great to see you too." I sidestepped him just as a black Mercedes pulled up across the street. We both paused, eyes drawn to the mammoth figure emerging from the driver's seat. This man, possibly the largest man I'd ever seen, reminded me of one of the contestants in the World's Strongest Man competition. He wore a short-sleeve button-down black shirt that seemed to blend into hairy forearms as thick as the steel cables of the Verrazzano.

Then out stepped a more familiar figure from the passenger side: Dante "Blue Eyes" Malaparte, the head of the Staten Island crime family. Compact yet imposing, his aura engulfed the neighborhood, casting a shadow over the street like a solar eclipse. He leaned against the hood, combing his Pat Riley–esque slicked-back hair, which seemed to match the sheen of his tailored gray suit.

Though Chickie would never admit it, even he seemed a bit starstruck. Despite Dante's citywide reputation, he was beloved on the island—the closest thing we had to a celebrity. Like Pablo Escobar to Medellín, he was our gangster. This was the first I'd ever seen him in person, and his presence in Travis was sure to get my neighbors chirping.

The duo made their way into The Linoleum, our sole tavern and a nod to Travis's erstwhile identity as Linoleumville, named after the factory that had once been the lifeblood of this community and the magnet for my Polish immigrant ancestors.

"An odd time of day to grab a drink," I finally offered.

Chickie, setting his boxes down, lit another cigarette, his facade of indifference melting away in the face of good gossip. He liked to put on a front like he was hard and unapproachable, but he loved nothing more than to kibitz about the neighborhood.

"They bought The Linoleum last weekend. They're setting up shop in town. Signed a contract to rent a bigger part of the dump."

"Why would anyone want to rent a piece of that?"

"Private trash disposal. Huge business for the ginzos."

"I know that, Chickie. I read the papers. I mean, the dump. Isn't it closing soon?" Rumor had it that the city planned to close the dump by 2001, a few years away.

"Don't believe it," Chickie said. "Those empty suits in Albany will never let it happen. Remember when they first built it? They said it would be temporary. Three years, they said. Now we're a few months away from its fiftieth birthday. You watch—that disgrace will outlast me. It may even outlast you."

Travis had a strange relationship with Fresh Kills. Though we loved to complain about it, we also took a perverse pride in our place as the final resting place for the refuse of New York City's eight million residents. My science teacher never tired of reminding us that the only man-made structures visible from space were the Great Wall of China and the Fresh Kills landfill. As far as we were concerned, those two were comparable—monuments to humanity's limitless potential. Sure, one may have been an architectural wonder and the other a festering mass of filth, but hey, they were both visible from orbit. At least we were first in something. I'd never be able to stomach the indignity of living atop the second-largest landfill.

Just when Chickie seemed about bored with me, the deli door swung open, catapulting a girl into the street, followed by Phene, Chickie's wife, in hot pursuit.

"Stop!" Phene's voice cut through the air, her hand firmly planted on her peroxide-touched perm to keep it intact.

At just the right moment, Chickie extended his foot. The girl tripped and slid across the pavement, shoulder first. He yanked her to her feet like a cop apprehending a bank robber.

The girl tossed her reddish-blonde hair to the side with a brisk flip of her head, revealing gas-flame-blue eyes. Instinctually, I took a few steps back, startled by the look of her. She had a creepy magnetism: all sharp angles and hollows—almost skeletal—and a knifelike nose that jutted like a blade. I thought I knew everyone in Travis, but I'd never seen her before.

"What did she do?" Chickie asked.

Phene pulled up, out of breath. "Check her pockets."

Chickie still had the girl by the arm, and she wasn't even trying to squirm to break free. If she was afraid or embarrassed, she didn't show it. She almost looked bored by it all.

"Out with them," Chickie demanded.

With her free arm, she pulled four Butterfinger bars from her blue Wranglers.

"I'll call Booch," Phene said over her shoulder as she walked back inside.

"Wait," I protested. "I'll pay for it."

"Do you know her?" Phene asked.

"Yes," I lied.

"Who is she, Raj?" Phene asked.

"I'm Georgia," the girl replied with a mouth of teeth that were a battlefield of misaligned soldiers, some standing proud, others deserting their posts in chaotic disarray.

"What's that accent?" Chickie probed, eyeing her with suspicion.

"Delta born and raised," Georgia scratched her cheek, which was covered in what appeared to be a combination of freckles and acne scars. "Moved here just last week."

"The delta of what?" Chickie asked.

"The Mississippi Delta," Georgia declared, a flash of pride cutting through her affected boredom. "Sunflower, Mississippi."

"Georgia from Mississippi." Chickie shook his head. "Why the hell would someone from Mississippi come to this godforsaken place?"

"My granny—"

"You know what?" Chickie gripped her arm tighter. "I don't care. We don't have time for this. Phene, go ring Booch. I'm sure she'd also be interested in why Raj here is playing hooky."

Phene disappeared back into the deli.

"Give her a break," I said. "She just moved here. She doesn't know any better."

"They don't pay for things down South?" Chickie asked.

"I bet it's more of an honor system down there," I said, looking to Georgia to take it from here.

"Yes . . . honor system," she improvised. "I planned to come back and pay her at the end of the month like we do back at the Sunflower General Store."

Chickie pulled Georgia toward the door. "It's too hot to sit out here and listen to this bullshit." By then, a curious crowd of sanitation workers had formed a ring around us. I wasn't going to reason my way through this, so I ran over and stood between Chickie and the entrance, facing his incredulous stare.

"What the fuck are you doing?" he seethed.

I produced a twenty with a shaky hand. "Here. This is more than four times what the candy is worth. And I know you don't want to spend the morning filling out a police report."

"Chickie, she's a kid," Phene offered from the open service window beside me. "Booch has better things to do than deal with this."

"All right," Chickie said as he let go of Georgia and grabbed ahold of my right shoulder. He was staring straight into my eyes. "Listen, you little shit. If your girlfriend ever sets foot in Phene's again, she'll be headed to the one-two-oh." The 120th police precinct had jurisdiction over most of the island's north and west shore neighborhoods.

"Understood," I said, shrugging off his meaty paw. "But she's not my girlfriend."

Leaning close, Chickie's voice dropped to a whisper. "I see how you're looking at her. Be careful. I'm not sure that one likes boys."

"Chickie, isn't he starting to look like Big Stosh?" Phene extruded her arm from the window and squeezed my cheek with surprising force. "So handsome."

I yelped and recoiled, the sting momentarily blinding me.

"He's soft, this one," Chickie said. "It's gotta be that half-Paki blood that makes him such a pussy. I bet his grandpa is rolling in his grave."

"Leave him alone," Phene said. "And watch your mouth."

Chickie and my grandfather, Big Stosh—not to be confused with Little Stosh, my uncle—had been best friends. They fought alongside each other in Korea in the infamous battle of Chosin Reservoir as part of a contingent of thirty thousand American and UN soldiers. They were surrounded by over one hundred thousand Chinese soldiers, triggering a brutal seventeen-day battle in legendarily freezing conditions. Those who made it out, like Chickie and my grandfather, were later nicknamed "The Chosin Few." When they returned, Chickie opened Phene's, and my grandpa opened a diner two blocks away called the West Shore Inn, now owned by Greeks from Queens.

"Why don't I pinch your cheeks, Chickie?" I reached toward him. "Wanna see how it feels?"

"Sure." He jutted out his chin. "If you wanna lose that arm."

Confident my threat was hollow, Chickie flashed a wild grin, grabbed his boxes, and walked into the deli. The altercations from the morning likely made his day. The guy clearly missed the action.

Georgia swept her fingers through her hair. "Thanks, Roger."

"It's Rajiv," I clarified. "Raj for short."

"Sorry," she said. "What kind of name is that?"

"It's Indian."

"That's cool. I've never met an Indian before, but my granny used to go to the Choctaw Casino in Pearl River."

"I'm a different kind of Indian, and only half."

"Oh."

I wondered what that "oh" meant, suppressing an eruption of insecurities.

"We should get to school," I suggested, the words feeling more like a plea than a proposal.

"It ain't gonna make a difference for me." Georgia took a seat on the curb in front of Phene's and pulled out a Butterfinger bar. "I already got my grades from back home. School ended a few weeks ago down there."

"The truant officers will pick you up if you stay out here. Trust me, you don't want them learning who you are."

She took a bite of her candy. "I've met them already."

"They got you?"

"They chased me," she said through a mouthful of Butterfinger. "Those guys are slow and lazy. Outran 'em every time."

Every time? She'd only been in Travis a few weeks.

"Sounds like you're catching on." I laughed. "The last day of school is usually fun, though. You should still come."

"I may." She held out a Butterfinger bar. "You want one?"

"No thanks. It sticks to these." I pointed to my teeth.

My braces were long overdue for retirement, but Mom couldn't take me to the orthodontist because she was delinquent on thousands in back bills. Val was convinced he could remove them for me, but my faith in him had limits.

"Fair enough." She deposited the bar in the front pocket of her flannel shirt.

"Can I ask you something?" I inquired.

"Shoot."

"Why did you steal that candy? Just to give it away?"

"I don't know. I just did."

I narrowed my eyes. *There had to be more to it than that.* "Those are good people, and now you won't ever be able to go back to the one good deli in town."

"You talk like an adult." The corners of her mouth pulled down slightly. "Like a teacher."

It wasn't even nine a.m. yet, and three different people had reminded me to lighten up. "Sorry" was all I could manage to offer.

"Don't worry about it," she said with a hint of a smile. "It's cute."

My cheeks blazed, and suddenly I was acutely aware of every awkward inch of my body.

No girl had ever flirted with me before. Who could blame them? At five feet nothing, with arms like pipe cleaners that mocked my weekly weight lifting sessions in Val's garage, I was hardly *GQ* material. And then there was the unibrow—a defiant black thicket that had resisted every attempt at taming. My last battle with the tweezers had left me looking like a confused goldfish.

It was all part of a doomed crusade to blend in with the Irish and Italian guys at my school. My olive skin and unruly curls could pass for a dozen ethnicities, but there was no escaping the neon sign of my name: Rajiv Patel. It clung to me like a second skin, a constant reminder that I'd never quite fit the cultural camouflage I so desperately craved.

The screech of brakes jolted me back to reality. The bus had arrived, my ticket out of this awkward moment.

—

"I gotta go!" I sprinted across the street.

"Hold up!" she yelled. "Where ya going?"

I offered her a hurried wave and boarded. Settling into my seat, an inexplicable sensation, like the faint touch of a cat's whiskers, brushed against my neck. My eyes, almost of their own accord, flicked to the grimy window.

There he was—Dante Malaparte, unnaturally close to the other side of the glass. Our eyes connected in a silent exchange, not menacing but strangely familiar, like meeting with an old acquaintance from a dream I couldn't quite remember. As the bus started to move, he winked.

CHAPTER 3

THE NEW SPRINGVILLE CREW

Later that morning

At the sound of the third period bell, the hallway emptied like a sinking ship. I removed the false bottom from my locker and grabbed my remaining CDs, spare cash, and a few TI-83 calculators I'd rented to upperclassmen at a premium. With heavy pockets, I planned to fill the remaining orders during lunch and cut the rest of my classes. Just six more CDs and I'd be in the clear.

The moment my locker clicked shut, the air behind me seemed to thicken with the rumble of deep voices. I sucked in a deep breath and braced myself for the inevitable storm.

It arrived in the form of Sal Longo, the leader of the New Springville Crew, and three of his goons. They were the apex predators of the island's teenage ecosystem—the largest gang in school. And they were large in every sense: the strongest, most numerous, and most aggressive. Their territory, New Springville, bordered Travis, separated by a section of the dump and acres of protected wetlands. Unfortunately for me, most of them attended my high school, and they'd been tormenting me since they found out about my CD business.

Sal swaggered up to me. I craned my neck to meet his gaze, a good ten inches above mine. "You guys smell that?" he asked his friends, who plugged their noses in unison. "Smells like curry." They laughed like this was the first time they'd heard that joke. Sal added, "Don't you people believe in deodorant?"

Even though I felt an ass kicking coming, I couldn't help but smirk at how ridiculous he looked. A gravity-defying fade topped his head, spikes jutting out like the quills of a porcupine—the *Dragon Ball Z* look," as I called it. Waxed to a Boy George level of thinness, his eyebrows stood out against his peachy-orange, tanning salon–baked skin. Draped over him was a black tee, the Armani Exchange logo so large it stretched all the way around to the back of the shirt because, god forbid, someone ever thought he bought it at Aeropostale or Old Navy. His entourage, a collection of similarly styled upperclassmen, were sculpted at the gym to a peculiar uniformity: huge biceps, burly chests, and underdeveloped backs perched atop scrawny legs. I liked to imagine that if I shoved them from behind, they would tip over like cows in a pasture.

Like an '80s movie villain, Sal clamped onto my shirt and pushed me against the locker. "What's so funny?"

"Nothing." I threw my hands up. "I smile when I'm nervous."

"Why are you nervous?" he asked, an odd question under the circumstances.

"I need to get to class." I made a halfhearted attempt to break free.

He yanked my bag from my shoulder and pulled out my CDs. "What's this? I told your Gandhi ass not to sell these anymore."

"Gandhi" was a common insult for Indians, which was like calling Black kids "MLKs." I never bothered to explain this irony to anyone, though, because whatever moniker they would replace it with was bound to be worse. Plus, I got a subversive pleasure every time someone used it.

Sal took my bag and handed it to his crew. As they examined its contents, I saw Georgia from the corner of my eye. She snuck up behind them and rummaged through Sal's bag, sitting on the floor. Once I realized what she was doing, I started to distract them further.

"Sal, I've been wondering. Where do you get your eyebrows waxed?"

At that, Sal delivered a wind-sucking blow to my stomach. As I fell to the floor, one of Sal's buddies snuck up from behind and locked me in a full nelson. I was now facing Sal with my eyes watering from the gut punch, my arms stretched out, and my head bent down from the pressure on my neck. I stared at Sal's shoes, wondering if he would kick me in the face.

Sal craned his neck down so his eyes could meet mine. He was so close that I could see the brown of his eyes underneath his blue contact lenses. "Talks so much shit, this guy. And cries like a baby at one punch."

Before he could land another blow, a voice on a bullhorn echoed down the hall. "Stop right there!"

Sal's goon let me go as Principal Ruffone charged down the hall, bullhorn in hand.

"Mr. Longo. Mr. Patel," Ruffone boomed through his bullhorn as he neared. "Let's break this up." He was handsome, with a perfectly coifed side part like a news anchor, yet his outfit was a hodgepodge: brown pants, a yellow shirt, and an orange tie.

The goons disappeared, but Sal lingered. Once Mr. Ruffone took his eyes off us, Sal delivered one final message. "We'll see you and your Victory fags tonight at the UA. Tell Val that my brother will be there to see him."

Val? What did he have to do with this?

As Sal walked away, he held up my CDs, calculators, and cash. That run-in set me back weeks, perhaps months. I turned to my locker and stared at the poster of John Starks, the lovable loser of the New York Knicks, dunking over Michael Jordan. Starks was my favorite player because he, like me, was a bit of a runt who got by through sheer determination. When I shut the locker and turned around, Georgia was standing there, watching me.

"You okay?" she asked.

I straightened my shirt. "Those assholes stole all of my stuff."

"I saw. If it makes you feel any better, you can have this," she said, tossing a yellow slab of plastic at me. It was the just-released Sony D-E705 Walkman, gleaming like a trophy.

My eyes widened. "Oh shit! Shock protection . . . Is this what you took from Sal's bag?"

Georgia's lips pursed in a rebellious slant. "There's also this," she said, producing a black Case Logic case, bulging at the seams.

I flipped it open, a gasp escaping my throat. Each page held six fat slits, row after row, easily twenty pages deep. This was a goldmine, eclipsing anything Sal had swiped from me. "Most of these masters I haven't even digitized yet. Thanks a bunch."

"It's nothin'," she said.

"Sal will lose his shit when he realizes these are gone."

"We can fuss about that later," she said.

"I thought you weren't coming to school." I slipped the case into my bag and started walking toward the exit.

"I changed my mind." She matched my stride. "Where are we going?" *We?*

"I can't stay here and risk running into Sal again." I reached for the door handle. "Plus, I've gotta find out what Val had to do with this."

"Who's Val?"

Before I could answer, a security guard emerged from around the corner. His uniform stuck to his broad frame like a second skin, yet he moved with surprising speed for a man of his size.

"You two, seniors?" he called out as he approached.

"Yes," I replied, trying to sound casual, "last class."

"Schedules," he demanded, the skepticism in his tone unmistakable.

I kneeled and pretended to search my bag for my schedule. That's when I caught Georgia's eye. A silent understanding passed between us, and in an instant, we turned and sprinted, a blur of flailing limbs and pounding sneakers as the guard roared obscenities in our wake.

We burst through the stairwell exit, racing through a cloud of smoke from a group of loitering upperclassmen. The guard was hot on our heels, wheezing but persistent. We reached the bus stop just as the doors of the 61 hissed shut in the guard's frustrated face.

As the bus pulled away, Wagner High School receded into the distance, Mr. Ruffone, Sal, and the whole sorry mess of my other tormentors shrinking in the rearview mirror. School was out, but that final sprint was just the starting pistol for a summer that promised to be way more terrifying than anything I'd left behind.

CHAPTER 4

THE VICTORY BOYS

The bus coughed and halted, discharging us from its air-conditioned interior onto the sizzling pavement in front of St. Anthony's.

Georgia paused, her gaze drawn upward at the church's frayed exterior as the bells tolled noon.

"The steeple . . ." She cocked her head.

"I know." I shaded my eyes from the sun. "They've been trying to raise money to fix it for years."

St. Anthony's was Travis's neighborhood Catholic parish. It was a humble structure with a crooked, rust-streaked steeple that towered above the surrounding trees, watching over us with concern like an aging parent. The white paint on its wooden body clung on stubbornly, revealing a map of weathered gray beneath.

For me, St. Anthony's was more than just a building. Its walls witnessed some of the most significant moments of my life; it's where I was initiated into the faith, my parents exchanged vows, and we said goodbye to my grandfather.

A patch of sun-bleached headstones poked like broken teeth through the overgrown fringe of the cemetery alongside the church. There, a figure emerged, tall and muscular, a water pitcher swinging rhythmically at his side. This was Val, my best friend. Where I was built of nervous tics and hangdog shoulders, Val was granite—a cool self-assurance chiseled into every inch of him. The kind of confidence that bordered on arrogance.

Each pour of water onto the wilted geraniums held a reverence that demanded silence. We shuffled closer, but seeing his focus, I knew better than to disturb him. Georgia, of course, didn't. "What's up with your hair?" she blurted, her eyes glued to his shaved head and the unusual blond hair gathered at the top. It wasn't quite a braid, more like a short, thick clump held together by a rubber band, standing defiantly upright like a tiny, spiky crown.

Val straightened, a flicker of something unreadable crossing his face before offering a curt nod in Georgia's direction.

"Val, this is Georgia," I said.

He grunted in response and continued his solemn walk toward another headstone, another parched bouquet.

As we followed, Georgia leaned in and whispered, "Isn't that a girl's name?"

"His full name is Valery. Air instead of err. It's a Polish name. We call him Val for short."

"He lives in that shed?"

"No," I chuckled. "He's the gardener for the church. When people drop off flowers at graves, they usually die quickly. Val tries to keep them alive as long as possible. He's kind of obsessed with plants."

"Isn't he a bit young to be a gardener? Doesn't he have to go to school?"

"Not anymore."

Val's mom and mine were best friends, so he and I had spent nearly every waking hour together since before I could speak. He was two years older than me, a brother in all but blood. None of us had it easy at home, but he may have had it the worst. When he was in the fourth grade, his father, a police officer, died of lung cancer. His mom had since become a functioning alcoholic. She spent her days selling magazine subscriptions at a telemarketing agency and her nights drinking at The Linoleum.

"Raj! Who's your girl?" Val finally said, still crouched on the ground with his back to us.

"I'm Georgia, and I'm no one's girl." She narrowed her eyes, the Southern sweetness in her voice giving way to a trace of steel.

"She just moved here," I explained, trying not to sound wounded.

"Welcome to our pile of trash, Georgia." Val spun and peeled off his gardening gloves, offering his hand. She shook it with a fleeting spark of intrigue in her eyes. Val had this effect on people, a charm so effortless he made nuns at St. Anthony's blush.

"Let's get out of the sun." Val waved us forward. "Come with me."

We followed him to the shed at the back of the lot. The building was in the twilight of a losing battle against the yard's advancing vegetation, with warped wooden walls and a tangle of weeds and vines snaking around its base. Hanging above the doorframe was a sign that read Victory Boys HQ in black paint.

"Who are the Victory Boys?" Georgia asked.

"It's just what kids in other neighborhoods call us," I said with a shrug.

Val gave the door three knocks and it flung open with a cloud of billowing pot smoke. Two familiar figures, one White and one Black, sat on buckets, sharing a blunt. The White kid was Mike Fannelli, whom everyone called Deadbolt because he lived in an apartment above the Victory Locksmith. He was rail thin with an aggressive underbite that drew attention to the large scar across his chin.

"Raj!" he said through the cloud of smoke.

"Puff puff pass, dude," the other kid said as he took the blunt from Deadbolt.

Like a younger Tyrese, he had a smooth charisma: shaved head, broad shoulders, and high cheekbones. His clothes reflected his passion for skating: JNCO jeans hanging low on his waist and a Quicksilver tee.

"That's Brian Tanzillo," I said, whispering to Georgia. "We call him Cheetah because he runs slow."

"I heard that," Cheetah protested.

Cheetah looked the part of a natural athlete but moved with a confounding lack of speed. Once, when a group of cops chased us out of Schmul Park for trespassing, we all got away except for Cheetah, who was run down and tackled by a decidedly rotund beat cop.

"Dude looks like he can run like Carl Lewis," Val told Georgia. "But he's slower than Carl Winslow."

"Don't start," Cheetah said as he took another hit. "I'll race you right now."

Val ignored the challenge. "This is Georgia," he announced. "She just moved to the neighborhood."

Cheetah and Deadbolt exchanged knowing glances.

"Don't be creepy," Val warned.

"What are you talking about, son?" Deadbolt protested. He talked and dressed like he was straight out of *Boyz n the Hood*, even though he was as White as anyone I knew. Such was the duality of Deadbolt and Cheetah. They both played against type.

"Take a seat." Val cleared some tools from a bench for me and Georgia.

"You're home from school early," Cheetah said.

"I had a run-in with Sal." I shot daggers at Val.

"Is that right?" Val asked, his eyes skimming past mine with a flicker of evasion. "About what?"

"He stole my CDs, my money, and my calculators."

"For real?" Deadbolt said. "Sorry, bro."

"Did you guys have trouble with Sal or the New Springville kids lately?" I asked.

"Not that I can remember." Val ran his pointer finger across his right eyebrow, a gesture he made when he lied.

"Fuck, you can't remember?" Deadbolt said. "It was just yesterday."

Deadbolt was the storyteller of our crew. Our neighborhood Jimmy Breslin, a living repository of every dumb trick we'd ever pulled. He had a talent for making seemingly routine events entertaining, the kind of person who would have been great at improv if that was a thing in Staten Island. But you had to be careful what you told him because he could not keep anything to himself.

Val tossed him a loaded look, but Deadbolt ignored it and launched into his story anyway. "Okay, okay. So, Val and I were at the mall yesterday, and we see Tara walking with a girl we didn't know at the food court, looking mad good. Val starts talking to her, telling her how much he misses her and all that shit."

"Relax," Val said with an uncharacteristic trace of embarrassment.

"What?" Deadbolt said. "That's what you were saying."

"Whatever, bro," Val muttered.

Deadbolt continued. "So, as he's talking to her, a bunch of New Springville juiceheads walk up to us and start asking questions—"

"New Springville is the neighborhood that those guys from school are from," I cut in, explaining to Georgia. "The ones who stole my stuff."

"New Springville," Georgia said, lingering on the "ing" like a new taste on her tongue. "Where is that?"

"By the mall," I said. "Not too far from here. Over on the other side of the dump."

"They're the only kids on this island as radioactive as us," Val added.

I gave him a shove. "Don't compare us to those 'roid-heads."

The New Springville kids didn't operate by the same code as everyone else. They routinely crashed other crews' parties, jumped anyone they outnumbered, and even used weapons. They were infamous for burning any drug dealer foolish enough to give them anything on credit. Unfortunately for me, many of them attended my high school.

"One of those wannabe gangsters is seeing Tara now, right?" Cheetah asked.

"Yeah, she was with Sal Longo," Val said.

"Wearing a fake Chinatown silver chain and a wifebeater," Deadbolt said. "Fresh from the tanning salon."

Everyone laughed except Cheetah. "I would love to get through this story by the time school starts up again in September," he said.

Georgia fiddled with Val's toolbox. I kept one eye on her to ensure she didn't pocket anything. I'd never be able to bring her back if she pulled anything like she did at Phene's. Val was even less forgiving than Chickie.

"You say that like you've actually been to school," Deadbolt said.

"Hey, I'm on track to graduate with Raj here," Cheetah said. "More than you can say."

Cheetah was one of the only members of the Victory Boys who still occasionally showed up to school. But he was too sporadic to offer me any help fending off rival crews.

"You want a medal for graduating two years late?" Deadbolt said.

"Better than not graduating at all," replied Cheetah. "What's your plan? Get promoted from Pathmark bagboy to the frozen aisle?"

"I already have my GED."

Cheetah and Deadbolt could bicker like this for hours.

Georgia held a level up to the light. "What's a GED?" she asked, her eyes locked on the small bubble suspended in liquid at its center. I was worried she was bored by the back-and-forth, but she had been listening after all.

"Something to wipe your ass with," Cheetah answered.

"A GED is a general equivalency degree," I said. "Basically, you take a basic math and reading test instead of finishing high school."

"Yeah, but Deadbolt couldn't even find it within himself to study," Val said. "So Raj here took the test for him using a fake ID." Deadbolt gave me a pound and a pat on the back. "My boy got every question right."

"I'm with Cheetah," I said. "Is there a story anywhere in our future? All I need to know is why Sal was so amped up about Val today. It cost me a lot."

"Calm down, son." Deadbolt leaned back on the bucket. "Where was I? At the mall, talking to Tara. Then Sal, his big-ass older brother Carmine, and three of his mutant buddies come up to us. Sal comes right up to Tara and hugs her, and then the two of them start making out right there. Anyway, then he turns to us and says, 'What are you herbs doing here? I didn't realize the mall takes food stamps.'"

"Damn!" Cheetah interjected.

"The balls on that kid." Deadbolt passed the blunt to Val. "Then Val calmly looks at Sal and says, 'And I didn't realize they found a cure for herpes,' and then winks at Tara!"

"She laughed, too." Val grinned as a lazy cloud of smoke climbed from his blunt.

"Sure did," Deadbolt added. "Anyway, at that, Sal's gorilla of a brother steps in front of Val and starts talking all kinds of shit. Two security guards had been watching this whole thing and stepped in to break it up. So they escort us out of the mall to different exits. But that's not the end of it. On the way home, we stop by Miggy's to get cigarettes. And guess who we see coming out as we pull up?"

"Noooo!" we all said in unison.

"Sal and his brother," Deadbolt said with a huge grin. "The others weren't with them. Val looks right at Sal, flicks his cigarette to the ground, and stares at him."

"Some Clint Eastwood shit," Cheetah added.

"And then we get into this negotiation about who should fight Val. I felt like Don King. I said Val should fight Sal, not his grown-ass brother. But after some back-and-forth, Val shrugged and said okay and handed me his beeper, wallet, and keys. Sal's brother then takes off his shirt and steps back with his hands up like a boxer, trying to intimidate Val."

"And he didn't have just a six-pack—more like a ten-pack," Val said.

"I've heard that dude's on the Ben Johnson meal plan," Cheetah added.

Everyone laughed, including Georgia. She was keeping up with all this new information or at least doing a good job of pretending to.

Deadbolt acted out the fighting motions. "So Val throws up his hands, and the brother charges at him, and he stops and throws an off-balance overhand right, and Val ducks and jumps on the dude's back like Blanka from *Street Fighter* and starts choking him out!"

"He fell on the floor while I held onto his back," Val said. "He was squirming all over the place, but I wasn't letting go."

"After a while, I was worried Val was losing his grip," Deadbolt said. "So I kicked the brother in the head."

There was a long pause as we took this information in.

"You what?" Cheetah said.

"I kicked him right in the head, and he was out cold right there," Deadbolt said with a note of pride. "And Sal looked like he was gonna shit his pants. He was watching with his jaw hanging out. Dude was in shock."

Val held up his bruised, cut hand. "Yeah, and Deadbolt caught a piece of my hand, too."

We were silent again for a few beats, staring at Deadbolt and Val.

"Dude," I said. "Why?"

"Val got up, we looked at each other, and bounced," Deadbolt added.

"That bitch Sal never said a word."

"This ain't funny, man," Cheetah said. "They won't let that shit go. We're never gonna be able to step foot in that mall ever again."

Deadbolt blew a stream of smoke in the air. "Who gives a fuck about that corny mall?"

"The mall is beside the point," I said. "I got jumped today because of this."

"How many neighborhoods are we gonna piss off in one year?" Cheetah added. "It already feels like *The Warriors* every time I have to leave Travis."

"Relax," Val said. "We'll be fine. And it was only a matter of time with those guys."

"Sal is going to be at the UA tonight, and he expects you to be there, too," I said. The parking lot of the theater would be particularly busy given it was the first night of the summer.

"Fuck that," Val said. "Waste of time."

"I have to be there," I said. "I have to go home and burn new CDs now that I lost the other ones to Sal. My best hope is to track down customers at the UA tonight. I have to deliver those before folks disappear for the summer. Like Jack Welch says, 'Inventory is the enemy of profit.'"

"Jack, who?" Val asked.

"Never mind."

"What time do you need me there?" Val asked.

I shrugged. "I don't know. Nine?"

"I should be able to do that," he said.

"Busy schedule?" Deadbolt asked with a hint of sarcasm.

"I've been growing some shrooms behind Schmul," Val said. "I want to test them out tonight." Schmul was Travis's only park, a mostly concrete playground with a large baseball field protruding from a section of Fresh Kills. It was an ideal place to trip because if the cops came, you could always flee into the service roads abutting the dump, where the cops wouldn't give chase.

"Behind Schmul?" I asked. "You mean in the dump?"

"It's not in the dump," Val clarified. "It's a little patch of field next to the pumping station. Deadbolt's been there with me."

Deadbolt took another long drag. "We've got enough shrooms up there to last all summer."

"The pumping station?" Cheetah asked. "That's beyond the fence line."

None of us had been on the other side of the fence before. Or so I thought. There were all kinds of rumors about what happened up there. No doubt, many of them were urban legends, but I'd never had the courage to test out whether they were true. Whenever I got close to the fence line, an unsettling feeling would pass through me, like the chill you get when passing a dark alley.

"Don't worry about it," Val said. "Just know I'll be at the UA tonight."

"Don't take a lot," I said. "Given the enemies we made, I don't need you guys bugging out tonight."

"Calm down," Val said. "These shrooms aren't that strong."

"According to who?" I asked.

"Roy," Val said. "I gave him some last weekend to test."

Roy was an older guy from the neighborhood in his early twenties who was everyone's conduit to psychedelics and raves. He claimed to have taken acid over two hundred times and was probably undercounting.

"When was the last time Roy said a batch was strong?" I asked. "Dude's tripped more than Jim Morrison. Electroshock therapy would feel weak to him."

Val gave me a reassuring pat on the back. "Don't worry about it, boss." He paused to watch Georgia pick a scab on her elbow and then taste the blood. "It seems like you have enough on your plate already."

CHAPTER 5

SHOWDOWN AT SHOWTIME

A s I opened the chain-link fence in front of Georgia's house, I heard a strange animal sound coming from inside. It sounded like a duck's quack but with a staccato rhythm, a series of abrupt notes forming a discordant musical pattern. I shimmied over to peer into the small diamond-shaped window into the garage where the noise seemed to emanate from, but it was too dark to see anything.

I rang the doorbell, and an older woman with dyed blonde hair came to greet me. She looked to be in her sixties, with a faded pink robe that poorly concealed a thin tube that snaked from her nose to an oxygen tank on wheels. I stared at the tank through the screen door for a few seconds before snapping to attention.

"I'm sorry to disturb you. You must be Georgia's, uh . . . grandma."

"Hi, precious." She opened the door. "Georgia didn't tell me she had any friends coming over." She looked me up and down. "Come in, dear. I'll get her."

"Oh no. That's not necessary; I can wait out—"

She opened the screen door and pulled me into the house by the arm. "Oh, don't you even think about it."

Their kitchen was immaculate but dated, with gold-flecked Formica counters and avocado-colored appliances that looked straight out of the '70s. I sat at the kitchen table in the shadow of a massive painting of Jesus, naked in a seemingly erotic pose with a leaf covering his penis.

"Georgia, your friend is here!" she shouted, dragging her oxygen tank across the kitchen like a sad dog. She grabbed a pitcher from the fridge and brought it to the kitchen table. "What's your name, sweetie?"

"Rajiv."

"Robbie is here!" she yelled.

"I'll be right there," Georgia shouted from an adjacent room.

"So, Georgia tells me you are Baptists," I said, staring at the Jesus painting. I was terrible at small talk, and this was the best I could come up with.

"By God's grace, we are. Do you worship?"

"Sometimes." I shifted in my seat as the comment hung in the air between us. I was clearly not impressing her. "Most of us are Catholics here. Georgia says you all go to El Bethel?"

"We do. You should come with us to service and see what you've been missing."

"Sure, I'd be happy to." I stole a glance at the clock as we sat in silence for a few beats.

"By the way, what's that animal noise coming from the garage?" I asked.

"Oh, that's Georgia's peacock. The folks over at the Staten Island Zoo gave it to her last week."

"They gave it to her?"

"Yeah, very nice of them. She's always making friends."

I fought hard not to laugh. It seemed that her grandma didn't know Georgia was a kleptomaniac. I wondered how someone would even go about stealing a peacock. That seemed like expert-level theft, not something you'd expect from someone caught stealing candy.

"Wanna see it?" Granny asked.

"Sure—if it's not too much trouble."

She walked me over to the door to the garage and stopped at the front of the steps. When she flipped on the lights, I couldn't believe what I saw. The garage looked like the stockroom for an electronics store. It was filled with all kinds of expensive items: multiple DVD players and PlayStations still in their boxes, a Pentium computer, a dirt bike, and a large cage in the corner with a blanket over it.

"Where did you get all of this?" I asked.

Before her grandma could answer, Georgia came barreling in, hurtling over the oxygen tank and planting a kiss on her grandma's cheek.

"Did you take your medicine?" her grandmother asked.

"Of course," Georgia said before turning to me. "I see you've met Granny." She then hit the garage door opener with her elbow and said, "Let's go."

"You two have fun," Granny yelled over the sound of the grinding gears of the garage door.

As we started to walk to the UA Theater, I was deciding where to start with Georgia. I had so many questions.

What medicine is Georgia taking, and for what? Why is she living with her granny? What happened to her mom and dad? What disease does her granny have that requires an oxygen tank? Why did she steal all that stuff in the garage? How did she accumulate so much so fast? Was she super religious like her granny?

But what I asked was, "Where'd you get that peacock?"

"The zoo."

"I know that. Your granny told me. I mean, how did you get it?"

"I've never been to a zoo before, so I went there the other night."

"They were open at night?"

"No. They were closed. I wanted to check out the sea otters."

"And took a peacock?"

"The otters were sleeping. I was yelling at their little cave to wake them up, and instead, I woke up the peacocks. Did you know they're not in cages?"

"I've seen them. If you go during the day, they're roaming around. I'm surprised they don't lock them up at night."

"They have these skinny legs. So, I turned my bag inside out, wrapped it around my arm, grabbed one by the legs, and flipped him upside down."

"Upside down? Why?" *Did she think everything was fair game?*

"It worked. He went crazy at first but then calmed down after a few minutes."

"How did you get it here? The zoo is far."

"Can't reveal all of my trade secrets." She stared at her fingernails as she kept walking. "What movie are we seeing, by the way?"

"We're not. We chill outside. That's what most kids do here on Friday nights."

"Cool. Kind of like the Walmart parking lot back home in Mississippi."

"Something like that."

—

We approached the UA Theater on foot from Victory, passing a group of kids blasting Ghostface Killah's "Winter Warz" from the back of a Ford Expedition. They looked to be seniors or older, but I didn't recognize them from school. The entire back of the truck was sodded with twelve-inch subwoofers that were so powerful you could barely hear the lyrics over the bass. The crowd was huddled together, sharing a blunt, and didn't even give us a look as we passed.

The lot was filled with groups like this. There must have been over a dozen cliques hovering around cars—mostly smoking up, drinking forties, and playing music. On most weekend nights, a cloud of hostility hung in the air at the UA from the tension between rival gangs who congregated there from across the island. But with school out, everyone seemed to be in good spirits. Most of the energy focused on getting drunk or high and hooking up. We passed one girl going down on a guy in the back of a Honda Accord. Though the windows were tinted, they hadn't even bothered to roll them up all the way. I knew the guy—he'd ordered a few CDs from me a few weeks ago—and I instinctively made eye contact with him and instantly felt embarrassed, darting my eyes away.

I tried to gauge Georgia's reaction to it all. She was mostly silent, glancing around and taking it all in. I couldn't imagine the Walmart parking lot in Mississippi was anything like this.

Even though this was our neighborhood, the Travis contingent was dwarfed by crews from other neighborhoods. Like a stranger at a party, I anxiously searched for anyone I knew well enough to hang out with. There was no sign of any of the Victory Boys.

After a few minutes wandering with a silent Georgia, I spotted Cheetah in front of the entrance to the Showtime Bowling Alley, which jutted out from the movie theater like the base of an L. He was on a skateboard doing tricks with Mercedes Morales, a buzzsaw of a foster kid.

I gave them each a pound and introduced Georgia.

Mercedes scanned Georgia's Wrangler jeans and red flannel shirt. "Interesting choice. Does everyone in Georgia dress like Woody from *Toy Story*?"

The last thing we needed was another fight. Mercedes had a short fuse. Her mom was serving five to eight in Ossining for grand larceny, and her father had been beaten to death by neighbors who felt, apparently with some justification, that he'd taken an outsized interest in middle school girls. The cops didn't bother to pretend to investigate his murder, and closed the case as a "domestic accident." Mercedes spent a short stint with a foster family in Travis before moving to Mariner's Harbor, a mostly Black and Latino neighborhood a few miles away.

"Hey. Be nice." I folded my arms. "And she's from Mississippi, not Georgia." What little I knew about Georgia suggested she didn't have much self-restraint, so this could escalate quickly.

"Then why is her name Georgia? That's confusing. That'd be like a New Yorker naming their kid New Jersey."

"You're funny," Georgia smiled. "My momma named me after the Ray Charles song."

All right. Georgia may be a thief, but she's not a hothead.

Mercedes furrowed her brow, likely confused about whether the comment was sarcastic or earnest.

"Where's Val?" I asked.

"I haven't seen Val since he went out to Schmul," Cheetah said.

"Damn." I frowned, scanning the parking lot. "Are the Springville kids here yet?"

"They sure as shit are." Mercedes pointed to the back of the parking lot. "I saw a bunch of those greaseballs over there."

I gritted my teeth, taking in the figures huddled in the dark. "You hear what happened yesterday?"

"Oh, I heard," she said. "Sounds like shit is gonna go down tonight."

It sure was, and we seemed about to face them with inferior numbers. "Val and Deadbolt have been tripping all day at Schmul. They better make it here ASAP."

"We were skating over there and didn't see them," Mercedes said.

"Fuck. Okay. Let's move over in front of Showtime." I started walking toward the entrance to the bowling alley. "At least we'll be near that security guard."

Mercedes pointed out an overweight middle-aged man in a security uniform. "You think that rent-a-cop is gonna protect us?"

"Why don't we go inside?" Georgia suggested.

"If we go in, we've gotta pay," Cheetah said. "And I ain't giving them five bucks to not bowl."

"Here we go." Mercedes bounced up and down like a boxer before a fight. "Here comes the JV mafia."

Sal and about a dozen of his crew were moving toward us. They all seemed to look straight at me, like a troop of lions spotting a gazelle. There wasn't a single girl among them.

"Should we run?" Georgia asked.

"Fuck that," Mercedes said. "Let them run."

The rest of us gave Mercedes the same exasperated look. Her swagger was entertaining when the stakes were low, but now, she was a liability.

I took a deep breath. "Let me do the talking." I didn't know what I was going to say, but I was confident I didn't want Mercedes leading our peace negotiations.

"You sure?" Cheetah asked.

No, I wasn't sure. We were all about to get our asses kicked. But I smiled and shrugged.

Cheetah rubbed his palms together. "Okay, I'll be right behind you."

We waited in silence while Sal approached at the tip of the spear along with a guy who looked like a professional bodybuilder. Based on their resemblance and the welt on the bigger guy's eye, I figured this was Sal's older brother, Carmine. The same brother who Val had knocked out the day before.

Sal stopped a few feet from us, his gaze still latched to mine. "Look at these Victory pussies."

Mercedes leaned around my shoulder. "Takes a lot of balls for you to call us pussies in front of your brother. After you wet yourself while he was getting stomped yesterday."

That took little time.

Sal turned to Mercedes. "Shouldn't you be playing in a tree house with the other little kids? Get the fuck out of here so we can deal with grown-up business."

Mercedes charged forward, but I was quick to block her path, while Cheetah, with a swift motion, caught her by the waist.

"Hold up," I intervened, facing Sal with raised hands. "What's up, Sal? What can I do for you?"

I was treating this like I did everything else: like a negotiation.

"Where's Val and Deadbolt?" Sal asked.

Good news. No mention of the stolen Walkman or CD case.

"The last I heard, they went to a rave in Philly," I said. "Will probably be back Sunday."

"Yeah, I heard that too," Cheetah added.

"Want me to pass along a message?" I added.

"Bullshit," Sal said. He pointed to the pay phone about ten yards away. "Why don't you beep them to this phone and see what happens?"

Carmine got in Cheetah's face. "And in the meantime, none of you are going anywhere." Carmine glared at Cheetah, nose to nose.

Cheetah smiled, pulled out a cigarette, lit it, and blew smoke directly into Carmine's face. "We've got no plans anyway. Wanna catch a movie with us?"

"Shut your monkey mouth," Carmine yelled in Cheetah's face, like a drill sergeant barking orders at a private.

"Look at this guy," Mercedes said. "A glass jaw and a filthy racist tongue. Your parents must be proud."

"He wants to be like us," Cheetah said to Mercedes as he stepped back. "That's why he spends so much time in the tanning salon trying to get brown."

Predictably, that comment hit a nerve. Carmine growled and pulled his T-shirt off—ready to fight. Shirtless, he appeared even more massive, with traps so big they looked like the buttresses on St. Patrick's.

I was at the pay phone but could see Mercedes clutching her skateboard from the corner of my eye.

"Carmine, aren't you Sicilian?" Mercedes asked. "You and T are basically cousins, anyway."

That got Carmine's attention, who turned toward her while she perfectly timed a direct shot with her skateboard across his already bruised face. Remarkably, Carmine stayed on his feet, clutching his jaw. I tried to get a peek at how badly she'd hurt him, but he melted away behind his friends.

That was the beginning of a full-tilt brawl.

Sal lunged at Cheetah, who somehow kept his cigarette in his mouth while he wound up and coldcocked Sal in the face. Three of Sal's buddies bum-rushed Cheetah to the ground, where they took turns pounding him while he did his best to block the onslaught.

The scene unfolded before me like a movie as I stood at the pay phone, until reality hit when some of Sal's buddies started approaching. Dashing toward Georgia, I found her pleading with the rent-a-cop who radioed lord knows who for backup. I glanced at the fight and could see Mercedes swing her board again, this time across the back of one of Sal's thugs, giving Cheetah an opening to crawl out from the pile.

Finally, the rent-a-cop decided he needed to intervene. He stepped forward with his arms out, serving as a laughably inept barrier between the Springville kids and us. At this point, Georgia and I had our backs to the bowling alley. Mercedes and Cheetah raced around the security guard toward us.

"Go!" Mercedes yelled.

I jetted into Showtime and sprinted down the narrow hallway entrance. I blasted past the cashier, who yelled something inaudible. Georgia, Mercedes, and Cheetah were right behind me, Cheetah catching up fast, and Sal and his crew a few yards behind the girls.

The bowling alley was packed, so I had to weave in and out of crowds. At one point, I crashed into a guy and his girlfriend, sending them flying into a garbage can. When I went to help them up, Cheetah grabbed me by the shirt and shoved me forward, shouting to keep running. Sal and his crew were closing in.

When we got to the end of the long room housing the lanes, Cheetah pushed open the side emergency exit door. Alarms blared while we raced out into the back parking lot. As we made our way across the empty lot—on weekends, everyone congregated in the front—we approached the back fence that bordered the dump.

A dozen Springville kids were maybe twenty yards behind me, out of breath but still trotting along like a group of offensive linemen chasing down a pick-six. They were precariously close to Cheetah, who, true to form, lagged behind. He had about a five-yard lead on the fastest of their group. Mercedes was a few steps ahead of him.

We all needed to pick up the pace or we were screwed.

Georgia was the first to scale the fence. I followed suit, catching a glimpse of her purple underwear peeking out from a hole in her jeans. We went up and over the No Trespassing and Hazardous Waste signs. I knew whatever was behind that fence was safer than what was in front of it.

When I reached the top of the fence, I straddled it like a horse. I wanted to make sure Cheetah and Mercedes were good.

Mercedes, perhaps sensing Cheetah wasn't going to make it—or because she wanted to divert the Springville kids—abruptly turned before reaching the fence, running at a forty-five-degree angle to the opposite side of the parking lot. Cheetah followed. Two of the Springville thugs peeled off to chase them.

I lost sight of them as I dropped to the ground inside the dump. With the fence separating the two of us, Sal walked up and stared at me, wheezing from the run.

"All that time in the gym, yet you've clearly never touched a tread-mill," I said, emboldened by the barrier between us.

He ignored my comment and looked up, pondering whether to scale the fence.

"Let's do it," his buddy said, pulling up behind him.

"Fuck that," Sal said, backing away from the fence. "I ain't trekking through that shit. We'll catch them next week." He turned away, leading his buddies back toward the bowling alley.

Satisfied that we were safe, I turned toward Georgia, but she was gone.

CHAPTER 6

THE WRONG SIDE OF THE FENCE

Alone, I slogged up the steep incline of North Mound, the tallest in a quartet of mountains that together formed Fresh Kills. The peaks had an unlikely majesty: they were the highest elevation points on the Eastern Seaboard, the Alps of garbage. But the valleys were as scary as the summits were breathtaking. In these canyons, even city light couldn't penetrate.

As I climbed, I took one careful step after another on the mushy earth, paranoid about sinkholes and garbage-eating creatures that burrowed under the surface.

When I finally reached the top, I settled on a firm patch of ground and took in the Manhattan skyline, an optical illusion that seemed almost touchable. On the opposite side, across the tidal strait, illuminated gas tanks marked New Jersey's Chemical Coast. From this vantage point, Travis seemed to command respect, asserting its place alongside the metropolis that mindlessly sent its waste to our doorsteps. The very trash we'd turned into mountains.

After I caught my breath, I began to descend the opposite side. Bottles and tangled pieces of metal slid down the mountain with every step. *How could one city produce so much trash?*

I started to lose hope of finding Georgia. I could look all night and never locate her—assuming she was still there. It was time to find a way out on my own. I wasn't about to head back to the UA Theater exit, not when the Springville crew could still be waiting for me.

Eventually, I spotted tire tracks that cut through the weeds. I followed the path past the gallery of torched cars, some still hot to the touch. Petty gangsters would routinely drive stolen vehicles up Victory, deposit them in the dump, strip them, and burn them. UA theatergoers were prime targets because the run time of movies gave thieves plenty of time to steal a car and drive it a half mile deep into the dump without having to pass a single traffic light or intersection.

A hundred yards into the path, a sharp prick hit my back, almost like a flick from an invisible hand. I spun around but found nothing. Then a second, harder shot stung the back of my head. The bushes started cackling, and out came Georgia.

"What the hell?" I shouted.

I could barely pretend to be outraged. I wanted to give her a hug but thought the better of it. The fractured moonlight pooled in the hollows of her face, turning her eyes into dark wells.

"Calm down," she said. "They were just little pebbles."

I dragged my fingers through my hair and then looked past the burned cars, up the mountain of trash, and down the long dirt road. "What's our best path out of here that doesn't lead us back to the UA?"

"Val says he knows where to go."

"Val?"

She pointed to a patch of trees and bushes behind us. "He's over there somewhere, peeing." She shrugged, like she'd just bumped into him at a Yankees game. "He was wandering up here all by himself, looking for water."

"Is he high?"

"I'm not sure. He didn't say much, really."

Val appeared from behind a tree, looking like a cat that had been pulled from a storm drain. He was sweaty, with his hair half out of his ponytail and hanging in his face. His shirt was shredded, and scrapes and cuts covered his arms as if he had run through a patch of thorns.

He looked up, and his eyes widened when they met mine. "Raj! You okay, man?"

"I'm fine. You?"

"Fried. Haven't eaten anything all day. But at least I found a place to take a shit."

"Congratulations," I said. "This is a dump; I can't imagine it was that hard. Why are you up here?"

"We wanted to watch the sunset from the top."

A rat scampered around a small mound, grabbed a candy bar wrapper, and sprinted into the woods. Why anyone in their right mind would choose to be in this stinking place, I couldn't imagine.

I frowned. "Did Deadbolt come in here with you?"

Val grinned over glassy eyes. "BJ did."

"BJ?"

"Yeah. He'll be back soon."

"Who's BJ?" Georgia asked.

BJ was Val's older brother, who'd died of cancer two years earlier. I didn't want to explain this to Georgia in front of Val, and I definitely didn't want to remind Val of that unfortunate truth while he was in that state.

"Val clearly hasn't fully come down," I told her. "We need to get him food and water, and then to bed."

"It's powerful shit, bro," Val moaned.

"If only someone warned you about that," I said, unable to resist the jab.

He gave me a blank look.

"Can we get the heck out of here?" Georgia asked.

"I saw light coming from over there." Val pointed into the trees.

It's possible that light was coming from his imagination, but there was no harm in checking it out. We followed him through a dense thicket of bushes until light started to show through the branches, and we heard two men arguing.

"Shit, stay down." I grabbed Georgia's arm, but when I looked back, Val was nowhere to be seen. "Where did he go?"

Georgia shrugged.

I shook my head. "Hang back." I slunk toward the voices, while, for once, Georgia stayed put. I made it to the clearing and hid behind a bush. About twenty yards ahead, an SUV was parked with the headlights pointed away from us, the bickering men standing in the beams of light. I couldn't identify who they were or what they were up to, but I could hear them.

"Hurry up!" I heard one guy yell to the other.

My throat constricted, a scream trapped inside. In the shadows, I saw what looked like a woman seated cross-legged, leaning against the rear left tire. She had her hands tied behind her back.

I nearly twisted an ankle rushing back to Georgia. "We need to get the fuck out of here now," I whispered.

"Why?" Georgia asked, a little too loud.

I put my finger over my mouth and glared at her with as much intensity as I could muster.

"I'm pretty sure those guys are burying a body."

"A body? Like a dead body? How do you know?"

"Because I saw a body!"

"I wanna see."

I shook my head. "No shot. Let's go before we wind up buried too."

Georgia narrowed her eyes and crept toward the clearing. I followed after her, even though my instincts told me to run in the opposite direction. I didn't owe her anything, and I should have found Val and gotten out of there.

She glanced over her shoulder and looked me up and down. "C'mon." She grabbed my T-shirt and pulled me close. "Come with me."

That was all I needed to override my urge to flee. Her hand was clenched around a wad of my shirt, my heart knocking against her nail-bitten fingers.

When we got to the tall grass, she let me loose and peeked at the truck through the tall strands. We'd been concealed in the pitch black of the brush, but if we made it any closer, we'd risk being seen.

Georgia seemed to understand this, stopping just short of the light. "Okay, so, where's this body?"

"Over there." I pointed toward the truck. "Back left tire."

Georgia continued to squint through the grass. "Wait a minute. She's not dead."

I pushed aside the grass and got a clearer look. Georgia was right. The woman was moving—squirming—trying to sit up taller with her hands tied behind her back. That didn't change anything, though.

"If she's not dead now, she will be soon." I flinched. I hadn't meant that to sound so cold, but Georgia had to see this for what it was. Those guys were going to kill that woman.

Georgia nodded. "You're right. We can't leave her there."

I flinched again. That wasn't exactly the reaction I'd hoped for. I mean, I didn't want to leave anyone to die, but I didn't want to put my own life in danger, either. These weren't bullies in the parking lot wanting to beat us up. These guys were grown-up thugs.

"Look." I pointed into the clearing.

The woman pulled against her binding three times before she turned toward us. Georgia stifled a gasp with the palm of her hand. The woman's mouth was duct-taped, and her eyes widened as she locked gazes with me. My stomach sank as she stared with such desperate, pleading eyes that both Georgia and I sidled back, sinking into the muck.

Our eyes were locked on the woman while the mud beneath our feet seemed to come alive, sucking us in like quicksand.

We couldn't just sit here. We needed to do something.

I gulped. "Let's go get the cops."

"She'll be gone before we get to a phone."

She was right. I tried hard to override my sense of panic, to think logically. "We have to assume these guys have guns. So how would we get her out of here without them shooting us in the clearing?"

"I'll distract them," Georgia offered.

I glanced at her. "How? And we don't even know how many there are."

"It's one truck," she said. "They got her up here. Couldn't be more than two or three of 'em."

"Two or three grown men. Armed grown men."

"I'll circle round to the patch up there." Georgia pointed to the wooded area on the opposite side of the clearing, behind the gangsters. "If I make enough noise, they'll come looking for me."

I didn't want them coming for her, but then again, the alternative was for them to come for me. "So, misdirection?" My head started to spin. "What if they catch you? Or shoot you?"

"I'm fast," Georgia said. "Don't worry about me. Your job is to grab that woman and run as soon as you hear me yellin'."

In the clearing, the woman was still gaping at us. She was alone, and we were her only chance. We had to give it a try. I turned to tell Georgia I was in, but she was already on the move, disappearing into the darkness.

I inched closer, trying to keep my head down. From my new vantage point, I got a better look at the arguing men. My breath hitched in my throat as recognition flooded into me. The guy digging the hole was the massive bald guy I'd seen in front of Phene's earlier. I'd also seen his pudgy sidekick outside of The Linoleum before. This was the only confirmation I needed: these were gangsters.

The woman let out a groan.

The pudgy guy shot her a look over his shoulder. "Shut the hell up."

The big guy wiped the sweat from his brow. "I don't know why you didn't just shoot her already."

"I just got the upholstery in my car cleaned. I ain't getting blood all over it."

"Why don't you just shoot her now?"

"Because then we'll get blood all over the dirt. This way, it will be harder to find her, you idiot."

The woman started to panic, groaning even louder—her eyes locked on me, begging for me to do something. My mind screamed at me to act, to help this woman, but my body refused to listen.

Then out of the darkness came shouting. The men whirled, startled. At first, I thought it was Georgia, but then I saw a male figure walking toward them.

"Shit," I muttered to myself. "Another one." We were outnumbered.

But as the third man walked into the light, I couldn't believe what I saw.

"Yooo." Val walked toward them with a smile. "Whatya doin'?"

Both men paused and looked at Val. "The fuck," said the shorter guy as the larger guy put down his shovel and reached his hand behind his back.

"Run," I yelled.

The next few minutes were chaos. The men lurched around and looked straight at me while Val ran in the opposite direction.

"Police!" came Georgia's voice in an unconvincing baritone. "Hands in the air."

There were three of us—spread out—and only two men. Puzzlingly, both men chased Val into the bushes instead of splitting up. I was about to pivot and take off when I saw the woman spring to her feet with her hands still tied behind her back. In the commotion of the moment, I had forgotten I was supposed to save her. I doubled back and grabbed her by the arm, holding her upright as we ran for safety in the opposite direction from where the gangsters had disappeared into the bushes chasing Val.

The woman and I darted through bushes on Georgia's tail. Georgia kept looking back, shouting for me to keep going.

Heading downhill, stumbling on loose spaghetti sauce jars and plastic cups, I tripped and fumbled while trying to stay upright with my arm locked around the woman's. Georgia doubled back, propping the woman up from her left arm while I held onto her right—like we were two officers speed walking a perp. The woman was at least half a foot taller than us, which meant we unintentionally served as an anchor, pulling her down and back with each stride.

Then a loud sound echoed through the air. Like a balloon popping. A gunshot. We sped up, except we were each accelerating at a different pace. Eventually, our legs tangled, and we tumbled down the hill through a wall of bushes and into a shallow pond. The stench wafted around me. I gagged and sprung to my feet, but the water was still up to my knees.

"Ugh!" Georgia said. "What is that smell?" She shook off her hands, heading toward the bushes.

I didn't have the heart to tell her it wasn't normal pond water. It was leachate: liquid garbage. People from Travis knew the term because, on rainy days, it would flow down the mounds and into our streets. The dump had an elaborate piping system that drained the leachate for years after trash was buried, dumping it into dark pools like the one we were standing in.

Every one of my senses went haywire. The smell burned my nostrils, the moon reflecting off the water fed me back my own panicked reflection, and a stinging pain from my jaw blunted my hearing.

The world spun, and I staggered toward the mystery woman ten yards away, who was struggling to her feet in the sludge water with her hands tied behind her back.

I tried to see if the goons were close, but the bushes lining the pond blocked the view. I helped the woman to her feet, guiding her out of the water and onto its bank. Then I peeked out from the bushes that concealed us. No sign of Georgia. We'd already made plenty of noise, so I didn't want to call out for her, risking the attention of whoever fired that gunshot. And I tried not to imagine Val on the receiving end of it.

I crouched in front of the woman, whose black eyes were fixed on me as I searched for the frayed edge of the duct tape on her face. She looked to be in her late twenties. She wore jeans and a once-white button-down shirt, now streaked brown with dirt and garbage water.

Strands of her long black hair were caught under the tape, which forced me to move extra slowly as I peeled it off, careful not to pull her hair out. As soon as I tugged the tape free, she made a loud, high-pitched wheezing sound, like she was having an asthma attack. Dangling from her hair, the tape hung across her chest like an ugly necklace. Without scissors, that was about as good as we could hope for.

I knelt behind her and went to work on her bound hands. My task was momentary relief from the chatter of my brain, screaming at me to run. To save myself. But I couldn't just leave her.

I ripped at the tape, but there were too many tight layers. Squinting in the dark, I felt for the seams, but there were none.

I leaned back. "Shit. I can't find the edges. I'm sorry."

"Just cut through it. Do you have a knife? Keys?" the woman asked in a hoarse whisper.

Hearing her voice—an adult—calmed me down.

"Keys. Um, yeah." I pulled my keys out of my pockets to saw through the layers. She was bound so tight it was hard to avoid cutting her skin. "Sorry. I know this probably hurts."

"Who cares?" she yelled. "Don't stop."

I kept sawing at the tape, ignoring the growing line of blood mixing with the trash water, until it finally gave.

When her hands were free, she moaned and clutched her ankle.

"What's wrong?" I asked.

She fanned out her hands, revealing her right foot. It was twisted at a brutal angle. It swelled before our eyes as if taking on water.

"They shoot horses for this," she said with a dour look. "You better get running, kid."

Then another gunshot rang out.

"They're getting closer," the woman added. "You have to go."

"I can't leave you here."

I tried to grab her under her armpits and pull her up, but she pushed me away.

"No," she shouted. "You'll die with me if you stay here. I need you to go so you can do me a favor."

"A favor?" What favor could be more important than saving her life?

"Twelve Mann Ave. By the 7-Eleven up Victory."

"I know the area." I cocked my head, breathing heavily. What was she getting at?

"Say it back to me."

"Twelve Mann," I repeated.

"Good. Second-floor computer. Password is Axl Rose. One word, no spaces."

"What about the computer?"

"Take it. You'll know what to do with it."

"Take it to the police?"

"No police."

"Then what should I do with it?"

Before she could answer, someone crashed through the bushes and tumbled onto the ground at our feet. I froze. They'd found us. Then I recognized the jeans and ripped flannel.

"What are you doing?" Georgia screamed over her shoulder as she leaped to her feet and kept running. "They're coming."

"Go!" The woman pushed me in Georgia's direction.

I backed away a step but hesitated. If I left her there, she was as sure as dead.

"Axl Rose!" she screamed at us.

"Axl Rose!" I screamed back.

Georgia was already out of sight, but I ran after her across the sewage pond and through the clearing on the opposite side. After a safe distance, I peeked back in the woman's direction. A silhouette loomed over her. A few seconds later, I heard a long, loud shriek—punctuated by a chilling hiss from where I'd been.

That was it. We'd tried, but that hadn't been good enough. Voices echoed through the trees. I couldn't understand what they said, but I didn't have to. They didn't want witnesses. The woman was dead, and now they were after us.

CHAPTER 7

THE LONGEST NIGHT

Deadbolt's eyes widened as he took in our chaotic appearance. "What the fuck happened to you two?"

Georgia and I had attempted a hasty cleanup at Schmul Park's water fountains. In hindsight, that was a waste of time, given we were on our way back into Fresh Kills in search of my Discman and to find Val. Under the unforgiving fluorescence of the service road lights, it was clear we didn't do a great job anyway. Mud clumps stuck to my legs like barnacles on the Staten Island Ferry, and Georgia's plaid shirt bore dark ambiguous splotches I silently prayed Deadbolt's addled brain would mistake for dirt.

I staggered over and slapped his hand with a quick pound. "We're fine, where've you been?"

Though Deadbolt had been in the dump that night with Val, he'd missed everything that went down. Fresh Kills was over two thousand acres, so vast it could swallow a person whole. I could see from the glassy and unfocused look in his eyes that the shrooms hadn't totally worn off,

which explained how he'd lost track of Val. He shook his head as if trying to jolt himself into sobriety. "Why are you here?"

I gave a rambling recount of our helter-skelter night, from the con-
frontation with Sal and his Springville goons to the face-off with mobsters
and our botched rescue of the mystery woman. I carefully omitted the
bit where Georgia might have killed one of the thugs.

"So, now we have beef with gangsters?" Deadbolt asked. "Full-on
adults?"

Georgia, already striding toward the entrance of the dump, threw
over her shoulder, "Let's go."

"Fuck that." Deadbolt fished his pager out of his pocket. "Did you
get this?"

He showed me the mysterious 173 message.

Matching him, I produced my beeper, echoing the mysterious digits.
"What's it mean?"

"The graveyard. One-seven-three Victory is St. Anthony's."

"Huh." That code should have clicked earlier. "Do you recognize that
number?"

"No, but who else would it be?"

I chased Georgia down. "Hold on a minute."

She kept walking. "We don't have time for this."

Gently catching her arm, I showed her the beeper. "One-seven-three
is the address of the church, the cemetery. It must be Val. We're going
down there to see what's up."

"And then what?"

I held my palms up to the sky. "Who knows? We should at least see
what he has to say and then decide what we should do."

Torn, she hugged her arms. "I don't know."

"It won't take long. If you still want to head back into the dump
after we go to the graveyard, I'll go with you." I wasn't fully prepared
to honor that promise, but I was fairly confident we'd find Val at St.

Anthony's. And he'd no doubt reassure Georgia of whatever our new plan was.

Finally, she nodded. "Whatever."

The service road eventually spat us out onto Victory, where we made our way to the cemetery. My mind couldn't help but picture a black Lincoln following us, windows rolling down, guns ready. Yet the night was quiet, almost unnaturally so. The windows of the houses were dark, the roads empty, and the sidewalks devoid of life, except for one lone figure: Sam, the town's perpetual drifter, parked on a bus stop bench. He hummed "We Didn't Start the Fire" by Billy Joel, the only tune he seemed to know.

Deadbolt couldn't resist as we passed. "Hey, Rain Man!"

Sam rocked gently on the bench, murmuring, "They're gone, gone for good. No coming back."

The three of us exchanged twitchy glances.

Deadbolt hovered over Sam. "Who isn't coming back?"

Sam ignored him and continued to hum the song while he patted his thighs to the beat.

I slipped between them and pushed Deadbolt back a step. "It's Sam. You know he talks nonsense. Don't be so paranoid." Though, in truth, Sam's comment freaked me out too.

Deadbolt's fists were now clenched. "I'm talking to you, Rain Man!"

Mercifully, we were interrupted by shouting from the cemetery. It was Cheetah, sitting on a gravestone, waving his hands.

"Where's Val?" I asked as we approached.

"I don't know," Cheetah answered with a bear hug. "I hoped he'd be with you." He examined me and, satisfied I was okay, moved on to Georgia.

Georgia waved him off. "I'm fine."

"Mercedes and I dusted those dudes," Cheetah boasted.

Deadbolt gave him a playful shove. "First race you've ever won."

"Fuck you," Cheetah shoved back. "What happened to you guys?"

Their relaxed mood made me more anxious, and the last thing I wanted to do was to repeat my story. "Let's wait 'til Val gets here for that." I took a seat on the grass. "By the way, who sent the one-seven-three messages?"

Deadbolt and Cheetah both shrugged.

"Must have been Val," I looked into the trees and nodded. "That's a good sign."

After a few minutes, we caught a glimpse of Val crossing Victory Boulevard, illuminated by the streetlamps. He looked like Verbal Kint as he walked, with a noticeable limp in his right leg. When he arrived, I eased him to the ground so he could lean against a gravestone, his injured leg fully extended. His pant leg was torn down the front, revealing a bloody knee.

"What was all that about up there?" Val asked.

Before we could answer, he rested his head on the gravestone and his eyes drifted up to the sky. I tried to shake him into consciousness, but he didn't respond. He was checked out at the moment I needed him most.

"Can someone please tell me what's going on?" Cheetah asked.

I launched into a full debrief of what we saw, again leaving out the crucial detail about Renzo, the gangster with a hole in his head.

Georgia paced back and forth like a basketball player eager to be subbed into a game. "We need to go back and see if the woman's alive."

"Sounds like she's six feet deep by now," Deadbolt said. "Which is where we'll be if we go back there."

"Six feet deep," Cheetah said with a mocking impersonation of Deadbolt. "Listen to this guy. Like he's some kind of mobster."

Deadbolt punched Cheetah's shoulder. "Fuck you."

"Neither of you was there." Georgia stepped between them. "Y'all don't have anything to offer to this conversation."

Deadbolt glared at her. "Who the fuck do you think you are? We don't even know you. You don't know shit about how things work around here, or who these people are."

Georgia brandished the stolen wallet. "I know more about them than they know about us."

"What's this supposed to mean to me?" Deadbolt flipped through the wallet like a critic flicking through a pulp novel.

I grabbed the wallet from Deadbolt and passed it to Georgia, who snatched it out of the air with one hand. "She stole it from one of the gangers—some guy named Renzo Razza."

Cheetah peered over Georgia's shoulder to get a look at the wallet. "How the hell did you do that?"

Georgia stuffed the wallet into her back pocket. "Don't you worry 'bout that. The important part is we know who they are."

Deadbolt lit up a cigarette. "Big deal." He blew a cloud of smoke in Georgia's face. "Anyone here can tell you who they are. A hundred bucks says they work for Dante Malaparte."

"They do," I said. "I saw one of them with Dante earlier in front of The Linoleum."

"See?" Deadbolt pointed the cigarette at her. "What's the wallet going to do for us?"

"We can bring it to the police," Cheetah said. "We can tell them everything that happened."

"We can't do that." I cocked an eyebrow at Georgia, who returned a blank stare.

Deadbolt caught on. "What's going on here? How exactly did you steal that wallet?"

"I hit him in the head with a rock," Georgia confessed, matter-of-factly.

For a long beat, no one spoke. I couldn't bring myself to look my friends in the eyes. This was a different kind of trouble than we were accustomed to. It wasn't a chase from the truancy cops or a spat with the New Springville crew. We were now well out of our depth.

After a few tense beats, Deadbolt sputtered through gritted teeth, "You hit who? The gangster?"

"That Renzo guy. I had no choice. He had me by the hair, pulling me up that hill like a rag doll. The rock was my only chance to break free."

Deadbolt shook Val. "Are you listening to this?" But Val just continued to stare at the sky, his head resting on the gravestone.

"Did you kill that dude?" Cheetah voiced the question I'd wanted to ask Georgia ever since we met up at Schmul. I'd hesitated because I didn't want to know the answer.

Georgia absentmindedly fiddled with a pile of twigs in her palm. "I don't know."

Between puffs on his cigarette, Deadbolt's face turned shades darker. "You seem awfully calm about this."

Georgia shot Deadbolt a look of genuine curiosity, like a cat discovering a new toy. "How would you want me to seem?"

"I don't like having to beg you for details." Deadbolt's agitation was bubbling like a kettle about to whistle, and Georgia's icy demeanor only seemed to make him more anxious.

Deadbolt had a point, though. We all deserved to know everything that happened because we were all in danger.

Yet Georgia didn't seem in a rush to share. She was still playing with her twigs. Deadbolt lunged to smack the twigs away, but her hand retreated with uncanny speed. A smile cracked her face. "What do you want to know?"

Deadbolt grimaced and let out a deep sigh. "Well, to start, how hard did you hit him?"

"Hard enough. Only once, then ran as fast as I could."

"Yet somehow, you found time to steal his wallet?"

Cheetah broke in, the eternal optimist. "Sounds like self-defense."

Deadbolt flicked his cigarette at Cheetah's foot. "Moron, self-defense only works if we go to the cops and tell them about it. Then she'll have to explain why she robbed him."

I stepped in front of Deadbolt and rested a hand on his shoulder. "We can't go to the cops. The woman said no police."

"The woman said?" Deadbolt nearly hyperventilated. "We're taking orders from a kidnapped woman now?"

I leaned in for effect. "Whatever she's got in that computer, she doesn't want the police to know."

"Then what do you suggest we do?" Val asked.

"We do nothing."

"What do you mean, nothing?" Georgia asked. For the first time, she seemed agitated.

I didn't want to disappoint her, but I knew how things worked in Staten Island. The best course of action was to mind your business. "If that woman doesn't want the police, then there's probably something illegal on that computer. Why do we want to get any more involved in this?"

"Raj is right," Cheetah said. "What if the cops show up while we're at the house?"

"Or Dante's crew?" Deadbolt added. "And do we even know she lived alone? We don't know a fucking thing about her, and I'd like to keep it that way."

"Didn't you promise her you would find that computer?" Georgia asked.

"She's dead," Deadbolt barked, his voice an octave higher than before. He was now up in Georgia's face. "Who gives a shit what Raj promised."

Georgia squared her shoulders and pointed at her own chest. "I give a shit."

"Don't be emotional." Deadbolt turned his back on her, addressing Cheetah and me. "We don't owe this girl anything either. Why are we protecting her? Let her deal with Dante."

"Deal with Dante?" I asked. "Just say what you mean. You know what he'd do to her."

"Better her than us," Deadbolt shouted, his voice ricocheting off the gravestones.

As the tension among us reached a tipping point, Val suddenly came to life. He unfolded his tall frame from the ground, slowly rising to his feet with a deliberate, almost majestic movement. Everyone, myself included, watched in silent astonishment. Just moments ago, he seemed lost in a world of his own, but now, here he stood, fully present and commanding.

"No cops, no Dante," Val declared, his voice steady and authoritative. "That's not how we do things. A rat is a rat. You know that. We handle this ourselves."

Val's ability to absorb the gist of the conversation while seemingly unconscious dumbfounded me.

"Thank you," Georgia said to Val.

"We've got your back." He winked at her.

When Georgia needed help in the dump, Val was lost in a drugged haze. Yet here he was, the hero, after I'd done all the work.

"But Val—" Deadbolt began to protest.

"Shut up," Val cut him off. "If you want to be a pussy, stay home tomorrow. We'll be fine without you. For everyone else, we can decide whether to return to the dump or this woman's house in the morning. Let's meet back here at ten a.m."

That settled matters. With no further discussion, we left in smaller groups to avoid attracting attention along Victory. First Val and Cheetah, then Deadbolt, then me and Georgia.

As we navigated the gravestones, Georgia started to pick up the pace. When I tried to catch up, she snapped, "I'm fine on my own."

My earlier acts of bravery were worthless now that I was the leading proponent of the "do nothing" strategy; I could feel her respect for me dissolve into the humid night air.

I watched her go, waited a few heavy minutes, then trudged up Victory. Just as I approached The Linoleum, a light flickered on—startling me into the bushes. My heart ricocheted against my ribcage as a dark figure appeared in the window, peering out as if searching for someone.

Every cell in my body screamed at me to run, but for the second time that night, my feet were glued into place. The shadow seemed to lock onto where I hid and then, after a few long seconds, retreated from view. And then The Linoleum's door creaked open.

My paralysis shattered. I burst from the bushes, sprinting down the back alley behind the West Shore Inn, hurtling fences like a fugitive. When my key finally turned in the front door of my house, relief washed over me. I had survived this horrible night. Now, I'd need all the rest I could get to survive the days to come.

CHAPTER 8

A NEW DAY

I n my nightmare, it was pitch black. I was in a hole in the ground while dirt dropped on my head like heavy rain. Over time, my eyes adjusted to the darkness. Shadows formed, swayed, and settled into definite shapes. Then a hand materialized out of the gloom, dispatching each shovelful with an eerie precision. I screamed at it to stop. The hand ignored me and maintained its mechanical cadence until the soil was up to my chest. I began to weep with such intensity that the dirt around me liquefied to mud. And then, just as the ground had nearly reached my chin, I caught a glimpse of my executioner. It was Dante Malaparte. His face was illuminated by a light that seemed to defy the surrounding blackness. And with no discernable emotion, he lobbed another batch of earth onto my face.

Panicked, I awoke in a cold sweat. I sat up in my bed, pulling in sharp breaths. I couldn't go back to sleep after that. For the rest of the night, I stared at the ceiling, my thoughts circling around the critical choice morning would bring. We could pay a visit to the mystery woman's house, though that would risk the wrath of Dante's crew and the attention of the police. We could head over to the dump to recover my Walkman before someone else did, though we'd have to cross back into the Fresh Kills crime scene. Of course, we could simply go to the police and trust adults to protect us. After all, Booch, a detective, lived next door. I could knock on her door right then and end it all. But could I trust her? What did I really know about Booch?

After hours of anxious rumination, I wound up where I'd started—believing the best course of action was to do nothing. At the first hint of dawn through the window, I peeled myself out of bed. A trail of dirt led from my side of the room to the shared bathroom—remnants of the prior night. I grabbed a towel and quickly wiped it up to avoid Uncle Stosh's scrutiny. As I scrubbed the floor, I noticed patches of dirt on my arms despite having halfheartedly showered the night before.

I stood in the bathroom and doused a towel with soapy water, my eyes drifting out of the window. Nothing appeared out of the ordinary. Just a typical Saturday morning with a neighbor out tending his lawn in a bathrobe and bunny slippers. The only car on the road was a beat-up old Geo Storm station wagon that crept along, spewing copies of the *Staten Island Advance*—the island's paper of record. The car belonged to my buddy Tommy Sessa, whose mom chauffeured him on his morning paper route. He had the aim of a drunken darts player, and his customers frequently complained that copies of the *Advance* found their way into hedges and flower beds.

I was exhausted and badly wanted to go back to sleep, but my pager buzzed in my pocket. It was from Val. A "123" followed by a "173," which I now knew meant to hurry up and get to the cemetery.

I cleaned up my mess and took a more thorough shower before changing into a Champion mesh tank top, cargo shorts, and old baseball cleats. If we decided to return to the dump or break into the woman's house, I had to be prepared.

On my dresser, I found my father's letter, unopened. In the chaos of the day before, I hadn't found time to read it. For a moment, I considered ripping off the Band-Aid right there and facing whatever revelation awaited. It was probably some grand promise he'd inevitably break. He was manic like that. When he was around, every now and then he would have some epiphany about what it meant to be a dad, embracing some short-lived manic frenzy. On one Saturday, he decided he needed to teach me to play baseball, even though he didn't know anything about the game. Undeterred, he dragged me out to Modell's Sporting Goods to buy new gloves and then to Schmul, where he forced me to play catch all day. Of course, he grew bored of this exercise after a few days, and we never played catch again. A few months later, he became convinced his role was to make me fit and strong, and he had me doing push-ups and calisthenics at my high school track for hours. Then it was literature— maxing out his credit card with a trip to Barnes & Noble, ignoring my suggestion that he just get me a library card instead.

I stuffed his letter into the pocket of my cargo shorts for later, along with my wallet and beeper. I hadn't eaten in over a day, so I ambled down to the kitchen, where, to my surprise, Georgia was standing at our stove in my mother's apron, flipping pancakes.

"Morning, sunshine." She leaned toward my mom's bedroom. "Do you want blueberries?"

A muffled "Yes, please!" came back through the wall.

"What are you doing here?" I whispered. "And where did you get these pancakes?" The only breakfast supplies we ever had stocked in my house were cornflakes and coffee. I considered it a luxury if the milk wasn't expired.

"I brought a mix from home." Georgia dropped three perfectly round cakes onto a plate and deposited it on the kitchen table with a chef's flair. "Sit."

I had so many questions, but the smell of the pancakes was alluring.

My mom appeared in her nurse's uniform. "Sweetie, I've gotta run." She patted Georgia on the back with uncharacteristic warmth. "If you don't mind putting my breakfast in the fridge . . ."

"Take it to go." Georgia began to rummage through the barren cabinets. "Do you have ziplock bags?"

"I've got it." I pulled an empty Waldbaum's bag from under the sink. "Saturday shift?"

My mom slung her purse over her shoulder. "Every week this month."

Georgia handed my mom her to-go bag. "My ma used to work weekends too."

That was the first I'd heard Georgia mention her mother.

"She's such a gem, this one," my mom gushed to me. "How come you never told me about her?"

It was an odd question from my mom. I never talked to her about any of my friends. Everything about her energy that morning felt fake, like she was acting the part of a bubbly sitcom parent.

"She just moved here."

"Oh, I know." My mom threw a playful smile at Georgia. "From Mississippi. We've caught up already."

Mom kissed the top of my head. "I'll see you tonight." And to Georgia, "Thanks so much for breakfast!" She waved as she headed out the door.

How long had they been talking? Did Georgia mention anything about the night before?

I shoved a few bites of the pancakes into my mouth. They were delicious, even better than the ones the Greeks made at the West Shore Inn. Once my plate was clean, I took it to the sink before I turned to Georgia. "What did you take?"

She frowned, taking my plate and washing it. "Take where?"

"From this house. What did you steal?"

"I wouldn't steal from you." Her voice was uninflected, no trace of offense.

"You stole from literally everyone we came across yesterday: Phene, Sal . . . even the mobsters."

She wiped her wet hands on her jeans. "I don't steal from friends."

I was relieved to hear her call me a friend, given how icy she was to me when she'd left me at the cemetery. "At some point, you're gonna have to explain your code to me."

She started drying the plate. "My what?"

"Never mind. We've gotta go." I grabbed a steak knife, wrapped it in a dish towel, and shoved it under my belt.

Georgia shot me an amused look—like a parent catching their toddler "shaving." "What's that for?"

"In case we run into trouble again," I mumbled, adjusting the makeshift weapon back under my shirt. I ushered Georgia toward the door, but our escape was cut short by Uncle Stosh lumbering down the stairs.

"Whoa there, Rambo," he chuckled, eyeing the bulge beneath my shirt. "Where are you going with that?"

I pulled down my shirt in a half-assed attempt to cover it. "We're going to the dump, and I just wanted something to protect us."

"The dump? What are you doing up there?"

"We're just exploring the patch behind Schmul. Not going too far."

He cocked his head. "Does your mom know you're going there?"

I shrugged my shoulders. "What do you think?"

"Raj, I don't need any trouble. Lori would give me the boot if she knew I was hiding stuff like this from her."

"Good thing I never told you."

He stared at me for a moment, then let out a deep sigh. "Fair enough. Just be careful. I heard there've been some coyotes roaming around. A knife won't do you any good against them."

It was hard to keep up with the rumors of wildlife sightings at Fresh Kills. The *Advance* had recently run a story speculating about a herd of deer based on the account of one sanitation worker who'd spotted tracks.

"This is Georgia, by the way." I nudged her forward. "The girl who moved into the Moseleski's house."

"Welcome to the neighborhood, kiddo." Uncle Stosh raised his hand for a high five.

She returned the gesture with a firm slap. "Nice to meet you."

Just as my hand touched the front doorknob, Uncle Stosh threw in, "Oh, almost forgot, someone came by for you earlier."

I gulped, releasing the door. "Who?"

Uncle Stosh scratched his chin. "Some kid I hadn't seen around before. Lanky fellow. Said he wanted to pick up a CD. I told him you were zonked out and to come back later. Didn't catch his name, though. Seemed like he was in a real hurry."

"Did you get a look at his car?"

"It looked like one of those Lexus SUVs. Black."

"Big nose? Spikey hair, faded on the sides?"

"Yeah. Odd-looking kid."

That could only be Sal Longo. He'd never been to my house before.

"Was he with anyone?"

"Not that I could see."

Sal was brazen to venture this deep into Travis without his crew. *Was this visit about revenge from the night before? Or did he discover his missing CD case and Discman?* Either way, I had bigger enemies to worry about. What seemed like an existential issue yesterday morning was now a sideshow. Perhaps this was courage—racking up ever-increasing threats and becoming desensitized to the smaller ones.

I grabbed the handle again. "Thanks. If he comes back, tell him I'm out of town."

"Out of town? Where?"

"Just make something up." I hurried out the door.

While we passed through the front gate, I scanned the yard next door. No sign of Booch or her car.

At the corner of Victory, Deadbolt's stepdad sat in a plastic chair on the sidewalk in front of Victory Locksmith—wearing nothing but his boxers.

"Is Mike home?" I asked, referring to Deadbolt's real name. Of all of the Victory Boys, Deadbolt was the one I was most worried about that morning. He was a bundle of nerves in normal times, and I couldn't imagine he held together well overnight.

Mr. Deadbolt took a sip of his beer while scratching his sizable gut with his other hand. "He headed out about a half hour ago."

"Thanks."

We'd walked for another block along Victory before I noticed a man walking parallel to us. After a few more steps, I mustered up the courage to take a more extended look and confirmed that he was staring right at us.

"It's Dante Malaparte," I whispered.

"Who?" Georgia craned her neck back to get a sightline, but I grabbed her by the arm and pulled her along. We were now walking at a brisk pace.

"What's wrong with you?"

I kept my voice to a whisper and my eyes ahead, deliberately avoiding any glance across the street. "He's the leader of the mobsters from the dump. The guy Deadbolt was talking about. Renzo's boss."

Georgia abruptly stopped and knelt.

"What are you doing?"

Pretending to tie her shoe, she snuck a glance across the street. "He's definitely looking at us."

"Shit." My heart raced as I picked up the pace.

Georgia started giggling and simply took off running. I followed after her. She beat me to the cemetery, where I collapsed on a patch of grass in front of Val and Mercedes.

Val looked down at us. "What are you doing?"

I was relieved to see him. To see both of them, even though they looked like they'd done ten rounds with Evander Holyfield. Val's leg was wrapped in white medical tape so sloppily applied that some of it stuck to the outside of his shorts. Mercedes was covered with cuts and bruises from the fight with the Springville kids. Only Georgia—who saw some of the most significant action of the night—looked unscathed.

"We thought someone was shadowing us." I popped back up. No sign of Dante. Just Sam the Wanderer strolling along Victory, muttering something to himself.

"Who was following you?" Val scanned the street. "Sam?"

"No, it was—" Georgia started to say.

"—probably just Sam." I shot Georgia a quick look, hoping she understood to keep quiet. Georgia tilted her head at me but didn't say anything.

Mercedes put her hands on her hips and scrunched her face. "I know you guys had a wild night, but you all sound crazy."

"You must not have heard much about last night," Georgia said. "Wild don't begin to describe it."

Mercedes dropped her hands to her sides. "My bad. They told me what happened. Sorry." I'd never seen her contrite before. I wasn't sure how much of our story they'd told her, but it had been enough to unnerve her. Another person to share the burden of our secret.

Val tussled my hair. "We'll keep a lookout for anyone suspicious, Raj."

"What's with the ridiculous outfit?" Mercedes looked me over. "Are those cleats?"

Val squeezed my puny bicep. "Never seen you in a tank top before," he said. "Looking jacked, bro."

I pushed them both away. "Shut up."

Georgia stood with her arms crossed and tapped her foot. "Are we ready to go?"

"Shouldn't we consider waiting a bit?" I asked. "We don't want to make this worse. And Deadbolt and Cheetah aren't even here yet."

"They aren't coming," Val said. "Cheetah's working at Pathmark and Deadbolt chickened out."

I nodded, mostly to myself. The smaller the group, the better. And I wasn't in the mood to deal with Deadbolt's angst.

"Let's meet back here in two hours," Val said. "Be careful."

My eyebrows rose. "What do you mean? Where are we going?"

"Mercedes and I are heading up to the dump," Val said. "You two are heading to the woman's house."

I swallowed the growing lump in my throat. "When was that decided?"

"Raj, we don't have time to fuck around."

I'd seen Val like this before. He'd made up his mind, and there was no sense in arguing with him. That didn't mean I wouldn't try, though. "Why would we split up?"

"The smaller our groups, the less attention we all attract."

"We won't attract any attention if we just stay here."

Georgia retied her laces. "You can stay if you want. It'd probably be better if I went alone anyway."

That comment stung. She seemed unmoved by my display of valor the night before.

"No," Val said. "Raj is the one who talked to the woman. He should go too."

She hesitated for a moment, looking me up and down like a captain forced to pick among scrubs at recess. "Fine. Just him."

I pulled Val aside. "You sure this is a good idea? You were pretty high last night. Do you even remember where we were?"

"I remember."

Just in case, I gave him a brief refresher on how to find the clearing where we'd been the night before and a description of where I could have dropped the Discman.

I then pulled the knife out from under my shirt and handed it to him. "Take this with you."

He grabbed the knife by the handle and examined it with a smile. "What the hell were you gonna do with this?"

"In case we ran into trouble again. Keep it. Especially since you're all crippled. You won't be able to run away if someone finds you and chases you."

Val paused for a moment, spinning the knife between his fingers. Then without warning, he tossed the knife across the yard, where it buried itself in a patch of dandelions.

"Mercedes"—he started walking toward Victory—"let's roll."

"Be careful," I shouted after him.

He held up his middle finger without looking back.

CHAPTER 9

BEHIND ENEMY LINES

An hour later, Georgia and I hunkered behind a rusted Ford Bronco parked at the end of a quiet cul-de-sac in New Springville, staring at a blue three-story shotgun house across the street. Twelve Mann Avenue—the address whispered to me in the dark by a woman about to die. Our task: to secure any files she had left in her computer.

Then what? We weren't sure. The little we knew about the woman suggested she had information that proved inconvenient for Dante and his crew. Her possession of that material probably related to why she'd been heading for a shallow grave in the dump the night before. Beyond that, we knew little else—her name, profession, or even what files to look for. Was she married? Did she have a roommate? There weren't any cars in the driveway or any signs of kids.

I peeked around the car for the tenth time that minute. "What's our move?" The block was deserted, but this was a perilous operation. We risked running into Dante's crew, who likely knew where this woman lived and could be on the hunt for the same digital prey. We also had to keep cops in mind, who may have already stumbled upon the woman's corpse in the dump. And then there was Sal's posse. We were well into their territory—two blocks from Sal's house—and we were alone out there without any of the Victory Boys to have our backs.

"We got two options: the front door or the back." Georgia stated the obvious. She stood up and leaned against the Bronco, back toward the house, arms crossed as she gazed down at my crouching form. She was short enough that the truck still blocked her from the view of the street. "Here's the plan. I'll ring the doorbell. If no one answers, I'll go through the back."

"What if someone answers?"

"I'll pretend to be a Jehovah's Witness."

"Aren't you a little underdressed for that?"

She wore cutoff jean shorts, a yellow ribbed tank top over a pink sports bra, and the muddy knock-off Converse from the day before.

"How's this?" She drew a rubber band from her pocket and efficiently fixed her long, chaotic ginger-blonde hair into a ponytail.

My eyes locked on the now-unobstructed view of her face. Her hands rested on her hips, radiating a sense of command and determination.

"What?" she asked, breaking my trance.

"Oh, yes, sorry. You look fine."

"You're the lookout. Warn me if anyone comes."

"How?"

"Make noise, yell, scream—whatever. As long as I know something's up. Or, better yet, distract them."

This was a replay of the events from the night before, with her charging into battle while I watched. The difference was this time, I'd be the bait.

"Ten-four." I smiled, mindlessly accepting the challenge. I was starting to dissociate as the air seemed to shift around me. With my slow, tangled thoughts, I'd become a passive observer of my own experience, like I was half-asleep, watching myself on TV. The distant feeling may have been a coping mechanism because the smart thing would have been to stay as far away from that house as we could. Yet, there we were, getting ready to go inside. Or, more accurately, Georgia was.

"Second-floor computer?" Georgia asked. "She didn't say anything else?"

"She gave us the password, but you won't need it. Remember: Grab the whole tower because we won't have time to sift through it."

Georgia nodded. "If there's any trouble, we need a meetup spot."

Good point. Chances were we'd get split up if things went bad. "Sicilian Swirls Ice Cream Shop. It's about five minutes that way." I pointed toward Richmond Avenue. "It's one block south of the bus stop. In a strip mall with a big sign of a fat man holding an ice cream cone."

She nodded again. "Sicilian Swirls."

And with that, she was off, beelining straight for the front door. She rang the bell and waited, occasionally glancing my way with a shrug. After a minute or so without an answer, she hopped the chain-link fence and disappeared into the backyard.

Noon approached, and the sun radiated off the Bronco, making it hot as an iron on laundry day. My tank clung to my skin, drenched in sweat, and my eyes began to grow heavy. I'd been running on adrenaline for the past twenty-four hours but was starting to buckle from the fatigue. After a few minutes, I stood and stretched out the stiffness in my legs before I shielded my eyes to get a clearer view of the block.

There wasn't a soul around—from the patch of woods at the end of the cul-de-sac to the cars buzzing past at the busy intersection of Victory Boulevard. *Smooth sailing.* Soon we'd be back on the bus with a computer, safe and sound again. I shifted my weight, getting hotter as I imagined squeezing next to her on the seat. Should I make a move on her? If I did, what would I even do?

Then I remembered my dad's letter. I fished the envelope out of my pocket and started to open the flap before several voices interrupted me, shouting and laughing at the top of the block. I stuffed the letter in my pocket and crouched back behind the Bronco.

It was a large group, maybe a dozen or so kids. I couldn't make them out, but only one posse would roll that deep in this neighborhood: the Springville Crew. They were a few hundred yards away and headed in my direction, likely aiming for the woods at the end of the block.

I took slow, steady breaths as their voices grew louder. My instinct was to stay hidden and hope they wouldn't find me, but then I remembered my orders: deflect attention from Georgia. I couldn't let anyone see her leaving that house, much less with a computer in hand.

I gritted my teeth, stood up, and walked right toward them—knowing full well I was probably stepping straight into the beating of my life. A day earlier, I'd have taken off, but these guys somehow felt less intimidating after what we'd seen the night before.

I spotted Sal wearing a yellow Laker's jersey, half flexing as he excitedly told a story. One of his buddies spotted me, and the crew went silent, stopping about thirty feet away.

I had to act fast. I slowly threw my hands up and stepped toward them, like a bandit surrendering to authorities. They looked shocked to see me in their hood. Alone. Too good to be true.

"I come in peace," I shouted. "With a proposal."

Sal walked out in front of his crew to meet me. He grabbed me by my mesh tank top and pulled me into a headlock. "What the fuck are you doing here?" He was spitting with rage. "And why are you wearing fucking cleats?" His buddies erupted in laughter, and I couldn't blame them. I looked ridiculous. And now that I wasn't in fact returning to the dump, they were totally useless.

"Our crew versus your crew," I yelled. "Monday night. Seven p.m. Neutral territory."

"Neutral territory?" He tightened his hold around my neck. "What is that supposed to mean?"

I'd forgotten who I was dealing with. I needed to dumb down my vocabulary a bit.

"It means somewhere outside of both our neighborhoods."

His grip tightened, and I gasped, starting to see stars.

Sal loosened up a bit. "Like where?"

Good question. I needed somewhere with open space—like the place we used for pickup games of tackle football. "How about the Alba House?"

"The Catholic convent in Westerleigh?"

He flung me to the pavement, and I tossed my hands forward to soften the blow. I quickly sat up and spun, facing Sal as his goons started to gather around me in a semicircle. I backed away in a crab walk, palms tingling from the gashes and heat of the concrete . . . until they closed the circle, and I had nowhere to go.

Sal crouched in front of me on the floor, picking up a piece of paper. My dad's letter. "What do we have here?"

"That's private," I said. "It's for my mother."

He unfolded the letter and scanned it. "Dear Lori," he began reciting it loud enough for the crew to hear. "I'm sorry I haven't written for a while."

Before he could finish, I lunged at him, snatching the letter from his hands and crashing back to the pavement. While seated, I hurriedly tore the letter up. I'd rather not know what was in it than have them make a spectacle of it.

"The balls on you," Sal said. "You must really want to get pounded."

"At least make it a fair fight," I pleaded. "One of you should be more than enough."

Sal's eyes narrowed as he scanned his crew before putting his arm around the shortest of the bunch. "Matteo, how'd you like to take care of this smelly Gandhi faggot?"

Matteo was about my height but had at least fifty pounds on me. He looked like a miniature version of Sal's brother, Carmine. He unfastened his silver chain and handed it to Sal.

"You can keep that on," I said. "This shouldn't take long."

That got a laugh from Sal's crew.

"This fucker," Sal said. "You think this is a joke?" He shoved Matteo forward. "Stomp this dot head."

"Get up," Matteo barked.

I stood and put my hands up in front of me, hunched in a defensive stance, closing my eyes as I prepared for a pummeling.

Except none came.

"Oh shit," I heard one of Sal's crew say, and then I didn't hear anything else. *Are they playing a joke on me? Waiting for me to put my guard down?* After about a minute, I peered out from behind my arms. They were all gone.

I wasn't alone, though. In front of me, leaning against a black Cadillac, was none other than the gigantic bald goon from the night before.

"Get in the car," he said.

CHAPTER 10

BLUE EYES

We rolled onto Victory Boulevard in silence. The goon's huge hand rested on the wheel while his other fiddled with the radio. I was alone in the back, staring straight ahead at the empty passenger seat, stealing glances at my mammoth chauffeur. He had to hunch to avoid bumping his head against the roof of the Cadillac. A thick gold chain, twisted like barbed wire, emerged from under his shirt collar, etching grooves into his skin like a choke collar on a pit bull.

This could be my last ride, I thought. A hearse transporting me to my final resting place.

For the time being, my strategy was to stay as silent and still as possible—and resist my usual urge to talk myself out of a jam. We stopped at a red light next to a white Ford Explorer just a few feet from my window. It had a Joe & Pats Pizzeria decal emblazoned on its front door and a delivery boy who nodded along to music behind the wheel.

A fleeting window of opportunity seemed to open before me. I could unlock the back door, run out in front of the truck, or try to crack the Cadillac window with my elbow and get the driver's attention.

If I did manage to get away, Dante's crew could easily find me. They may already have known who I was. I could go to the cops, but then I'd have to explain what I was doing in front of that woman's house. Then again, whatever the police had in store for me would be preferable to whatever the mobsters had planned.

The light changed just as I'd worked up the courage to make a move. The Cadillac started rolling through the green light while the pizza delivery man hung a right and disappeared, along with my last hope.

Music started playing from the car speakers, and I snapped my head back and fixed my eyes straight ahead.

The goon turned up the volume to a song I recognized, though not one I would have predicted for a middle-aged mobster. He began singing along, hitting the notes with impressive harmony, his voice raspy yet more falsetto than I expected.

We rode along while he serenaded me for a minute or so before he turned the music down.

"You know this song?" he asked, eyes trained on me through the rearview mirror.

He'd noticed me reflexively mouthing the words.

"It's Mad Season," I said. "'Long Gone Day.'"

"Interesting. Do you know their story?"

Of course I did. This was a relatively obscure band, but it was my job to know as much about music as possible. "That's Layne Staley's supergroup." I referenced the lead singer of the band Alice in Chains. Staley and Mike McCready, a guitarist from Pearl Jam, formed Mad Season as a band exclusively composed of musicians recovering from drug addiction. Their goal was to use music as a catalyst for recovery, but the group lasted only a few years before Staley and the group's bassist relapsed and died.

He nodded, seemingly impressed. "I'm glad not all kids listen to garbage." As insane as it sounds, that compliment from my kidnapper stroked my ego, and I began to calm down, which could have been precisely what he was going for. "Maybe you're too young to be listening to this? It's dark stuff. But I guess it's better than that hood music you all love."

Here he was, possibly on his way to execute me, yet he was lecturing me on my generation's music tastes. I should have just let the comment go, but I couldn't help myself.

"They're just describing the world they know." I was suddenly confident. We were on my terrain. I could bullshit about music all day. "Those grunge guys are from Seattle, where the sun never shines, and everyone seems to be on drugs. Wu-Tang is from Park Hill, which I'm sure you know is a messed-up place. They're all broken in some kind of way." I gestured to the rundown buildings and townhomes along Victory. "They aren't lucky like you and me. They don't get to spend their time in beautiful Fresh Kills."

He smiled and turned up the music. I stared out the window, wondering where Georgia was. She had to have gotten away. Otherwise, she'd be in the car with me. Was she waiting for me at Sicilian Swirls?

We were heading toward Travis, which eased my nerves a bit. If he wanted to kill me, he wouldn't bring me back to my hometown to do it. Then again, he could be taking me to the dump to do to me what he likely did to that woman the night before.

We drove through the heart of town, past St. Anthony's. The streets were completely empty—the heat and humidity nudging all of Travis to their air conditioners and above-ground pools. If I could find one friendly face, I could pound on the car window and make a scene.

To my relief, we stopped at The Linoleum halfway through town. This was directly across the street from Phene's, but we were in the back driveway, obscured from view.

The goon parked in front of the back door and pulled the key out of the ignition. "I'm Ugo," he said, breathing heavily, "with a *U*, not an *H*."

"I'm Raj."

"I know who you are."

I could have interpreted that as a threat, but it didn't come across as one.

"I don't need any trouble," he continued. "I'm going to come around to your door and let you out. We're going to walk casually into the bar together. Can I count on you to do that, or will I need to take you somewhere else?"

I nodded and followed him out of the car and through the back door. The last time I'd been in The Linoleum was the previous fall, during a Sunday afternoon Giants game. Then it was filled, as it usually was, with Travis's least responsible adults: the alcoholics, cokeheads, and gamblers. Now it was totally transformed. There were two older mobsters at the bar smoking cigars and reading the newspaper, a bartender who looked to be installing an espresso machine where the old margarita mixer used to be, and a table of younger guys at the front in wifebeaters playing cards. One had a gun in a holster on his belt.

Ugo sat me alone at a table across from the bar. "Keep your mouth shut," he ordered me before disappearing into a back room.

The two older men at the bar were in the middle of a heated argument about the news. Mayor Rudolph Giuliani had announced fresh "quality of life" measures that week, which essentially meant another slate of policies aimed at micromanaging New York City's residents. That sparked a debate about who they preferred: former Mayor Dinkins or the current mayor. Giuliani was a bit of a puzzle for the mobsters because he was Italian American, but he'd led the prosecution of the mob before running for mayor. That made Rudy, according to these guys, a traitor to his people. On the other hand, Dinkins was Black, which to one of the older gangsters, was more of a mark against him than anything Giuliani did.

The discussion turned to a business news story. A rival crew had bought up a series of medical clinics, which seemed to puzzle the two men.

"What would those Brighton Beach boys want with clinics?"

"Anthony told me they'd also bought up some medical supply company in December."

"Are they going legit?"

"Get the fuck outta here. We'd go legit before those Russians ever would."

"Gotta be a wash operation."

"Why health care, though? If you're gonna wash, why pick businesses where the government's all up in your ass with regulations, inspections, and all that shit?"

I should have kept my mouth shut, but I had their answer. "Medicare."

Not only did that comment stop the men at the bar but it also turned some heads at the poker table at the front.

"Who the fuck are you, kid?" one of the men asked. "Didn't I hear Ugo tell you to shut your mouth until he returned?"

"I—"

The other man cut in before I could answer. "Wait, what do you mean, 'Medicare?'"

"May I?" I asked the other man. He looked at his friend for a few seconds, skeptical, before nodding to me to proceed.

I stood up and gave a mini-lecture about everything I knew about nursing-home fraud, which I learned from my mother, who'd witnessed it firsthand at one of the homes she'd worked at. The stolen Medicare numbers, fake licenses, and false claims. I was no expert, but it seemed a more straightforward and lucrative scam than the garbage business.

"So the beards are ripping off the government?" He referred to the Orthodox Jews, who've long dominated the nursing-home industry in New York City.

"They are at my mom's nursing home. And if they're doing it there, then why wouldn't they do it elsewhere?"

"The Brighton Boys must have picked up on that and decided to get in on the game. They all live in the same neighborhoods."

I shrugged. "That'd be my guess."

"Then why medical suppliers?"

Before I could answer, I heard that familiar abrasive falsetto behind me. "What the fuck are you doing?" Ugo stood behind me but directed his question to the men at the bar.

"This kid is smart, Ugo," one of the men protested. "Maybe we should put him on the payroll."

And just like that, with blazing speed, Ugo reached behind the bar, grabbed a bottle of vodka, and smashed it across the man's face. Unfortunately for the man, the bottle was full, so it didn't break, acting more like a heavy club. It knocked him off his stool and sent him flying against the wall across from the bar, depositing him on the floor. Nobody lifted a finger to help him. Everyone in the room just stared silently at the unconscious heap.

Ugo dragged me to the back of the bar by my shirt into what used to be the billiard room. He sat me down at one end of the folding table and left without saying anything. The space had been completely transformed. Gone were the pool and air hockey tables. The room had a spartan feel, with a folding table and plastic chairs. The Budweiser signs and dartboards had been pulled from the wall, now painted white instead of the emerald green it used to be. Only one picture hung on the wall: a sketch of an old, scary-looking man with sunken cheeks and black eyes.

The only object on the table was what looked to be a foot-long U-shaped golden object. I ran my fingers along its surface, trying to see if it was, in fact, real gold. Not that I had any idea what real gold felt like.

"Do you know what that is?" a voice asked from the doorway.

Like a toddler touching a hot stove, I pulled my hand back and jerked my head toward the entrance. "I'm sorry, sir," I said. "I shouldn't have touched it."

Dante Malaparte stood just within the frame in a gray suit and his trademark slicked-back dark hair. The papers made him out to be a titanic figure, but he wasn't that much taller than I was and probably didn't weigh much more, either.

"I asked you a question." Dante's voice boomed deeper and louder than what you'd expect to come from a small body. It's almost like he and Ugo had swapped voices. "What is it?" He sat across from me at the folding table, not breaking his stare. His tidy face was muscular, clean-shaven, and devoid of color, save for the dark bags below his eyes. His high cheekbones and long eyelashes gave him a mildly feminine look— like an aged former lead singer of a boy band.

Ugo stood against the wall, arms folded in front of him like a bouncer at a club.

"I don't know," I said, flustered. "A horseshoe?"

That got a laugh from Dante. "What kind of mutant horse would need a shoe like that? Ugo, you said this kid was smart?" Ugo looked at me and winked, a puzzling gesture from someone who'd just abducted me and smashed a man in the face for speaking to me. Whatever mind games these guys were playing, they were working. I was unsure what to expect next: an ice cream cone or a bullet in the head.

Dante pulled the object off the table and ran his fingers along the inside of the semicircle. "It's a toilet seat. I had the boys coat it in gold. They thought it was some kind of trophy for our dominance of the trash business. But that's not quite what it is."

He stood up, lifted the shades, and pointed toward Fresh Kills. "Like you, I grew up next to the dump. Arden Heights. My dad was a sanitation worker, an honest man. Operated the bulldozers up there. Died of cancer before he could even cash his first pension check. My ma tried to sue the city because she had this crazy idea that a man who'd never smoked a cigarette could have only acquired his cancer from breathing in sewage for ten hours a day. The city sent men to my house and threatened her that they'd block the pension checks if she didn't drop the suit. So, of course, she did as she was told."

"I'm sorry about your dad," I mumbled.

Dante's face relaxed for a barely perceptible moment. It felt like a peek behind a mask, a glimmer of humanity. "Me too." His eyes narrowed and jaw clenched, the mask back on. "But sorry doesn't get us anywhere, does it?"

He again sat down across from me. "The politicians have promised the city for fifty years they'd close this thing, but they never will. That's why we need to take it."

"Makes sense." I wasn't exactly sold on Dante's intentions, but I didn't want to anger him.

"Every day of my life, the fat cats in Manhattan have sent us all the shit they don't have to deal with: their dirty diapers, rotten food. Never give it a second thought. That ignorance is our advantage. If they don't want to know what happens to that stuff when it leaves their house, that makes it a perfect business for us. Better to pick a trade that's out of sight and out of mind. That's why I had them make this toilet seat for me. To remind us of the value in other people's waste."

This was a goofy villain origin story if I'd ever heard one. Only Staten Island could produce a gang whose symbol was a golden toilet seat. I found myself briefly sympathizing with Dante. Then I thought of the woman tied up the night before and the countless press accounts of the growing list of his enemies and competitors who've gone missing. I found it hard to look him in the eyes, so I let my gaze wander around the room, eventually locking on the one picture of the stern-looking old man hanging on the wall.

"Is that your father?"

Again, he laughed. "No, that's John Brown."

I studied the picture one more time. "The guy from the history textbooks?" We'd read about Brown in social studies class. About the abolitionists' failed raid on Harper's Ferry. Dante didn't strike me as a history buff.

"I bet they taught you in school that he was crazy, right?"

"We didn't really spend too much time on him if I remember right. It was a few sentences in the Civil War unit."

"That's a shame. He was a revolutionary. Even Frederick Douglass said Brown was more dedicated to the cause than he was. Brown knew the most important lesson for outlaws like us: that your code is only meaningful if you're willing to die for it."

He ran his hand through his hair, then pointed a greasy index finger at me. "That brings me to my first question: Do you know why you're here?"

"No, sir." I wondered what he meant by that creepy transition, what his question had to do with dying for a cause.

"That's a lie," he said without emotion or hesitation. "We'll call that strike one. Try again."

I had to choose my words carefully. "Well . . ." I gripped the underside of my chair, my sweaty thighs sticking to the cheap plastic. "Because I was at the dump last night."

"Correct." He pulled from his suit jacket my yellow Discman and laid it on the table in front of me. It was covered in mud from the dump and placed inside a ziplock bag. I stared at it, wondering how he'd so quickly linked it back to me. "Second question: Why were you in the dump?"

I told him about Sal and his crew and how they'd chased me into Fresh Kills.

"Why not stay and fight?"

"I would have gotten my ass kicked. Better to live to fight another day."

"That's the coward's way," he snapped back.

I didn't know what to say to that. "I may not be a hero, but I'm not stupid either."

"Another honest answer. You're learning. And what did you see?"

"I saw two of your men digging a hole and a woman tied up next to them."

"How'd you know they were my men?"

"Well, Ugo drove me here. I'd also seen him and the other guy outside this bar earlier that day. So I put two and two together."

"I see. So tell me, why does one of my men have a hole in the side of his head? He was in the hospital all night getting stitches."

Stitches? So he wasn't dead? That was a huge relief and explained why I was still alive.

"I tried to save the woman." I deliberately omitted any mention of Georgia and Val. "Your guy chased me."

"Why save her? If you know anything about me, you must know not to get mixed up in our business. You must have known I'd find you."

"I wasn't really thinking."

"Clearly." He paused for a few beats and looked me over like a cat would a cornered mouse. "Yet, you left her."

"She hurt her leg. Your men were coming for me. She told me to go alone."

"How did you know to go to her house?"

"She told me to before I left her."

"What else did she tell you?"

For a brief second, I held eye contact with Ugo, who was watching me with some concern. We'd reached a critical point in my interrogation. I had to tread carefully.

"Not much." I searched for the right words. "She said to get her computer but didn't say what was on it. She also said I shouldn't go to the cops."

"Why did you listen to her? Why not leave it alone? After all, you aren't a hero. You said so yourself."

"I'm a curious person. I wanted to know what could possibly have gotten her in such trouble."

"Do you really want to know?" Dante pulled out a cigarette and lit the tip before he sat back and took a long drag, never taking his eyes off me.

I shot another glance at Ugo, who ever so slightly shook his head.

"That's okay," I said. "I've had enough excitement for one weekend."

"Smart boy," Dante said. "Who else knows about what you saw?"

I thought long and hard about this one. I didn't want to give up Georgia, but I wasn't sure what these guys already knew. I still had two strikes left, so I decided to take a chance.

"Just me."

"Strike two," Dante said. Ugo slouched and stared at the floor. He'd probably witnessed Dante's wrath enough to know what would happen next.

"Okay, okay," I clarified. "A few of my friends know about last night."

"A few?"

"Four of them."

"I'm going to need their names. Especially the name of whoever hit Renzo with that rock."

"How do you know that wasn't me?"

"A hunch."

"None of my friends know what's on the computer."

"At least one of them might. My men chased a girl out of that house. She scaled a ten-foot fence carrying a desktop. Strong girl. My guy busted up his knee trying to keep up with her. That's two of my men in the hospital, in case you're counting."

I didn't know what to say to that. Georgia had racked up quite the casualty list.

"Who is she?"

I couldn't be sure what they would do to Georgia if I gave them her name. But if I didn't, I was pretty sure what they'd do to me. That meant only one thing: I needed to buy time and find a third option.

"Given this is baseball and all, can I have a foul ball?" I asked.

Ugo's face twisted into a confused grimace.

Dante smiled. "A foul ball?"

"Yes. I won't lie and say I don't know who she is. But I can't tell you the truth either."

"Sure you can."

"Remember what you said about John Brown, that he had a code?"

"I do. He died for that code."

"I don't want to die for my code, but I will," I said, surprised by my own words. "Among my crew, we don't rat each other out. That's our number one rule."

"Your crew?"

"Yes. We call ourselves the Victory Boys."

Dante erupted in laughter. "The Victory Boys? Ain't that something? How cute. I see. But she's a girl."

"She's new. Not officially a member, but the same rules apply."

"You like this girl?"

"I do."

"You're trying to impress her?"

"Right now, I'm just trying to stay alive."

"Do you love your mom, Raj?" He emphasized the *J*—using my name for the first time. "What's her name?" he asked, looking at Ugo. "Oh yes, Lori, right?"

"That's her." I shifted in my seat. "How did you know that? And how do you know my name?"

"Don't insult me." He stood, leaned against the windowsill, and took another long drag of his cigarette. "Part of me says I should have Ugo twist your testicles and see how long your code lasts. The other part of me is curious whether you'd find this girl faster than we would. It's hard to find good help these days. And given you haven't gone to the cops yet, I'm inclined to spare your little nuts for now. I'd also rather not disappear two teenagers if I can help it. It wouldn't be the first time, believe me, but I try to keep the harsher parts of this business between grown-ups. So, I will let you go, under one condition: that you find this young lady and bring me the computer. If I'm convinced that neither of you has copied the contents of the computer or plans to go to the cops, I will forget we ever crossed paths. How does that sound?"

"It sounds great, but I have one question."

"Indulge me."

"What about your man with the stitches? Won't he want revenge?"

Dante looked at Ugo. "This kid, he likes to reach right into the wood chipper." He looked back at me. "That *gavone* is my cousin Renzo. He's a bit embarrassed he got his ass handed to him by a bunch of kids. Never mind if it turns out, as I suspect, that it was a little girl who put him there. He says he tripped and hit his head. He's fortunate he didn't have many brains to lose, and even more lucky Ugo here can keep a secret. If word got around, no one would take him seriously again."

I stood. "Thank you, Dante. I mean, sir. I'll make sure that doesn't happen."

"Sit down. I'm not finished."

I gulped, easing back into my seat.

Dante continued. "Let's get one thing straight. If, for some reason, you fail in this mission, then Ugo here will take you, your lady, and your mom on a short ride up to the dump. We have a giant hole up there; we can either throw the computer in there or, well, you get the picture."

I grabbed the arms of my chair, trying to keep from shaking. Getting myself killed was one thing. Dragging my mom into this was something else entirely. I took a deep breath and tried to keep my voice steady. "Understood. Can you give me a week?"

"You have forty-eight hours. That means Monday. What time is it?" he asked Ugo.

"3:13," Ugo said.

"I'm feeling generous. Let's round up. Monday at 3:14. Can you remember that?"

"Yes, sir." I saluted. "3:14. Like pi."

"You're an odd little freak. Let's hope I don't have to kill you."

CHAPTER 11

THE
(WO)MANHUNT

The Linoleum spat me out like a chewed piece of gum onto the sidewalk. My pupils, dilated from the dim bar, were now assaulted by a sun that seemed to punch my retinas with fists of light. As my vision cleared, Travis materialized before me like a developing polaroid. Everything looked more vibrant, more alive—as if the neighborhood had a fresh coat of paint. I'd survived another close call, but there was no time to savor the moment. I had to find Georgia.

Across the street, Chickie leaned against a telephone pole outside Phene's, a lit cigarette dangling from his lips. Our eyes locked for a fleeting second, and any relief I felt morphed into a deep sense of shame. My new mission implicated me in the cover-up of whatever happened to that mystery woman. I didn't know who she was or what, if anything, she'd done to deserve her fate. Just because I had little choice in the matter didn't make it right. Like me, she could have been an innocent person caught in the middle of something beyond her control.

It had been a mistake to leave through the front door of The Linoleum. While I could bullshit most people, it would be hard to spin Chickie on why I was in a mob bar on a Saturday afternoon. I had no time to squabble with him, so I stayed on my side of Victory and speed walked in the opposite direction.

Dante's men could be following me, and I didn't want to lead them to Georgia's house. My legs were on autopilot, propelling me in the opposite direction of her—and my—house. They stopped at a worn duplex of plain brick and white aluminum siding: Val's place. These houses sprouted up in the '80s when the island's quirky zoning laws prevented the construction of anything with more than two units under one roof. The west shore of Staten Island, once a swampy wasteland, had been transformed into a sprawling landscape of ugly townhomes, each unit identical to the next—like a scrunched-together, low-income Levittown. Though Travis resisted the full-scale redevelopment of neighborhoods like New Springville, those cheap duplexes like Val's dotted our blocks like spots of acne.

Val's mom, Pattie, sat in a lawn chair on the small patch of brown grass that comprised their front yard. She was sunning herself in a bikini, listening to Phil Collins on a radio perched at an open window. No kid in Travis would say so to Val, but she was hot. And not just hot for a forty-something-year-old. She had that Goldie Hawn ditzy blonde look that didn't crack with age. Every eligible bachelor in Travis—and quite a few married men—had pursued her at one point or another, but she never so much as went on a date after Val's father passed.

She sat up and straddled the chair. "Hey, hon." Her tanning oil–soaked skin was glistening in the sun. "Did your ma make it to work okay?"

"You know it." I kept my eyes low, trying to avoid staring at her chest.

She and my mom had been best friends since high school and still hung out on the rare occasions my mom was up for it. Pattie was always game, and it seemed from her question that the night before must have been one of those rare occasions.

Unlike my mom, Pattie hadn't pulled it together and gotten a job after her husband was gone. Instead, she'd spiraled into alcoholism. She'd spent many nights in The Linoleum before Dante took it over, while her bills went unpaid and their house went into foreclosure. They went on welfare and were forced to move from their large home with a half-acre of land on our block to this decrepit townhome closer to the dump. If I were Val, I wouldn't be able to get over the riches-to-rags turnaround, but he never so much as acknowledged it.

"She's a saint, that Lori," Pattie said. "No one works harder. You know how lucky you are?"

"Very." My eyes were still fixed on the ground.

"Don't forget it."

"I won't, Pattie. Is Val home?"

"Out back."

I found Val in what passed for their backyard. He was shirtless with a hose aimed at his mom's '83 white Chevy Monte Carlo. It was a beautiful piece of Americana, with sleek, curved lines and a long, wide hood. But the car was a money pit and a death trap—with rust that spread like a rash from the fenders to the wheel wells. Because it had belonged to Val's dad, his mom refused to sell it.

Val directed the stream of water at my feet, chuckling as I tap-danced in my cleats to avoid it. As annoying as he could be, it calmed me down to see him in a lighter mood.

"Funny." I made my way to turn off the hose's valve.

"Mom's letting me use the Monte tonight." He spun the hose like a lasso, uncomfortably close to my face. "A bunch of Todt Hill kids are throwing a party tonight."

Todt Hill, with its multimillion-dollar mansions and sweeping views of the Verrazzano and Manhattan, was the enclave of Staten Island's elite.

"Academy jerk-offs?" I'd never met a kid from Staten Island Academy I liked.

"Academy chicks. It will be good to get the crew out to party. They need it. You can invite the girl." We had more pressing business to discuss, but it wasn't lost on me how eager he seemed to invite Georgia.

Val proceeded to fill me in on his and Mercedes's return to the dump in search of my Discman—an operation that, of course, failed because Dante's crew had gotten it first.

"Our mission was a lot more action-packed." I told him about my trip to the mystery woman's house with Georgia, the run-in with Dante, and how Renzo was alive.

"That's huge. So, we're golden?"

"Golden? He threatened my mom. He knew her name, my name, too. Said he had a hole already dug for us up in the dump."

Val tossed aside his hose with a pensive expression as he perched on the hood of the car. "Then we don't have much choice, do we? We gotta find Georgia and get Dante that computer."

Joining him on the hood, I mulled over an alternative. "There is one more option. We could still go to the cops. To Booch." Up until my meeting with Dante, I'd thought we could ignore what we'd seen and hope nothing would happen. That was no longer an option. Now that my mom was in danger, I was starting to think we had to acknowledge we needed help.

Val drew out a cigarette and took a deep drag. "We could do that. We're talking about Dante Blue Eyes, though. No telling who on the force he's got on the payroll. What do they call him? The Crisco Don? Nothing ever sticks to him."

"You think Booch is on the take?" The possibility of Booch playing both sides had been on my mind and was probably what drove my nightmare. Of course, I didn't have any evidence to implicate her, but we couldn't put her past Dante's reach.

"Who can say? How well do you know her?"

A fair question. Though she was my next-door neighbor, we weren't close. She never socialized or so much as shared any personal details with anyone in the neighborhood. What little we knew about her Brooklyn past was from unreliable neighborhood gossip. Even if she was clean, which I wanted to believe, she seemed like the type who was so by the book that she might inadvertently tip off the wrong person in her precinct.

I reached for Val's pack of cigarettes. "Give me one."

He pulled the box away before I could grasp it. "One of what?" He knew full well what I meant. Like any teenager on the island, I'd smoked cigarettes before. Though I wasn't a regular smoker like most of my friends—and most adults in Travis, for that matter. They made me light-headed, which seemed appealing at the moment.

"Just give me one, you dick."

He stuffed the pack in his pocket. "Hold yourself together, Raj. We have a simple task. We find Georgia and take that computer to Dante. When the time comes, I'll go with you to deliver the computer to him."

That comment put me at ease. It was reassuring to think of this as a team effort. I straightened up and pulled my shoulders back.

"There's only so much he can do if we're all together in this. Even a psycho like him ain't gonna disappear a bunch of kids."

"He doesn't need to kill all of us, just me. That would send a message to all of you to keep quiet. One day I'll be crossing Victory and *bam*, a hit-and-run."

Val smiled. "I can see you've put some thought into this."

"It's not funny."

"Let's find Georgia, and then Dante won't have any reason to do anything. Where do we think she is?"

"I told her that if there was trouble, to meet me at Sicilian Swirls. I doubt she'd still be there, but we can check there first."

He slapped the hood of the car. "I'll take the Monte. You should go home, shower, get something to eat, and change out of those ridiculous clothes. We'll have this solved by the end of the day, and we hit that party tonight."

That sounded appealing, but I wasn't ready to split up again. And part of me didn't love the prospect of Georgia and Val spending time together without me. "No. I'm coming with you."

"Whatever you say, boss. Hop in."

"Wait, they may be following me. Dante's men. You leave in the Monty, and I'll hop this fence and meet you on Marble," I said, referring to the street behind Val's house. "Drive around the neighborhood a bit to make sure you don't have a tail, then pick me up if you're certain you're clear."

Val threw on his tank top. "Smart. I'll take this down the service road for a spin, then come back around. A half-mile straightaway. No way to tail me there without being seen."

"One more thing. When I ran into Sal and the rest of the Springville boys, I told them we'd fight them Monday night."

"We?"

"Our crew versus their crew."

"We've got other shit to worry about, Raj. Why the fuck would you promise that?"

The tone and insinuation of his question almost set me off. We wouldn't have been in this mess with Sal's crew or Dante's if Val hadn't picked a fight at the mall the week before. He's the one who should have been answering questions. But I needed Val and didn't want to risk pissing him off.

"I was trying to distract them. We were in front of the woman's house. I didn't want them to see Georgia coming out with the computer."

"I see. Where and when is this royal rumble?"

"The Alba House," I said. "Seven p.m."

"Why the Alba House?"

"I didn't exactly have much time to think it through. I figured we know the area, and the Westerleigh kids are our boys, so if we run into trouble, they'll have our backs."

We'd been playing the kids from Westerleigh in tackle football at the Alba House for years, and we'd often stick around to drink and party with them. Though we'd recently stopped because the nuns started calling the cops on us. The Westerleigh kids also had beef with the Springville kids, which could come in handy.

"I'm not even sure Sal is gonna come, though. Dante's guy showed up before we could confirm the details."

"Then, as far as I'm concerned, there is no fight."

I wanted to let the subject go, but I couldn't help myself. "We gotta stop fighting. I take the brunt of this stuff. You won't always be around to protect me."

"I'll always be around, even when I'm not."

"What does that mean?"

"It means stop being a pussy. I'm not going anywhere. Even if I'm not at Wagner, I've got your back. I'll come up there myself and kick Sal's ass every day next school year if I have to."

"I don't want that. All I want is to be left alone. To run my business."

"You think you'll be left alone if we didn't start shit with those guys? They are predators. Without us, you'll be a defenseless gazelle." He playfully patted me on the head.

I swatted away his hand. "You should come back to school."

Val crossed his arms and looked away. "Fuck that." This was a sore subject for him.

With both of our moms at work most of the time, Val and I had a lot of time to cook up schemes. At first, this meant typical seasonal stuff that occupied most kid entrepreneurs: mowing lawns, shoveling snow, and raking leaves. Val was a natural at anything related to landscaping and would go above and beyond to provide a service better than adult companies often did. I had a knack for the business side, consolidating the neighborhood kids and fixing the prices of standard kid jobs. By the time I was in eighth grade, most of the boys in our neighborhood worked for us. It was that cartel of sorts that originally earned the Victory Boys name.

Our work quickly morphed into more risky trades like a short-lived business selling recycled exams that I was forced to fold after a Travis kid raised suspicion after going from straight Fs to perfect grades. That's when I pivoted to the black-market CD business. By then, Val had dropped out of school just as our venture started to attract the attention of rival crews. Needless to say, it was a hostile business climate.

"Seriously," I pressed. "You're gonna be eighteen in no time. Then what?"

"Tree climbing."

"Tree climbing? I said eighteen, not eight."

"I'm serious. My cousin Jeff has been learning it. They go up in tall trees and trim the branches. Makes over a hundred an hour."

"Over a hundred? Dollars?"

"Per person."

"Seriously? That's brain surgeon money."

"He and I are saving up to buy a bucket truck. Like the ones Con Edison has with the arm that stretches way up high—with the little basket thing at the end."

"Those must be expensive."

"We found a used truck for fifty thousand. Jeff has fifteen saved up, and I have fifteen now. We're getting close. Then we can hire our own crew."

"You've done this tree climbing?"

"Jeff's been teaching me here and there. While you're over there adding up fractions and shit, I'm learning how to do real work."

"Here I was thinking you guys were doing normal landscaping."

He pulled open the driver's side door. "Fuck that. Lawn mowing is chump change."

I know he was just messing with me, but that comment stung. I was a bit jealous that he and Jeff were hatching a workable business scheme without me.

"It got you that GT Comp," I said, referring to the BMX bike Val bought with our lawn mowing proceeds two summers before.

"We're past that kid shit," Val said, depositing himself in the driver's seat and slamming the clunky metal door. "Enough with the career counseling. Let's get moving. I'll meet you on Marble Street in five."

With that, he fired up the engine and sped out of the driveway, spinning up a wave of muddy water in my face.

—

Val's five minutes stretched into a half hour. I'd been waiting in the middle of Marble Street, one of the denser blocks in Travis. On most summer Saturdays, kids would fill the street while adults relaxed on their stoops. Yet it was uncharacteristically deserted that day, perhaps because of the record humidity. It was the kind of silence that felt like a warning.

The empty houses, packed closely together, seemed to lean on each other like they were sharing secrets.

My beeper's battery light pulsed red, a ticking clock. If we didn't link up soon, we'd have no way to communicate. As I waited, my anxiety morphed from irritation and concern. Where was Val?

Just when I'd started to lose hope, a car turned the corner and cruised toward me. I squinted against the sun's glare, expecting to see Val's Monte. Instead, a dark blue Crown Victoria lumbered into view. It bore all the hallmarks of a "DT"—a detective car: tinted windows, steel wheels with hubcaps, and inconspicuous antennae on the roof. The car zipped past me, only to decelerate and halt about twenty yards ahead, then reverse, coming to a stop directly in front of me. The tinted windows rolled down.

"What are you doing?" Detective Booch had both hands firmly on the steering wheel.

"Um, me?" I asked, trying to buy time. Booch didn't typically patrol the neighborhood, no less on a Saturday afternoon. Something was clearly up.

"Yes, you," she said, uninflected and stone-faced.

"I'm, uh, playing capture the flag."

"Capture the flag?"

"My team's flag is in Val's backyard, so I'm guarding the rear entrance to his house."

She eyed me skeptically. "Is this your capture the flag outfit?"

I looked down at my muddy cleats and stretched-out mesh tank. "Cleats give me better traction for climbing trees."

She didn't return so much as a smile. "I see. How many of you are playing?"

I hesitated, sensing a trap. "All of us. Val, Deadbolt, Cheetah, Mercedes, the new girl, the Kowalski kids." I had an unfortunate tendency to yammer and get overly specific when I lied.

"All of you?" She looked around at the empty street. "Funny. I haven't seen any of them around."

I swallowed hard. "Our boundaries are pretty big. We go all the way to Schmul. Victory is our dividing line." Again, more information than necessary.

She stroked her chin and tilted her head back. "Have you seen anything unusual around here this morning?"

I blinked. "Unusual?"

She leaned in. "Unusual."

"Like what?"

"You tell me." A trained interrogator at work—careful, concise, wielding silence as a weapon.

"Can't say I have, but I'll keep an eye out."

"How about last night? See anything strange then?"

"Last night?" I tried to shorten my answers to avoid saying something suspicious.

"Yes."

"I was at the UA. Everyone was." This was not technically an answer to her question.

"Nothing strange around there?"

"Just the usual." *Other than the goons who chased us into the dump or the likely murder we witnessed.*

"The usual?"

"Yes, ma'am. Last day of school. A lot of hanging around."

"Did you see anyone go into the dump?"

The lump in my throat ballooned, and a sense of unease washed over me. *What did she know? Did they discover the woman's body? Did she hear about our sprint through the bowling alley?*

"To the dump?" I stammered. "Why would anyone go up there?"

"Do me a favor." She ignored my deflection, and her voice softened. "If you see or hear anything, let me know."

"I'll keep my eyes peeled." The eagerness in my voice failed to convince even me.

I expected her to drive off just then, but she sat there and stared at me—her eyes narrowed to slits—as if she had something to say but was unsure whether she wanted to.

Just as I thought she was about to come out with whatever was on her mind, an indecipherable call went out over the radio. She picked up the handset. "Booch here, I copy. En route." Without another word, she drove off.

On cue, when she disappeared around the bend, Val rolled up in his Monte with the windows open, blasting Pantera. I'd say it was perfect timing if he wasn't so late.

I turned the dial down to zero when I got in the passenger side. "Are you crazy? We're trying to avoid notice."

"Acting normal is the best way to avoid notice."

"Whatever. Where've you been? I almost went home."

"I thought someone was following me, so I went on the highway, got off, and turned around."

"*Was* someone following you?"

Val turned the wheel, depositing us onto Victory. "If they were, they aren't anymore."

"What made you think someone was following?"

"A green Ford Explorer got off at the service road at the same time I did and followed me onto the Expressway. Didn't take my exit though, so probably just a coincidence."

I told Val about my encounter with Booch, and he suggested we check the news. I fiddled with the radio, turning to the only AM news station I knew.

It's a big day for New York sports fans, with both the Knicks and the Yankees in action. The Knicks are facing off against the Indiana Pacers in game six of the NBA Eastern Conference Finals at Madison Square Garden. The series is tied two and two, and the winner of this game will . . .

"Put on the news, not sports talk," Val barked.

"This is the news. Ten-Ten. Hang on."

After a few minutes on the Knicks, the news lineup reset itself.

You're listening to Ten-Ten News. Give us twenty-two minutes, and we'll give you the world. We have some breaking news out of Brooklyn. Yesterday, prosecutors dropped charges against nineteen-year-old Ramon Cable of Queens, who had been accused of opening fire at the Fulton Mall on May eighteenth, wounding eight people. According to a law-enforcement official, speaking on condition of anonymity, a security videotape placed Mr. Cable in an elevator about twenty miles from the mall within thirty minutes of the shooting. Prosecutors felt that such evidence warranted Mr. Cable's release.

The charges were dismissed without prejudice, which means they could be reinstated if new evidence comes to light. Patrick Clark, a spokesman for the Brooklyn District Attorney's office, says investigators will continue to look for clues as to who fired the shots. In other news, a state supreme court judge yesterday issued a ruling that could have major implications for the city's taxi industry. According to lawyers for both the city and an industry group suing to overturn the rules, the Taxi and Limousine Commission apparently violated the state's open meetings law . . .

I lowered the radio. "If they found the body of a woman in the dump, they wouldn't lead with the Taxi Commission."

We made our way down Travis Avenue, a lonely road slicing through protected marshland that skirted the dump's border. I stuck my head out the window. It felt like we'd been spirited away to a remote wilderness. The landscape surrounding us was stunning, with towering grasses swaying in the breeze and birds flitting in and out of the foliage. It was hard to believe that such natural beauty could exist in the world's biggest city, a few miles from the largest accumulation of waste known to man.

I pulled my head back in. "Are we going at this wrong? Should we try to find this woman? Or at least find out more about her?"

Val sighed. "We need to stay in our lane. We've only got forty-eight hours to get that computer to Dante. We gotta protect you and your ma first."

"She could still be alive, that woman."

As we reached the end of the road, strip malls and duplexes gradually appeared, jolting us out of the idyllic scenery of Travis Avenue and into the gaudy aesthetic of New Springville.

Val flicked the turn signal. "Dante didn't say anything about her?"

"Not much."

We turned down Richmond Avenue, New Springville's busiest thoroughfare—their equivalent of Victory.

"Well, let's find Georgia as fast as possible, then we can figure out the rest. How long has it been since she was supposed to meet you at Sicilian Swirls?"

"Over two hours now."

"She strike you as the type to wait around?"

"No, but we're here, so we may as well check."

We pulled into the parking lot of Sicilian Swirls. It was a large compound whose main attraction was a small ice cream stand in the front adorned with a white, green, and red awning and a cheerful sign bearing a cartoon of a rotund Italian man holding a soft-serve cone. It was also uncharacteristically empty for a Saturday. It seemed like the entire island was in hiding.

Val and I walked up to the stand's window and out popped the head of Klodian Kadare, the owner's son. Everyone called him "Klo." His family was part of a growing trend on the island of Albanian food entrepreneurs who tried to pass as Italian.

"The Victory Boys. To what do I owe the honor?" He was tall and lanky, with long black hair and androgynous, angular features. He looked and carried himself like Keanu Reeves from *Bill & Ted's Excellent Adventure*.

"Klo!" Val tussled Klo's hair. "How've you been, brother?"

"Same old, same old. School's out, so my dad's got me on this grind."

"I hear you," Val said. "You hitting the shore at all?" Klo was an avid surfer, and his family had a house on the Jersey Shore. That made Klo popular around the island, especially as summer approached and everyone wanted a weekend invite.

"Dude, not this summer. My dad rented out the house. Says it's time for me to learn the family business."

"Brutal," Val said.

I'd lost my patience with the banter. "Klo, we're in a bit of a rush. Can I ask you something?"

"Raj, always all business." Klo chuckled.

"Sorry, man," I said. "But did you see a young girl hanging around here earlier? My age. Like five feet. Dirty-blonde hair. Blue eyes."

"Oh man," he said. "This morning was busy. What was she wearing?"

"Jean shorts and a yellow tank top. She was supposed to meet us here a few hours ago."

He thought about that for a second. "Sorry, guys. Can't say I remember her."

We were interrupted by the screeching sound of tires from Richmond Avenue. A car careened into the parking lot, skidding to a stop across two handicapped spots. It was a shiny, new two-tone Mitsubishi Eclipse, sporting a bold red upper body and sleek silver side skirts. The car was an absolute stunner, with a low-slung profile, a streamlined, aerodynamic shape, and pop-up headlights.

The driver-side door flung open, and out stepped Ornela Kadare, Klo's sister. Like Klo, she had sharp features, with cheekbones like blades cutting through the air and a jawline strong and chiseled like the edge of a cliff. But she had none of Klo's easygoing charm.

"Hi, Raj," she tossed off, without even looking me in the eyes, and then swiftly planted a kiss on Val's cheek.

"I haven't seen you around school in a while." She tilted her body slightly away from him.

Val leaned against the ice cream stand with his arms crossed. "I've been busy."

It was like watching two prize fighters sizing each other up at a weigh-in. Neither wanted to give an inch while they attempted to assert dominance.

"Any fun plans tonight?" She twirled her dark flowing hair, which tumbled down her back in loose waves.

"We're heading to Todt Hill for a party," Val said.

"Todt Hill? You chasing Academy chicken heads now?"

"Woah there, you don't have to—" Val halted midsentence, catching a subtle shake of the head from Klo that warned him not to venture further.

"Don't have to what?" Ornela's deep brown almond-shaped eyes suddenly flashed with fire.

"I think what Val means to ask is whether you want to come with us," I said, jumping on the grenade.

"We'll see," she said. "Val, you have my number?"

"I don't think so," Val said.

He definitely had her number.

"Klo can give it to you." She approached her brother at the window. "You can give him my pager number, too. Hit me up before you head there."

"Anything else, Your Highness?" Klo asked.

"Yes. I need two hundred bucks."

"For what?"

"None of your business."

"It is my business when I come up two hundred dollars short later and have to explain it to Pop."

"He told me it's fine."

"I'll let you two work this out," I interjected. "Do you mind if we look around back in the lot for any trace of our friend?"

Klo waved us in. "Go ahead. And help yourself to anything in the fridge room."

We stepped through an opening in the gate into the yard where they stored dozens of ice cream trucks. The lot was more extensive than I'd imagined, with rows of empty parking spots on the grass toward the front. Given it was a summer Saturday, most of the trucks were out on a route, but there were a half dozen still left in the lot, most of which appeared to have been sitting there for years, covered in rust and peeling paint.

We made our way to the middle of the lot, where we noticed a small workshop area that they seemingly used for truck repairs. A stack of spare tires was piled up next to a brand-new hydraulic jack, its red-and-black frame gleaming in the sunlight.

Val ran his hand across the cylinder, which was several feet tall. "This is some heavy-duty shit."

I ignored him and walked over to a stout, windowless, free-standing concrete structure at the far end. The door was unlocked. I stepped in and flipped the light switch, illuminating a room lined with shelves full of boxes. On each box was scrawled in black marker the name of a different candy. I rifled through them to confirm they did, in fact, contain what they'd advertised: Nestlé Crunch, Reese's Pieces, Nerds, gummy bears, and even more obscure candies like gourmet lollipops.

"Holy shit." Val stepped in from the yard.

I threw him a Snickers, his favorite candy.

He pocketed it and made his way straight to a steel door to the room's right. "I bet this is where the good stuff is."

I followed him into a freezer stacked with giant white buckets. Val pulled off one of the buckets' caps to find vanilla ice cream as untouched as snow on a winter morning. Apparently unimpressed, he capped the bucket and moved deeper into the freezer.

"Let's get going," I said, my breath misting in the cold air. "The clock is ticking."

"Hold on." He slid a box into the middle of the room and dug his hand inside. "Check these out." He brandished two WWF ice cream bars with a wild grin.

"No way." I grabbed one from his hand. "I haven't had one of these in years."

I tore open the packaging and held the bar up to the light. They still had the same look I remembered: rectangular, with vanilla ice cream coated in chocolate, with one side dark chocolate and the other a yellow-ish-brown color with a sketch of a wrestler.

"I've got Stone Cold Steve Austin," I told Val. "Who've you got?"

"The Undertaker," he bragged, holding his up to my face. I went to snatch his out of the air, but he pulled it away.

"Remember when we used to keep buying them until we got the Ultimate Warrior?"

Val sunk his teeth into the bar. "They aren't even that good," he said. "I think they tricked us."

I took a few disappointing bites. He was right; it tasted like cardboard soaked in sugar. I threw the rest in the trash and shoved the box back from where it came.

As we exited back into the lot, something caught my eye.

"Hey, hold up," I told Val. "Check this out."

I walked over to the back right corner of the lot, where I spotted a jagged opening in the fence, at least ten feet wide.

Val joined me. "They're asking for someone to rip them off."

"Strange," I said, running my fingers along the sloppily cut fence.

Val picked up what appeared to be oversized scissors. "Wire cutters."

"Why would they cut a hole in their own fence?"

Val walked through the hole and crouched down, inspecting the ground. "Fresh tire tracks." He pointed ahead. "Right through the brush." The path cut straight toward Travis.

"You don't think . . . ?" I wondered.

"Would you put it past her?"

My gaze drifted to the ground, where I saw, stuffed into one of the slits of the fence, a Butterfinger wrapper. I pulled it out and held it up to the light. "Georgia's favorite candy."

"Fuck," Val growled, making his way back into the lot.

I followed him. "Where are you going?"

"We need to find this girl before she gets us killed."

CHAPTER 12

NAKED JESUS RETURNS

Val and I ascended the steps to Georgia's front porch, dodging a minefield of cardboard husks.

"When did they move here again?" Val's hands brushed against the soggy boxes.

"A few weeks ago."

"Why Staten Island? Why Travis?"

Good question. The rare people who moved to Travis had some connection to the neighborhood, usually a relative or a job at the dump. No one drifted there by chance.

"No clue. They don't seem to know anyone here."

"There's something strange about that girl."

"Wait 'til you meet her grandmother . . ." My voice trailed off as we eyed the mat at our feet.

> *You will be blessed when you come in*
> *and blessed when you go out.*
> *(Deuteronomy 28:6)*

Val shook his head. "We gotta get that computer from her and be done with this."

I squared up to Val and delivered a pregame pep talk. "Don't provoke her. Let me do the talking. She can be stubborn. If we're too aggressive, she may do something crazy."

"That's why we need to get that computer from her."

"We will."

"Whatever you say." Val rang the doorbell.

As we waited, a helicopter cut through the sky above us. My eyes traced its trajectory, captivated by the contrast of the black aircraft against the perfectly blue sky.

The spell was broken by the creak of the door. Granny emerged, draped in a polka-dot muumuu, a delicate tube connecting her nose to the faithful oxygen tank at her side. "My, you boys look like hell."

"We were, um, um, playing baseball, ma'am." I stuttered over the lie. "I'm sorry to bother you, but is Georgia home?"

"She's out. But please come in. You both look like you could use a cold drink and cookies."

"That's okay. We've gotta—"

"—We'd be delighted." Val yanked the screen door open and flashed me a sharp grin.

"What the hell," I said.

"Trust me." He breezed through the doorway, and I reluctantly followed. The interior was just as spotless as it had been before. Granny guided us to the kitchen, where naked Jesus maintained his watchful presence.

As we took a seat at the kitchen table, Granny pulled a plastic pitcher of iced tea from the fridge and poured us two glasses, her eyes lingering on Val. He had a look of doe-eyed innocence he reserved for special occasions.

"Goodness, what a strong young boy you are," she purred. "What's your name?"

"Valery." It was the first time I'd heard Val use his full name. He ignored me, focusing his attention on Granny. She'd pulled up a chair and sidled up next to him, crossing her legs, nearly turning her back to me.

"What a beautiful name."

"Thank you."

She poked her index finger against the dragon tattoo on Val's bicep. "Did this hurt?"

"It wasn't too bad. Not nearly as bad as the one on my stomach."

"Ouch." She cast a flirtatious glance at his torso. "Valery, how do you know Georgia?"

"Raj introduced me to her yesterday."

"How nice. I bet you and Georgia get along good."

"They get along fine," I said, impatient with this creepy courtship. "Listen, Granny, do you have any idea where Georgia is?"

Val stood up. "Do you have a bathroom I can use?"

"Sure, honey. Just right through there, second door on the right."

I shot him a glare, mouthing a silent plea: *Don't leave me here alone.*

He smiled and patted me on the back before disappearing into the back of the house.

With Val out of sight, an uncomfortable silence settled between me and Granny. I reached for my iced tea, taking a slow, exaggerated sip, before mustering the courage to engage her on my own. "Do you have any idea where Georgia could be?"

"Beats me. I've given up tracking her comings and goings a long time ago. She's like a catfish in muddy water. No matter how tight you squeeze, she'll eventually slip away."

"I can see that."

"Back home she'd go off into the woods and come back days later covered in scratches and bruises."

"I bet its beautiful down there."

She had a far-off look in her eyes. "Like a dream."

"What brought you two here to Staten Island anyway? To Travis?"

"In their hearts, humans plan their course, but the Lord establishes their steps."

I let out a sheepish chuckle and rubbed the back of my neck.

"Proverbs 16:9, dear. We never know where life might lead us."

"Of course." I squirmed. She clearly wasn't ready to share, but I made one last effort to pry her open. "Do you like it here?"

"I'm settling in, hon. So far, everyone's been friendly."

It's not often you hear Staten Island described as friendly.

"And Georgia? Does she like it here?"

"Far as I can tell. She's been different ever since she got out, you know."

Got out?

Before I could dig deeper, Val returned. "Beautiful house you have here."

Kiss ass.

"Why, thank you," Granny said. "A work in progress. My first order of business is to replace these dreadful cabinets."

Val examined the counter with an appraiser's eye. "I do some contracting work if you need help. I also noticed that the tree in the backyard is brushing up against your windows. I could take care of that for you, too."

"I'd love that," Granny gushed.

I sprang to my feet. "Well, we should really get going. We've got a movie to catch."

"Understood." Granny's smile drooped like a balloon losing air. "You've got better things to do than hang out with an old hag like me."

"Oh stop it." Val grabbed hold of her hands and locked into her like Bill Clinton charming a swing voter. "I'll come back next week, and we can sketch out your kitchen remodeling."

"Come any time. I'm not going anywhere."

Granny ushered us to the door, her arm now wrapped around Val's torso. "Be careful up there at the theater. With all that commotion at the dump."

Val and I exchanged the same knowing glance, and in unison, we both asked, "Commotion?"

"You two haven't seen? It's been all over the news. They are digging something up out there."

I stopped at the doorway. "Digging up what?"

"They didn't say. Seems like an army of police are out there."

Val and I beelined back into the house. "Do you mind if we turn on the news?" Val called over his shoulder as he headed for the living room.

Her eyes danced with excitement as she waved us back inside. "Be my guest."

The living room was a window into another time and place. An overstuffed floral-print sofa held court in the center of the room, accompanied by a matching armchair. The coffee table, shielded by a yellow doily, showcased an assortment of knickknacks—from a snow globe to a row of ceramic angels. A decorative bowl filled with potpourri infused the room with the gentle scent of lavender. The wall was adorned with a large, framed needlepoint sampler with Old-English lettering that said "Don't let your halo choke you" beneath the sketch of a creepy shepherd with a shadowy, crooked halo.

I sank into the couch while Val wrestled with the bulky, wood-encased television in the corner. The set flickered to life, and Val flipped to New York One, the city's twenty-four-hour news network.

—

We leaned in as they came back from a commercial break. After a few run-of-the-mill stories—one a robbery in central Brooklyn and the other a trade rumor from the Yankees—we were starting to get antsy. Then the anchor's voice hardened as he confirmed our worst fears.

"Let's bring it back to the scene of a grisly murder in Staten Island," the anchor said.

"Shit," I gasped.

"Quiet," Val hissed.

They cut to Melissa Russo, one of their intrepid correspondents, stationed at the entrance to a service road leading into the dump. Police tape fluttered behind her as uniformed officers bustled in the background.

"Good heavens." Granny covered her mouth with her hand. "That's dreadful."

Russo continued, "Police have cordoned off a vast area of the dump as they scour for any scrap of physical evidence. They're using police dogs, helicopters, and dozens of officers to comb the scene. Authorities haven't divulged many details yet, but we're joined by the lead detective on the scene, who may be able to shed some light."

Then, as the camera panned out, a familiar figure.

"Booch," Val said with a tired whisper.

There she was, looking imposing in her NYPD windbreaker and baseball cap.

"Detective Bucciero, do you have any suspects yet?"

"Given the location, we suspect mob involvement. But it's too early to say for sure."

"Have you identified the victim yet?"

"We can't say much yet. Our forensics team is collecting as much physical evidence as they can, and we will make an identification as soon as possible."

"Okay, thank you, Detective. Good luck."

"Thank you, Melissa."

The program cut to commercial, and we stood there, frozen in stunned silence. Then suddenly, a new voice came from the kitchen. "What are y'all doing here?"

We spun around to find Georgia standing there with a desktop computer propped under her arm.

CHAPTER 13

A FORK IN THE ROAD

The sun's waning light stretched shadows of Val and me across Georgia's grass. We settled into weathered plastic lounge chairs and, for a moment, allowed ourselves to relax. The humidity of the day began to relinquish its grip, and just then Travis came alive. The sky overhead transformed into beautiful shades of orange and purple. Neighbors emerged, watching from yards and stoops, their eyes fixed on the horizon as if an alien spacecraft hovered above.

Val traced the gradient with his finger. "Where do you think that comes from?"

"The colors?"

"It's not normal."

"Uncle Stosh explained it once. Something called Rayleigh scattering. Apparently happens when there's little particles in the air. They bend and refract the light in different directions."

"Particles . . . ," Val echoed.

An understanding silence blanketed us for a few moments. It was a paradox: something so stunning, yet so lethal. Those minute particles, the unseen painters of this vibrant dusk display, had been stealthily invading the vital organs of our loved ones and neighbors for decades. Those beautiful assassins took Val's brother and father, just as they took my grandfather.

Georgia plopped down on a patch of grass in front of us. "Granny's makin' more iced tea."

I leaned forward. "Where's the computer?"

"In my room."

"What happened back at that woman's house?"

We were interrupted by a shrill yelp coming from the garage.

Val nearly jumped out of his chair. "What the hell is that?"

The peacock. I'd neglected to fill Val in on the full details of Georgia's kleptomania, which was likely for the best given his general skepticism toward her.

"Probably a horny cat or something." I cast a conspiratorial glance at Georgia, who returned a faint smile.

Val caught that exchange and cocked an eyebrow at us.

Georgia continued, "Anyway. Wasn't hard to find the computer. She doesn't have that much stuff. Doesn't even have a bed. Just a mattress on the floor."

"Then?" Val asked, impatient.

"As I left, two guys came through the back gate. They were fat and slow. I dusted 'em."

"You went to Sicilian Swirls like we said?" I asked.

"I waited there for you forever."

"Dante's men picked me up."

Georgia shot up. "They got you?"

"They didn't do anything to me. But they know about you. Sort of."

"I'll be fine. You sure you're okay?"

"He's fine." Val shifted in his seat, unable to bear not being the center of attention.

"They let me go," I continued. "Most importantly, that Renzo guy is alive. Stitches. He's probably already out."

"Cool." Georgia's voice was flat and unemotional. She plopped back down on the grass.

"Aren't you relieved?" I asked.

"Relieved at what? He's a killer. He deserves to die."

Val threw me a bewildered look.

"They gave us a deadline," I said. "Dante wants you and the computer. By Monday afternoon. 3:14 p.m."

"3:14?" she asked.

"Not important," I said. "Did you hear me? He wants us to bring you in."

"Who cares what he wants. I want a pony. We can't always get what we want."

That got a laugh out of Val.

"Guys, this is serious."

"Settle down, Raj," Val said.

I could see Georgia's demeanor softening toward Val. His whole cool guy schtick may have been working with her, but it was wearing thin with me.

"It's easy for you guys," I said. "Dante knows who I am. He threatened my mom. By name."

"I hear you," Val said. "I'm just messing with you. We can bring the computer back this afternoon and be done with it."

"Who says?" Georgia snapped, her eyes igniting with a fierce blue flame.

"Georgia," Val said. "You don't want to mess with these people."

"Is that so," she said. A statement more than a question. The warmth toward Val was instantly gone.

Val smiled and looked at me, his eyes almost pleading, as if to say *Your turn*. He was used to getting his way, but Georgia was proving to be a challenge even for his charm.

"What happened at Sicilian Swirls?" I asked, opting for a temporary change of subject.

"I waited there over an hour," she said. "I needed to get the heck out of there, but I didn't want to wait at a bus stop while those guys were lookin' for me. So I borrowed one of their trucks."

"You stole one," Val corrected.

"No one was using that old thing," she said. "Had to have been layin' around for at least a year collecting rust."

"How'd you get it out of there?" I asked.

"First, I had to pry open the steering column cover with a flathead screwdriver. That was easy. Then I found the red and yellow wires and stripped off a bit of the insulation from the ends of the wires with a screwdriver."

"How do you know this stuff?"

"My older brother was a mechanic."

Was? I filed that comment away.

"What do the red and yellow mean?"

"The red is the battery and the yellow is the ignition. Usually. I had to be careful not to cut the wire itself, just the covering. Then I twisted the exposed ends of the red—"

"Stop." Val finally lost his cool. "I don't give a fuck how you stole it. I care where you left it."

If I hadn't agreed with Val, I'd have found the whole scene amusing. He rarely lost his temper, and when he did, it was the stuff of legend. Usually, it meant some unfortunate kid was on the receiving end of an ass-kicking. But there was no one to hit. He'd never lay a hand on me or a girl.

Georgia, unfazed by Val, continued to recount her journey with mechanical precision. "I drove it out the back onto a dirt path, but I didn't make it far. It broke down a half mile away, in the middle of a field. The suspension was too low to off-road."

"You left it out there?" I asked.

"Didn't have much of an alternative."

"You know that truck belongs to friends of ours," Val said, a hard edge to his voice.

"Sorry," Georgia said, seemingly genuine. Val and I leaned in, waiting for her to say more, but she didn't.

"You've gotta find a way to return it," Val insisted.

"That thing ain't moving."

Val tightened like a coiled spring. "That's your problem."

Before things could escalate further, the screen door creaked open and out stepped Granny, balancing three tall glasses of iced tea on a tray. Her oxygen tank was wedged in the doorway.

Val sprang to his feet. "Let me take this."

"Thank you, dear," she said, passing him the tray. "Y'all got fun plans this evening?"

"We'll probably go the movies," Georgia said, ushering Granny back into the house. "Thank you."

"I don't know if I can drink another one of these," I told Val. "After that last one, my heart felt like a wild animal trapped in a cage."

"It's a Southern thing." Val took a gulp. "Extra sugar."

Georgia returned with a package of Chewy Chips Ahoy! in one arm and the desktop computer in the other. We each took a sleeve of cookies to ourselves. I hadn't realized how hungry I was until then.

"How did you get back here after you broke down?" I managed to mumble through a mouthful of cookies.

"I walked," she said.

"Glad you're safe," Val said with a note of sarcasm. "Now, let's get this computer over to Dante and be done with this."

"What about that woman?" Georgia shot back. "Are we just going to forget about her?"

"She's gone," Val said.

"How do you know?" Georgia asked.

"The news," I said. "While you were gone, they reported that the cops found a body at the dump."

"Are we even sure it's that woman?" Georgia asked.

"No," I said. "But Dante basically said that we aren't going to be seeing her again."

A heavy silence dropped between us. I caught Val staring at the ground. Maybe he was more affected than he let on.

He eventually shook off whatever doubt he'd been harboring. "Let's walk that computer over to The Linoleum right now."

"No." Georgia was firm. "If they killed that woman over this, I want to know what's on it. It's the least we can do for her."

"For her?" Val scoffed. "She's dead. There's nothing we can do for her."

Georgia stood up and poked at Val's bicep tattoo. "You're supposed to be the tough guy, aren't you? Now that you've got yourself a real fight, you're gonna give up so fast?"

Val let out an uncomfortable, raspy laugh. "Nice try. I see what you're doing. This isn't our fight. We've got other things to worry about."

"Oh, I see," Georgia said. "Fighting over girls and tripping your face off."

"Precisely."

Georgia had enough. She walked over, picked up the desktop, and made for her door.

"What are you doing?" Val asked, walking after her.

"None of your business," she said, ascending the steps.

Val went to grab her by the arm to pull her back, but she tripped and fumbled the computer on the floor of her patio.

I raced over to them, examining it. There was a deep crack along the side. "Guys! It serves none of our goals if we break this thing."

Georgia and Val huddled around me as I examined it like a surgeon in the ER.

"Will it be okay?" Georgia asked.

"No internal damage from what I can tell," I reported back. "But I'd need to open it up to be sure."

"I'll get a toolbox." Georgia disappeared back into the house.

While she was gone, Val crouched down next to me. "This is our chance. Take this to Dante and be done with this."

"No way. Georgia would go nuts if I did that. She risked her life to get this; she deserves a say in what we do with it."

"She had her say. She's outnumbered."

As much as I hated to admit it, he was right. We couldn't afford a stalemate or for Georgia to go rogue and put us all in danger.

I stood up, girding myself for the mission. "What will you tell her?"

Val hoisted the desktop into my arms. "Let me worry about that. Just go now and walk fast. Once Georgia finds out you've taken it, she'll come find you."

I did as told, speed walking through the gate and down toward Victory without looking back. By the time I reached The Linoleum, my back was screaming at me. I carefully placed the desktop at my feet and took a breather, hands on hips. This was my last chance. I could be a hero and go back to Georgia. We could solve the mystery of the woman together. Or I could end this now and save us all—Georgia included.

I was genuinely torn, but the memory of Dante's menacing words about my mom swayed my decision.

Bile rose in my throat, and I pulled in a sharp breath, steeling myself for what was to come. I lifted the computer and stepped into The Linoleum.

The place was empty, save for the lone figure of Dante nursing his whiskey at the bar. My footsteps echoed in the empty room as I approached. I set down the computer in front of him and felt an immediate sense of release as if unshackling a chain.

Dante's eyes slowly lifted to mine, holding a momentary stillness before he offered a faint nod of approval. "Good boy. You made the right choice."

I was naive enough to believe him.

PART 2

1999

CHAPTER 14

SOPHOMORE NO MORE

A year had wandered by since that fateful weekend. My life had since reshaped itself within familiar bounds like water finding a new path down a familiar hill. On the surface everything was recognizable, but nothing felt right. The way strangers took notice while friends ignored me. The doors that opened as others shut. The sense that reality had flexed and mutated.

It wasn't all bad, just . . . different.

My locker, a hoarder's paradise, was the only hurdle separating me from summer break, one I hoped would be less eventful than the last. I tossed stacks of mostly useless notebooks and texts but saved my marked-up orange copy of Gordon's *World History* because my notes in the margins were too valuable. I held up my dog-eared Barron's *Regents: Chemistry* for any freshman takers. "Anyone want this?" Nobody bit. Into the black trash bag it went. "Your loss."

The bell rang its final toll for the day, for the year. With that sound, I officially earned the rank of upperclassman. I was told this would be a big deal, the halfway point of high school. Yet, I felt as green as I did on the first day of freshman year.

I swung the locker door shut and knotted the trash bag. The hallways looked post-apocalyptic—crumpled papers, violated textbooks, discarded gym clothes. My classmates, already tasting summer on their lips, couldn't even bother to use the trash cans. The custodians were in for a long night.

"Need me to get rid of that for you?" The voice, unmistakable, came from behind.

Sal Longo. Yes, even he was my friend now. A lot can happen in a year.

"I can handle it." I lugged the bag a few yards over to where a makeshift pile had formed.

Sal caught up. "Sweet chain." He tilted his head and gazed at my neck. "Is that new?"

"Sort of." I tucked the silver chain under my shirt. "Where's the rest of the Backstreet Boys?"

He snorted. "No one else came today." He took in the chaotic hallway. "Last day they'll ever need to be in school, and those morons couldn't even make it."

"Well, congratulations on finishing." I patted him on the back. "What's next?"

He shrugged. "Work for my dad at the pizzeria this summer, then who knows. He wants me to enroll in CSI."

The College of Staten Island, or CSI, was the local campus for the City University of New York. It was a four-year university but functioned more like a community college—a place for the striving and aimless alike.

"What would you major in?" I had a hard time picturing Sal in that setting.

"What do you mean?"

"Major. As in, what would you study?"

"I don't know, man. Whatever they choose for me."

Sal appeared to think CSI would be like high school. "They have a solid nursing program," I offered.

"Nurse? The fuck do I look like?"

"They make a lot. Some over seventy k a year."

"I don't care if they make a million. I ain't doing no broad's work." He brushed the topic off with a wave of his hand. "Enough with all this college talk. I'll worry about that in August. Tonight, I'm gonna party like a motherfucker."

"I'm sure you will." I started to retreat. "Have fun and keep in touch."

"Always in a hurry, this guy," Sal said to himself. "Are you going to Klo's party tonight?"

"Maybe," I shouted over my shoulder. "We'll see where the night takes me."

I paused at the water fountain for a sip. As I leaned over, I caught a glimpse of Georgia. She was a classroom's distance away, tossing books into a trash can. She sunk several shots and then, suddenly, looked right at me. Her face was unreadable, a frozen pond. My heart kicked against my ribs. She'd been absent from school for weeks, and I was surprised to see her on the last day. I lifted my hand in a tentative wave, but she swiftly gathered her things and walked away.

I threaded my way toward the exit, maneuvering past a knot of rising sophomores whose laughter echoed across the hallway. From the group's periphery sprang Declan McBratney, his cheeks flushed and his eyes eager as ever.

"Wait up." He latched onto my arm and shoved a crumpled wad of cash into my palm. "Got rid of all but one."

I'd stopped selling CDs at the beginning of the year because I no longer had the time. But the equipment and clientele list had found a new home with Declan, a redheaded firecracker from the outskirts of Travis who'd proved himself a hard worker during a landscaping gig a few summers earlier. Profit was split fifty-fifty, even though he put in one hundred percent of the effort.

I smoothed the bills, counting the worn green faces. "Nice haul." I kept one eye on his eclectic posse. One was a blonde wearing baby barrettes and an oversized No Doubt shirt. She whispered to her friends, who traded glances at me.

Declan flashed a goofy smile. "Do you want me to introduce you to her?"

I ignored the question, holding up the newly organized wad. "How many times do I have to tell you? Keep your money organized."

"I know, I know. It's just been a busy few days."

"Small bills on the outside and big ones on the inside. That way—"

He launched into a poor impression of me. "That way people don't get talking about how much money I'm carrying. I got it."

I placed a hand on his shoulder. "The way you do anything is the way you do everything. Every detail matters."

I started to pocket the cash but reconsidered. "You know what? You take this." I handed him back the money.

"For what?"

"You've worked hard. From now on, you should keep it all."

"Are you sure?" he asked, his mouth open.

"Dead serious." I didn't want to embarrass him, but I'd heard his dad had lost his job at the Unilever plant in New Jersey. The McBratneys could use every penny. "Listen, I've gotta bounce, but have a great summer. And don't be a stranger. Beep me if you need anything, okay?"

"Thank you!" He went in for a hug, and we clumsily embraced, my arms patting his back like a diplomat unsure of the proper protocol.

Leaving Declan and his friends behind, I walked over to the bus stop as seniors poured out of school, congregating at their cars. I settled into the worn bench of a graffiti-marked bus shelter and cracked open my history book. Flipping ahead to next year's chapters, I landed on the

French Revolution. I was slated to take my second year of AP World History with Mr. Galli, who was everyone's favorite teacher.

A honk broke my concentration. Ornela Kadare peered out from behind the wheel of her Eclipse, wearing sunglasses and a black leather jacket, even though it was ninety degrees and cloudy. "Who studies on the last day of school?"

I tucked my book under my arm. "I'm not studying, I'm reading."

"Need a ride?"

I glanced at the empty bus stop. "I'm all set. Bus should be here soon."

"Hop in."

I gave in and climbed into the passenger side. "Can you drop me at Phene's?"

"Of course." She pressed down on the gas.

My head jolted back. "Where's Klo?"

"He's got his own car now. Seeing that I am graduating and all."

"What did he get?"

"My dad's Corolla."

"You get the Eclipse and Klo gets the Corolla? I'm surprised that car even still drives."

"I think it's an eighty-nine. My dad enjoys testing Klo. To see if he can get to him."

"Has he succeeded?"

"You know Klo. Nothing bothers him." She shifted into laid-back surfer tone. "A pebble in the river, the water flows over him."

I laughed. "That's why everyone loves him."

"Nobody hates him," she said. "That's different. Anyway, are you coming to our party tonight?"

"I don't know."

"Why not?"

I slumped deeper into my seat. "There's a lot going on."

She ruffled my hair with her right hand while keeping her left on the steering wheel. "Don't play cool with me, Raj. I remember you when you were a brace-faced loser."

"I only got them removed in January. I'm surprised anyone noticed."

"I know at least one person who's noticed."

"Who's that?"

"Antonella."

I didn't know what to say to that. Was she kidding? Antonella was Ornela's best friend. The two looked and dressed alike and were often confused as cousins. Though Antonella was shorter and curvier. She wasn't out of my league; she was out of my galaxy. Her last boyfriend was a star linebacker for the Wagner football team.

Ornela flipped a U-turn on Victory that sent my head snapping back. "Thoughts?"

"What do you mean she noticed?"

"Don't worry about that."

I folded my arms. "Then I have no comment."

Ornela stopped the car in front of Phene's and threw the car in park. "It's time to grow a pair. You're a junior now."

"And she'll be a senior."

"So what?"

I opened the door and placed a foot on the pavement. "Thanks for the ride, Ornela. Really. And congratulations."

"You're impossible," she said.

I slammed the door shut. "Maybe I'll see you tonight."

"Antonella will be there," she shouted.

The Eclipse peeled away, leaving me choking on exhaust and something that tasted suspiciously like hope.

Phene's was bustling with workers from sanitation and Con Edison. Deadbolt was in charge at the deli counter, jotting down orders on brown paper bags with an oil pencil and passing them back to Chickie in the kitchen. Like a well-rehearsed dance, Chickie promptly assembled the sandwiches, wrapped them in white paper, and placed them on the counter that separated the kitchen from the front.

It was almost Soviet in its simplicity. Coffee was either "regular" or "black." Cheese options were limited to having it or not; there was no Swiss, cheddar, or mozzarella. And no wheat bread, multigrain, or sourdough. Everyone got the same roll.

When I made it to the front of the line, Deadbolt reached his long arm over the counter to give me a pound. "Look who decided to grace our presence."

"Looking sharp, man," I said. It was great to see him in rhythm. He'd found work he was proud of. There were very few jobs at the deli, given Phene always worked the register and Chickie the kitchen. It was a huge mark of faith that Deadbolt won them over. And they paid above minimum wage, which was rare for deli work.

Chickie poked his head through the gap between the kitchen and the counter. "This isn't a social club. Get moving." He shot me a contemptuous look before vanishing back behind the counter. We hadn't exchanged any meaningful words since last summer when I took a job with Dante.

"Two regular coffees, please," I called out to Deadbolt.

"Coming right up."

As he handed me a paper bag, I asked, "What are you doing later?"

"Not sure," he said. "Probably hang in Val's backyard."

He neither invited me nor asked about my plans; he knew not to.

I took the bag to Phene at the cash register. She looked up at me over the rim of her reading glasses. "Don't take it personally. My husband just wants what's best for you."

I swallowed hard. "I get it."

"He knows what you are capable of. We all do."

Guilt tightened around my heart like a vise. "I know," I said, rushing out the front door, unable to look her in the eye.

I crossed the street and walked into The Linoleum. Three men sat at a table in the middle of the room, smoking cigarettes and reading the paper.

"One of those for me?" a man asked, fixing his eyes on me above his reading glasses. He was a slender, elegant man with a well-trimmed gray mustache and perfectly parted gray hair. This was Neri, Dante's consigliere—his closest adviser. People called him Neri the Knife, a nickname largely earned from his early years as a hitman for the Gambino crime family. After the family's leader was gunned down, Neri joined up with Dante to form the Staten Island crime family, marking the emergence of the first new Italian crime syndicate in years.

I pulled a Styrofoam cup from the bag. "Your lucky day."

"That's my boy," he said, patting me on the head.

Another man paused his writing in a ledger. He tilted back in his chair and folded his arms. "And me?"

"Sorry Renzo," I said. "Next time."

That got a chuckle from the men at the table. Renzo's eyes narrowed as he forced a smile. Though I could tell he wasn't amused. I made a mental note to get three coffees next time. Renzo was sensitive, and I hadn't given up on winning him over. He'd never gotten over how Georgia humiliated him last summer—and never forgiven me for it by proxy.

I navigated to the office in the bar's rear and flicked the lights on. The bulbs hummed to life overhead. Settling into my chair, I eyed the pile of folders on my desk, mentally tallying the work hours they represented.

As I booted up my desktop, the door flung open. Ugo was carrying a box. "Kid, give me a hand. Two more in the car."

Rising to assist, I halted at the sound of another voice.

"He doesn't have time for that," Dante said. "He's got work to do."

CHAPTER 15

A DISCOVERY

My desk still held a defiant stack of invoices as the clock nudged eight p.m. As usual, I was the last person left in the back office. My only companions were the quiet hum of an aging computer and shouts from the barroom.

I was at the center of Dante's river of cash, one that flowed in from the darkest corners of the city—places where the law was just a suggestion. You can't shove that kind of money under a mattress. It had to be laundered crisp and fresh through a maze of bank accounts, then served up to Uncle Sam. Because, as Dante liked to remind us, the feds nailed Capone with a calculator, not a smoking gun.

The play was simple in theory: Forgers whipped up false invoices in some back room in Chinatown, all stamped with the supposed legitimacy of Dante's waste management empire.

My role? I was the conductor of this crooked orchestra. I didn't just order the invoices; I crafted a symphony of lies—dates, amounts, and names all carefully composed to not ring any alarm bells. We couldn't use fake customers because Dante was paranoid about a state audit. That meant I had to rely on Renzo for customer names and dates since he oversaw most of the businesses in question.

The most important part of my daily grind was the books—a digital ledger I kept on clunky software. Each entry required careful consideration, ensuring that every dollar of Dante's shadowy income flowed seamlessly through our accounts, maintaining an appearance of legitimacy. That night, however, as I sifted through the final folder, I stumbled upon an anomaly—a series of invoices, all echoing the same details, all marked with the same date, all for identical "services." It was the sort of irregularity that could easily disrupt our carefully constructed financial facade, drawing unwanted scrutiny to our operations.

Armed with this discrepancy, I made my way into the barroom in search of the one person who could help me resolve it. The room was packed with mobsters playing cards and telling stories. In the corner, through a haze of cigar smoke, I spotted Renzo. His eyes were narrow slits, focused on the cards in his hands like they held the secret to life. I nudged his shoulder. "Not now, kid," he growled without glancing up.

I hovered on the fringe, letting another hand play out. Dante was behind the bar, his ear glued to the phone, Neri beside him playing chemist with a highball glass. Ugo, propped against the wall by the door, seemed fixated on his yo-yo.

Renzo tossed his cards down with a shrug. "Got nothing." He followed the confession with a gulp of gin and a new cigar, fished out from his shirt pocket like a magic trick.

I reached for his shoulder again. "Renzo, I need—"

He spun with a viper's swiftness, his eyes slicing through me. "I told you I'm busy. Now get the fuck out of here. This room is for grown-ups."

The room went silent except for the clink of ice against glass from Neri's direction. A hundred eyes, sharp as daggers, pinned me in place. Ugo's yo-yo came to a standstill. At the bar, Neri leaned in, whispering something to Dante. But Dante stayed locked in his call, oblivious to the small drama unfolding in his orbit.

Heat flared in my cheeks, a tide of embarrassment flooding in. I locked my eyes to the floor, made a beeline for the back room, and threw the door shut with a thud. The barroom at night was a minefield, and Renzo, after a few drinks, turned into a homing missile aimed right at me.

Sinking into my chair, I contemplated taking the Renzo problem up the chain to Ugo or Dante as I stared at the invoices scattered on my desk.

My fingers had barely grazed the keyboard when the door burst open. Ugo hauled Renzo inside, gripping the fabric of his pants like a parent with a misbehaving child.

"Get your fuckin hands off me," Renzo spat out.

Ugo released his hold, and Renzo squared up, fists clenched, ready to launch himself at Ugo's towering frame.

Then Dante stepped into the room, and the fight drained out of Renzo like air from a punctured tire.

"What is this?" Renzo's voice shrunk to a plea as he looked to Dante.

Dante leaned against the doorframe, arms crossed. "I was going to ask the same thing."

"The kid interrupted my game," Renzo grumbled. "There was a grand on that play."

Dante's gaze slid over to me. "What did you want with Renzo?"

I hesitated. "It's nothing, really." I didn't want to antagonize Renzo, nor did I want everyone to think I ran to Dante every time someone messed with me.

Dante strode to my desk, his fingers tracing the spines of my meticulously organized folders. He took in the forest of sticky notes on my wall.

"This kid is the only one around here who knows what it means to work hard."

Ugo grunted.

Dante's lips twitched into a smile. "Okay, maybe not the only one.

But, Renzo, I haven't seen real hustle from a single member of your crew."

"My boys have spent nearly every day in Port Richmond dealing with that Mexican problem," Renzo shot back.

"The only reason why we have a Mexican problem is because your men got hammered and beat the shit out of one of their men."

Renzo's jaw tightened. "One of them was sniffing around my girl."

Dante raised an eyebrow. "Your girl or your wife?"

"What's the difference?"

"The difference," Dante said, his voice low and calm, "is discipline. Something you've forgotten. Your men mirror you, Renzo. They're why your outfit's bleeding money and my patience."

Renzo appeared as if he might argue, but a look from Dante clamped his mouth shut.

Dante turned his attention back to me. "Raj, drop the books. Take a break tonight."

I looked at the ledgers, the numbers waiting to be tamed. "Sir, we're nearing the end of the fiscal year. I really should—"

Dante's expression shifted, a silent command hanging in the air. "I'm not asking."

My hands pulled away from the keyboard and reached for my bag. Work could wait.

—

Ugo pulled up in front of a series of white pillars. He looked up from the front windshield. "Who are these people?"

I unclicked my seatbelt. "The Kadares. Albanians. Ice cream business."

He squinted at the mansion. "I know this place. This was Paul Castellano's house, wasn't it? The mob's White House."

I looked up from the front windshield. "Are you sure?"

"Positive. Hard to forget a house like this. Dante and I came once. They served caviar."

Dante came up as part of Castellano's crew and talked about him often. He was the boss of bosses. He ruled over the five families before his reign ended in a hail of bullets in front of a Manhattan steakhouse in the '80s. Ever since then, it'd been anarchy. Each family for themselves.

"Fascinating." I shouldered the car door open. "Thanks for the ride. What are you up to for the rest of the night?"

"I'm going over to—"

"—Actually, I don't want to know. See you tomorrow."

I slammed the door shut. A crowd of upperclassmen I didn't know were gathered in front. They stared at Ugo's Cadillac as it rolled away. I walked through them to the entrance to the house, and they parted like I was a shark and they were the minnows. This was how most kids treated me ever since I started working for Dante. I'd gone from being invisible to being feared.

The front room of the house was a spectacle, full of teenagers grinding to bass reverberating from a DJ stationed on the second floor atop a winding staircase. There must have been at least a hundred people there—mostly kids I'd recognized from around Wagner. I wasn't much of a dancer. The thought alone sent a battalion of butterflies storming through my stomach. So, with the skill of a seasoned wallflower, I slid away, escaping down a hallway that spilled me into the kitchen. It was a vast, shining example of Staten Island new wealth opulence. It was larger than the entire first floor of my house and was adorned with cherry-wood cabinets, a six-burner professional-grade stove, and a double-door stainless steel refrigerator my mom could only dream of. The central island commanded the room like an aircraft carrier in the sea. It was at this impressive edifice that a group of a half dozen preppy-looking guys were perched under recessed lighting, taking turns snorting lines of

cocaine off the gleaming granite surface as casually as if they were sharing a six-pack. Staten Island Academy kids.

"Is Ornela here?" I asked them.

One of the boys wiped the powder from his nose and pointed to the
backyard. "Somewhere out there."

The patio was alive with a tight-knit throng circling a rectangular
pool, all gripping their cups as if they held on to summer itself. And just
past this gaggle, perched like an oasis, bubbled a hot tub crammed with
girls. Ornela, amid the froth and limbs, flagged me down with a beck-
oning hand.

I swallowed a mouthful of my drink and pushed my way through the
throng, receiving occasional pats on the back.

As I approached, Ornela leaped from the hot tub, ready to embrace
me.

I raised a hand in protest. "You're drenched."

She grabbed a towel. "It's just water."

Through the haze of steam rising from the water, I heard my name.
"Hi, Raj." It was Antonella, half-submerged like a lily in a pond. I
couldn't tell if she was wearing a strapless bathing suit or none at all. Her
eyes met mine, conveying a wordless invitation.

I acknowledged Antonella with a halfhearted wave before turning
back to Ornela. "Is she naked?"

Ornela arched her eyebrow. "Why don't you go find out?"

"Maybe later." We both knew I wouldn't make a move.

She placed a hand on each of my shoulders, leveling a stare that
reminded me of the way my little league coach used to look at me. "You
know, you aren't the brace-faced, short, pimply loser anymore. You
should be more confident."

"Um, thank you." I guess that was a compliment. I'd grown a few
inches in the past year—five foot eight the last time I checked. Still, I

couldn't tell how much of my newfound attention was because of how I looked versus who I worked for.

Mischief flashed across her eyes. "Antonella isn't the only girl who's noticed you."

I shook her off, changing the subject. "Great party, by the way. But aren't your parents going to be mad when the neighbors tell them?"

She shrugged. "Who cares? It's Klo's problem. I'm off to college at the end of the summer."

"Where did you wind up deciding to go?"

She twisted her face. "Albany."

I offered a weak cheer. "The Ivy of the SUNYs."

"Binghamton is the Ivy of the SUNYs. Albany is a pit. But my dad said he'd pay for my school if I went to the best college that accepted me, and Albany was it. His money, his rules."

"Not a bad deal." I changed tack. "Where's your brother hiding?"

She nodded toward the shadowy edges of the garden where the carefully sculpted hedges bled into the expanse of a vast, manicured lawn. "Over there, with your old crew."

Squinting, I saw mingling silhouettes materialize into my closest friends. Klo shared a blunt with the gang—Cheetah, Deadbolt, Val, and . . . Georgia. My pulse stuttered. Val, cozy with Georgia, arm looped around her like they were the last two pieces of a puzzle.

Ornela's voice broke into my thoughts. "You still got a thing for her?"

"For who?"

She rolled her eyes.

"She won't even talk to me. It's been almost a year now."

"What about Val?"

"We're fine."

We weren't fine. Val didn't get mad at me for working for Dante like Georgia did. Technically I'd been the one avoiding him. There was no dramatic moment. Once he started seeing Georgia, it made it hard to hang out both because she wouldn't talk to me but also because I still had feelings for her. Val tried to make it work; he did everything right. He'd asked my permission to date her and had been apologetic about it. But my resentment for him kept growing until I couldn't stand to be around him anymore. We still said hi and talked occasionally, but we'd drifted apart.

Ornela shoved me in their direction. "Go over and talk to them. Don't be a weirdo."

I kept my feet rooted. "Maybe later."

"Maybe later, maybe later. You need to stop avoiding things that make you uncomfortable. My dad always says, 'Run into the fire.'"

"Why would someone run into a fire?"

"A firefighter would."

"Everyone else runs away from a fire."

"Whatever. Rip the Band-Aid off. Dive in head first. Pick your cliché. You either go talk to them or jump into this hot tub with Antonella."

Antonella waved at me through the steam.

At this point, Cheetah had peeled off from Val and the crew to get a beer at the keg. This seemed like a safe enough option.

"Be right back," I shouted to Antonella.

Ornela scoffed. "You're such a pussy, Raj."

I held up my middle finger as I made my way to Cheetah at the keg. He greeted me with a hug. "Mr. Big Shot. Where've you been?"

We both knew where I'd been. "You know, just hustling as usual."

"Any fun plans for the summer?"

I shifted from one foot to the other, hands finding my pockets. "Not really. Work. You?"

"Got a job with some telemarketing company out on Bradley Avenue. Seven dollars an hour plus a MetroCard and free lunch."

I gave him a pound. "Nice. What are you selling?"

"Magazine subscriptions mostly." I could feel the energy leave his body.

"Cool," I muttered, scratching the back of my head.

Cheetah's hand was steady on the keg, coaxing out a smooth cascade of beer into the red Solo cup. "Hold this," he said, handing me a full cup before filling another. "Your mom. How's she been?"

"Really good, actually. Got her a new car. Well, a new used car. New to her. A Chevy Cavalier. Has saved her a ton of time off her commute."

As we talked, I felt a sudden jolt, and my feet left the ground. Someone had me by the waist, pulling me up.

A familiar voice. "Raj!"

When my feet landed on the ground, I pried myself loose and spun around to see Val.

He squeezed my shoulder. "Look at this guy. Getting jacked."

"I know." Cheetah playfully shoved Val. "He'll be bigger than you soon."

I rubbed the back of my neck. "How's business?"

"Killing it. We're booked through July. Should be able to hire a second crew and buy another bucket truck by the end of the summer."

"I'll leave you guys to it." Cheetah carried two beers back to the group.

"How about you? Has Dante made you a captain yet?"

"Shut up."

"Seriously. What does he have you doing?"

"You know, hijacking trucks, shaking down bookies."

"I bet."

"I know you hate it."

The warmth in Val's eyes faded, and his smile disappeared. "I want whatever's best for you, Raj. If you think this is it, I am happy for you."

"Not everyone feels that way." I gestured to Georgia, who was now kicking a soccer ball back and forth with Klo.

"She'll get over it."

We both knew she wouldn't. A few days after I returned the computer to Dante, the news identified the missing woman as Natalia Ragosta, a reporter from the *Staten Island Advance*. She was unmistakably the same woman we saw that night at the dump. Throughout the summer, the island had come together, chasing one dead end after another in search of her killers. Friends and family—including her ailing mother and distraught fiancé—would plead for help at news conferences that stretched throughout the summer. Those weeks were hard on all of us, especially Georgia, who never forgave me for returning the computer. Once I took the job with Dante, she stopped talking to me altogether.

"It's not just her. Chickie treats me like a stranger. Deadbolt has been weird. Half of Travis won't look me in the eyes."

"They're scared, Raj," Val said softly. "Scared of Dante. They aren't mad at you." He ran his pointer finger across his right eyebrow. His tell.

"There's nothing to be scared of. He doesn't care about Travis."

"I hope you're right." Val patted me on the back. "I've gotta get back to the crew. Come with me. I'm sure everyone would love to hang like old times."

"I've gotta go. I left The Linoleum before finishing my work. You know me. Can't leave the job half done."

He patted me on the shoulder. "Whatever you say. Just don't be a stranger."

"I won't."

Georgia's eyes flicked to us as he turned away, a silent dart of something like curiosity wrapped in a shroud of indifference. It was gone before anyone else could catch it.

After a quick call to Ugo from inside the mansion, I stepped out and waited by the grand gate. I checked my beeper, expecting the car any minute. When I looked up, Antonella stood in front of me, appearing seemingly out of thin air. She wore a bikini top with straps—confirming she had indeed been topless earlier—and a towel around her waist, no shoes. "Leaving so soon?"

I paused for a moment as I revised my earlier memory of her in the hot tub before shaking it off. "Let me guess. Ornela told you to come get me."

She grabbed my hand and traced a line down my palm. "Don't worry about that."

I couldn't bring myself to meet her gaze, my eyes fixed on the safe neutrality of the ground. "You aren't wearing any shoes. Aren't you worried about cutting your feet?"

She gently nudged my chin up with her other hand. "You're nervous."

The music inside the house seemed to get louder. And I began to shout, words tumbling out. "I guess I'm not in the partying mode. I have to be at work. A cab is coming."

"Your cab isn't here yet." Her voice was closer, and her hand now at the small of my back. I closed my eyes, a rush of something unfamiliar and thrilling surged through me like electricity sparking life into long-dormant wires.

Before I knew it, her lips were on mine. And then her tongue was in motion, erratic and searching. I followed awkwardly, unsure of the rhythm—far from the smooth, cinematic kisses I'd envisioned. My jaw stiffened from the effort, but I held on, determined not to pull away first.

A familiar shrill voice sliced through the night from an idling car. "Raj Patel, you dog."

I jerked away as if caught mid-heist.

"Who's that?" Antonella asked, annoyed.

"That's Ugo. My, uh, driver."

"You have a driver?"

"My friend, I mean."

"He's like fifty."

"Watch it!" Ugo protested from the car.

I clasped Antonella's hand. "Get my beeper number from Ornela. Let's hang out this week."

"When?"

Ugo leaned on the horn.

"How's Monday night?"

"It's a date," she said, a quick kiss sealing the plan.

Ugo could barely contain himself as I deposited myself in the passenger seat. "What was *that*?"

I waved at Antonella as we drove off. "What did it look like?"

"Were you trying to suck the life out of her? Who taught you to kiss a woman?"

No one had, obviously.

"Just drive, Ugo."

"You know, you can always take a taxi."

"What? Too busy shaking down delinquents?"

"Yes, actually."

Ugo caught me up on his evening. A contractor from the South Shore had refused to give a kickback to Dante. There was an informal rule that if you built a house on Staten Island, you paid $10,000 to Dante. This guy got zoning approval for six houses, and flat-out refused to pay a dime.

"Honestly, he doesn't sound like a delinquent. He sounds reasonable. Why should he pay you guys if he's doing all the work?"

"Pay *us*, you mean."

I still hadn't admitted to myself I was officially part of the crew, even though everyone else—from Val to Georgia to Dante to strangers all saw me that way. As a gangster. I couldn't accept what that would say about the person I'd become. I merely saw myself as someone doing hourly work to support his mom.

"Whatever." I pulled my beeper out of my pocket. It was nearly one a.m. "What did you do to the guy?"

An uncomfortable smile tugged at the corner of Ugo's mouth. "You really wanna to know?"

"Actually, never mind." I turned the dial to K Rock, the city's alternative station. Ugo's favorite. We drove off without exchanging another word until we reached The Linoleum.

Ugo dropped me off and drove himself home. The place was nearly empty. Only the bartender, a hunched geriatric everyone called "Lente," Italian for slow. He was there wiping down the tables and collecting trash.

I took a seat at my desk and started working through the remaining invoices, taking notes on revisions we'd have to make to avoid suspicion. The thought of broaching the subject with Renzo had my stomach in knots.

I was on the last ledger when Lente framed the doorway. "Raj, could you lend an old man a hand?" His voice, a scratchy tune, always seemed to play at the edge of apology.

"Of course. Whatever you need," I said, rising.

He walked me over to the back of the bar and pointed at a beer keg that had been disconnected. "Do you mind bringing this down to the basement before you head out? I nearly blew my back out last week moving these."

I gave him a firm nod as I rolled up my sleeves. "Of course. I'll see to it. You go home."

"Thank you, Raj." Gratitude warmed his eyes, and he clasped my shoulder. "I don't know what we'd do without you."

I hauled the keg downstairs, adding it to the collection with a thud. Then I turned to the back, where the liquor was stashed on sagging shelves. Box by box, I searched for a bottle of rum for my Monday night date with Antonella.

That's when I saw it: a computer, dusty and forgotten, wedged behind a box. It was cracked on the side, exactly where Georgia had dropped it.

A surge of disbelief hit me—this was the very machine we gave to Dante last year. He should have destroyed it.

My heart skipped. To find it then and there felt like an omen. This computer had cost a life. There, among the stench of stale beer and metal, I sat on a crate like a judge in a court of my own conscience. The easy move was to push the computer back into its dusty tomb. The safe move. Yet, Natalia's eyes haunted me—not the smile frozen in time on the TV screens, but the scared woman I abandoned at the dump. Her memory clung to me, a silent accusation every time I stepped foot into The Linoleum.

I made up my mind with a heavy resolve. Retrieving black trash bags from a corner closet, I double bagged the computer, shrouding it like a body for burial. Then I threw it over my shoulder and climbed the stairs. Each step was a declaration, and each echo in the empty bar was a warning of the reckoning to come.

CHAPTER 16

REUNITED

Under the cloak of night, I lugged the computer to the home of the only person I trusted enough with the secret: Val.

I slipped into his backyard, placed the bag gently on the grass, and tossed pebbles at his second-story window. It was nearly two a.m.

His figure, half-hidden by shadows, appeared through the second-floor window. "Raj? What the hell are you doing here so late?"

"Come down here," I shouted.

"Can't it wait? I'm fried."

"It can't."

He disappeared into his room. While I waited, I took in the scenery. I hadn't been in his backyard since last summer. He now had a huge bucket truck parked in front of his Monte and a new shed with the name Out on a Limb Tree Care emblazoned on the door.

He emerged from his backdoor, shirtless and shoeless. "This better be good."

"I have something to show you." I pulled open the bag, revealing the cracked desktop.

Val crouched down, his fingers tracing its scars. "Where did you find this?"

"In the basement of The Linoleum." I hovered over him with my hands on my hips.

His eyes widened and a crease formed between his brows. "Why?"

"What do you mean, why?"

His hands clenched and unclenched at his sides. A vein bulged in his neck. "Why everything. Why does it still exist? Why did you take it? Why did you bring it here?"

I could smell the beer on his breath. Ideally, he'd be sober for this conversation, but I didn't have the luxury to wait. "I don't know why they kept it. I don't know why I took it," I admitted, my voice almost a whisper. "I can bring it back, but . . . I thought we might want another shot at this."

"Another shot at what? We took care of this last summer."

"Did we?" I pressed, dropping down to his level, our faces inches apart, forcing him to confront the truth he'd been avoiding. "I don't know about you, but I have nightmares. Horrible ones. Every. Single. Night."

Val's eyes shifted away, unable to hold my stare. *He's having nightmares too.*

I leaned in. "We can turn this around, you know. But it has to be now."

From above, a voice sliced through the tension. "Listen to him, Val."

We both cranked our necks skyward. I blinked hard. It was Georgia, leaning out from Val's window.

Jealousy hit me like a gut punch. I knew about them, sure, but the sting of reality was sharp. I could feel my jaw tighten, the muscles working overtime to sculpt what I hoped passed for a smile. "What, are you two playing house now?"

Val looked at me, his eyes a mix of caution and something like pity. *He knew how I felt about her. Of course he knew.* I'd never said it out loud, but he was my best friend. Sometimes words aren't necessary. "Just the weekends," he said. "Her granny's place during weekdays."

I managed a mumbled response. "That's awesome. I'm happy for you two."

Val shot me a look you'd give a wounded animal.

I chewed on the inside of my cheek, stealing one last look up at the now-empty window. Georgia was gone. "Yeah" was the only sound I managed to push past the lump in my throat. I hoisted the bag over my shoulder, feeling its weight like a sentence, and started to walk away.

Val stood there barefoot. "You sure you're good, Raj?"

The words "I'm fine" came out of my mouth, automatic, a reflex to hide the hurricane inside. I kept moving.

"Morning," he called out, his voice trailing behind me. "I'll come by early, alright?"

I nodded into the darkness, letting the distance swallow his words and my reply.

—

Victory Boulevard lay empty as I trekked with the bag slung over my shoulder, my thoughts a jumbled mess. Side streets would've been smarter, but I'd left logic behind in Val's backyard. It was the middle of the night, which meant no one was outside, not even Rain Man. If anyone had driven by or woken up, I'd be the only one they'd see.

The Linoleum's dark form slumbered as I crossed Victory. St. Anthony's stood watch like a weathered lighthouse guiding me, a solitary vessel lost at sea. I took a moment to admire the graveyard, bathed in moonlight. Suddenly, a shifting shadow streaked from the corner of my eye. My heart skipped a beat, catapulting into my throat.

Georgia came at me like a storm, her hair wild and knotted—and her flip-flops slapping the concrete. Val's black Adidas pants hung off her like drapes.

She fell into step beside me. "What's your plan?"

I said nothing, just kept walking. The sight of her should have stirred something warm in me—it had been a year without a word, after all. But I was nursing overpowering jealousy that her sudden appearance only aggravated.

"Come on, let's check it out now," she pressed, her voice spiking louder than she probably intended.

I stopped, pulling her into the shadows of an alley by St. Anthony's rectory. "Keep it down," I whispered.

Then she hit me with it: "You look good, Raj." It came out of nowhere—a compliment, tied with a look that almost seemed like joy at seeing me. I was ready to stand my ground, keep the barriers up, act tough. Yet, there was something about the way she looked at me, that unguarded, almost happy-to-see-me look. It was like the sun melting through ice. My defenses didn't stand a chance.

"You too," I choked out.

"You don't have to lie," she smiled. "Be honest. I look like a scarecrow."

I held back a laugh. "It's not funny."

"What isn't?"

"A year, Georgia. A whole year, you've ignored me."

Her smile wilted. "I ignored you cuz you sold out."

The accusation was a kick to the balls. "I didn't sell out. I had to take care of my mom."

She crossed her arms and leaned against the damp bricks of the alley wall. "Everyone has someone to take care of. You don't think Granny needs help? If it weren't for Val, she wouldn't get the treatment she needs."

I'd been so consumed with my own petty emotions that I'd forgotten about Granny. I swallowed my shame and recovered. "How is she doing?"

Turning her head, Georgia let the alley's shadows cloak her face, her voice barely above a whisper. "Hanging on."

I pushed off the wall, moving a half-step closer, offering a lifeline we both knew Georgia would refuse. "Anything she needs, I'm here."

She turned farther from me, her shoulders rising slightly as if warding off the offer. "Thanks, but your help ain't something I can take."

The distant rumble of an engine interrupted the sting of her words, sending us instinctively ducking behind a pair of rusted trash bins. Through the gaps, I could see only the headlights. The car was moving slowly, like it was looking for something.

Georgia tried to sneak a peek. "What is it?"

"Don't know. Seems like they are looking for someone."

As the car reached us, its engine cut off. I breathed a sigh of relief and stood up.

"Get in," Val ordered from the front seat of his Monte.

Georgia ran to the car but halted halfway. "Come on, let's go."

I shook my head. "I'll walk."

Val's voice turned sharp. "Don't be a dick."

"I'm serious. Get out of here before we attract attention."

"Come on, Raj," Georgia pleaded. "Don't be stubborn."

As I waited, Val began to get impatient. "You have ten seconds to get in here."

"Or what?"

He started counting down. "Ten, nine, eight . . ."

I just stood there.

"Seven, six, five."

"What are you going to do? Run me over?"

"Four, three, two." Val leaned on the horn, and the night exploded with the sound.

"*Stop!*" I screamed, with my hands up.

The lights of the rectory flickered on. As did many at the houses lining the street.

I yelled over the noise, "*Stop!*"

Suddenly, lights flicked on up and down the street. Georgia, quick on her feet, looped her arm in mine.

I kept up my protest. "Tell him to cut it out," I shouted.

An evil grin spread across Val's face as he persisted. Dogs began to bark, and I started to make out indistinct yells from neighbors who'd been woken up. I didn't want to be blamed for this, especially given the cargo I was carrying. I relented, vaulting into the back seat of the Monte and hunching down just as the engine roared to life.

"The band is back together," Val crowed as he hit the accelerator and peeled away.

CHAPTER 17

THE SECRET

I n the dark sanctuary of my bedroom, we huddled around the computer like at a campfire. I tapped the power button, which sent a low thrum through the silence. The monitor flickered to life with a Compaq logo replaced a moment later by the Windows 95 welcome, whose progress bar inched across the screen like a slow-moving train.

When the password prompt demanded attention, Georgia gave a subtle nod. I typed in the password: "axlrose" and hit Enter. The computer responded with a beep and the prompt shook as it flashed a warning message that declared "Incorrect password. Please try again."

Val leaned so close that I could feel his breath on my neck. "Try it with spaces."

We had the room to ourselves while Uncle Stosh was at a gig in Manhattan—giving it the air of a secret hideout.

I kept my eyes on the screen. "She said one word, no spaces."

Georgia tilted her head into my periphery. "You sure you remember that from a year ago?"

"I'm positive."

Val gripped my shoulder. "Just try it with two words."

"Whatever you say." I retyped the password, this time as "axl_rose," but the stubborn warning message reappeared.

I experimented with various combinations of capitals and lowercase, but nothing worked. These old machines could be fickle, and who knew how many wrong attempts would lock us out. Frustrated, I spun to face Val and Georgia.

"Damn," Val said. "Maybe we got the wrong computer?"

Two lines appeared between Georgia's eyebrows. "I searched that whole house. This was the only one there."

I stroked my chin. "And it was on the second floor? Just like she said?"

"Yes," Georgia confirmed, hands planted on her hips.

I stood and paced. What did I get wrong? With a space, without a space. Lowercase. Uppercase. Then it dawned on me. "When I gave this to Dante, I also gave them the password. They must have changed it."

Georgia's face twisted. "Why would you give them the password?"

"The same reason why I gave them the computer," I answered honestly. "They asked for it."

"Unbelievable," she said.

"I'm sorry," I mumbled. "This means they know about whatever's on here."

Val planted himself in my path, his voice dropping to a murmur. "Maybe we ought to chuck this thing. I bet they won't even notice."

Georgia wasn't having any of it. "We're keeping it." She squared up to Val, their faces so close her nose was nearly poking his chest. "We promised this woman we'd do this."

"You didn't even talk to her." Val took a soft tone, grabbing her by the waist. "Raj did."

Georgia recoiled. "Don't matter who spoke to her. She's dead cuz of whatever's on there. We're gonna find out why."

"Hold up," I broke in, wedging my hands between them like a referee calling time. "I have an idea. We can pull the hard drive from this computer and access it externally."

"You know how to do that?" Val sounded disappointed.

"I don't, but Uncle Stosh does. I've watched him do it before."

Val's face fell. "We're not involving anyone else in this mess."

"He's my uncle. And my roommate. I trust him."

"We're not telling Stosh," Val said.

Georgia pressed on, undeterred. "You saw your uncle pull a hard drive before?"

"I did."

She clasped my hand, and her blue eyes peered into me. "Raj, you're the smartest person I know. If you saw your uncle do it, you can do it."

My pulse rammed against my ribs. I knew she was manipulating me, but I couldn't resist. "I guess I can." I ran my hands through my hair. "It's pretty straightforward."

Georgia clapped her hands like a coach rallying the team. "Let's do it, then."

Val slumped down on my mattress. He knew where this was going and clearly didn't like it.

"All right, grab that toolbox for me."

I tipped the desktop on its side, removing the screws and exposing its inner components.

"Now, we just need to find the hard drive." I pointed to a rectangular metal box tucked inside the case. "This is it."

Carefully, I disconnected the cables from the hard drive, making sure not to touch any other components. "We'll need one to connect this hard drive to another computer."

With Georgia at my side and Val laying in protest on my bed, I gathered the necessary pieces from around my room. I had an old computer with a parallel port, perfect for connecting the hard drive externally. I removed the hard drive from the Compaq and connected it to the parallel port of my old computer using a data cable.

The drive icon appeared on the screen, bypassing the password. "We're in," I announced, exchanging a triumphant high five with Georgia. Val reluctantly rejoined us, and the three of us huddled together as I began to sift through the files and folders. Our eyes darted across the screen, hunting for any indication of the elusive unknown file we were so desperate to find. I clicked on My Computer and began to systematically search through each directory, starting with the C drive. Natalia was a reporter, so she had hundreds of articles on her computer. But there was nothing personal in nature. It must have been her work computer. The topics of her articles ran the gamut from beat reporting at city hall to stories on run-of-the-mill crimes. Nothing we could find involved Dante, his crew, or organized crime generally.

"Maybe Dante's men deleted anything involving him?" I asked.

"That would make sense," Val said.

Then I remembered a trick we used to try to conceal files from the teacher in computer lab. It seemed like a long shot, but I tried it, enabling the "Show hidden files and folders" option in the folder settings. As I did that, a previously invisible folder materialized on the desktop. It was labeled Fresh Kills.

I double-clicked and the screen flickered for a moment before the folder filled our view. It was organized into subfolders: Research, Outlines, Interviews, and Drafts. One document stood alone and was titled "Fresh.Kills.Final.Doc."

Bribes and Backroom Deals: How the Mob Keeps Fresh Kills Open

By Natalia Ragosta

STATEN ISLAND, NY - In late September 1990, the New York City Council Committee on Sanitation and Solid Waste Management convened in a dimly lit chamber to determine the future of the Fresh Kills landfill. The stakes for the forgotten borough were high, as the city weighed whether to extend the landfill's life for yet another decade. Environmentalists and community activists, bolstered by naive optimism, believed they'd secured a promise from key leaders to shutter the landfill and replace it with an alternative plan that would distribute waste across various locations via barges.

That alternative plan, championed by a coalition of local ecologists and Staten Island luminaries, would have utilized cutting-edge waste-to-energy technology and recycling initiatives to reduce the burden on landfills. This shift was a culmination of years of research and collaboration, and the activists believed it was the perfect solution to address the city's insatiable appetite for trash while minimizing environmental and health impacts on the island.

But in a twist that left onlookers in the gallery gasping, Sanitation Commissioner Liam McGovern, with a furrowed brow, read from a prepared statement advocating for a ten-year extension of the landfill. He offered a thin justification, arguing that the alternative waste-disposal plan was unfeasible. While some council members questioned McGovern, most showed little fight.

"While this news saddens me, I know you and your team did your very best to explore alternatives," lamented Chairman Anthony Cappetta, a representative for the Staten Island neighborhoods bordering the landfill. "We have no choice," he added.

But Councilman Cappetta did have a choice. *The Staten Island Advance* has unearthed evidence that suggests Cappetta and at least half a dozen other current and former committee members had accepted cash payments from associates of Dante Malaparte, the reputed head of the Staten Island Mafia. The bribes allegedly totaled a staggering $750,000. Multiple sources, who asked to remain anonymous for fear of their safety, told the *Advance* that Malaparte wielded his influence over the committee to prolong the operation of Fresh Kills and suppress an environmental assessment that detailed the landfill's alarming health consequences.

continued

The report, commissioned by the New York City Council and carried out by the New York City Department of Health, revealed that cancer rates in neighborhoods adjacent to Fresh Kills were more than five times the city average. The study also found elevated levels of respiratory illnesses and increased rates of low birth weight among infants. In a curious development, the report's lead author, Dr. Miriam Rosenberg, abruptly retired just two weeks before the September 1990 hearing, the very forum where her findings were to be disclosed to the public.

The extension of the Fresh Kills landfill was a windfall for Malaparte and the Staten Island Mafia. Since the early '80s, they've steadily expanded their grip on city waste-disposal contracts related. Although the landfill is city-owned, private contractors oversee most daily operations, including waste collection, disposal, staffing, and maintenance. Companies with ties to Malaparte have reportedly received at least $100 million in payments from the city for contracts connected to Fresh Kills since 1986. This was when the Staten Island Mafia allegedly wrested control of the waste business from the Bonanno crime family amid a bloody turf war that left dozens dead. The conflict, which lasted for several years, was characterized by a series of gruesome murders, mysterious disappearances, and brutal reprisals as the two crime families battled for supremacy in the lucrative waste-disposal industry.

Sources confided to the *Advance* that Malaparte's bribery and strong-arm tactics reach far beyond the city council. "Dante owns city hall, One Police Plaza, the One Twentieth Precinct, and even the local FBI," alleges a law enforcement insider who requested anonymity for fear of retaliation. "He's not the Crisco Don because he's lucky; he's bought his immunity."

The extent of Malaparte's influence suggests a possible explanation for why city officials, law enforcement officers, and even judges have appeared to turn a blind eye to the illegal conduct of the Staten Island Mafia. In one notorious case, a high-ranking police officer was caught on tape discussing the details of an ongoing investigation with one of Malaparte's lieutenants. Despite the damning evidence, the officer was merely reassigned to a different precinct, while the case against the foot soldier was inexplicably dropped.

The scope of the impunity reached deep into the city's bureaucracy. Several city inspectors responsible for monitoring the operations at Fresh Kills routinely ignored safety violations and underreported the amount of waste being dumped at the landfill. In exchange for their silence, these inspectors allegedly received envelopes stuffed with cash from Malaparte's henchmen, as well as other perks such as expensive vacations and luxury cars.

In the autumn of 1990, following the announcement by the sanitation commissioner to extend Fresh Kills, the city witnessed a handful of lackluster protests before swiftly moving on. This muted response was in part due to the pervasive sense of hopelessness and resignation among the residents of Staten Island, who had long grown accustomed to the stench, noise, and health hazards associated with living in the shadow of Fresh Kills.

For decades, the city implemented half-hearted measures in an attempt to mitigate the impacts of Fresh Kills on the surrounding communities, including installing odor-control systems and constructing noise barriers. This window-dressing did little to alleviate the suffering of the residents, who continued to bear the brunt of the city's waste-disposal crisis.

The city council will soon reconvene to debate another ten-year landfill extension. Most observers anticipate that the city will finally shutter Fresh Kills, with the mayor and governor all but guaranteeing it. But the city's current sanitation commissioner is Dominic Cappetta, brother of Anthony Cappetta. Our

continued

sources reveal that Dominic, much like his brother, has been accepting bribes from Malaparte since he was first elected to the council in 1992.

As the decisive day approaches, a new generation of activists has emerged, promising to fight for the closure of Fresh Kills. Armed with a renewed sense of urgency, these concerned citizens have mobilized support from a diverse collection of Staten Island civic leaders—staging rallies and demonstrations to raise awareness about the burdens of the dump.

With the future of their community hanging in the balance, the residents of Staten Island will watch closely to see whether the city will finally rid itself of the infamous landfill. The mayor and governor's promises have provided a glimmer of hope. Yet the specter of corruption and a sense of earned cynicism continues to cast a dark shadow over the proceedings. As the city council prepares to make a decision that will impact the lives of thousands of residents, it remains to be seen whether justice and the public interest will finally prevail.

Val and Georgia stared at the screen while I sank to the floor beside them. I tucked my knees to my chest, overwhelmed by the scale and significance of what I just read. Each line of this article stoked a growing fire that began to rage in the cold pit of my stomach. These weren't just statistics or nameless victims, they were our neighbors.

Cancer cast a long shadow over Travis, where tumors spread like strawberry plants in an untended garden. Every other gravestone at St. Anthony's stood as a testament to the disease's power, including my grandfather, who died of lymphoma. Few had it worse than Val. His father was taken by lung cancer, and his older brother, BJ—his only sibling—waged a long and futile battle against the disease. BJ, who had been even stronger and more athletic than Val, endured endless rounds of chemotherapy and bone marrow transplants that zapped his energy, took his hair, and cut his weight in half. By the end of it all, when BJ finally gave in, he looked like he'd spent years in a concentration camp.

Val's voice broke through the silence. "Those motherfuckers," he said, his words laced with anger. "They knew all along."

I readied myself for the storm, expecting him to tear my room apart in a rampage. Instead, he slumped down next to me and crumpled like a paper boat in a pond. He cradled his head in his hands and wept. I'd never heard him cry before. He sounded like a wild beast caught in a trap, raw and gut-wrenching.

Georgia, untroubled by Val's outburst, settled in front of the computer and began sifting through the remaining files. They were a strange couple, and in that moment, any jealousy I had was replaced by pity.

I patted Val on the back in a futile effort to lend support.

"I'm sorry," I repeated again and again.

Eventually, he sprung to his feet with fists clenched and approached Georgia.

"What do you have?" he asked, his voice flat and focused.

"I don't know yet," Georgia said. "Raj, I think it's best if you saddle up. You'll understand this better. I've gotta pee."

She disappeared into the bathroom as I took her seat and girded myself for a long night of reading.

I could feel Val's breath on my neck. "What do you see?" he asked.

"I don't know, man. I'm not a robot. I need more than a second to digest this all. This could take a while."

Val gave a slow nod. "Take all of the time you need."

The weight of what we'd uncovered began to press down on me. A heavy fog of doubt and guilt rolled in. I worked for those mobsters. Over the course of the past year, I'd become culpable. The fear gnawed at me, too—the fear of what would happen if Dante discovered we had the desktop. The secrets it held threatened the most powerful people on the island and many others across the city. Not just Dante but the entire political establishment.

I gave voice to my anxiety. "We can take this out back right now and bury this in my yard. Dante won't ever know we took it."

Val leaned in with a defiant spark in his eyes. "Dante's going to know we took this. Because we're going to use it to take him down."

CHAPTER 18

ADULT SUPERVISION

I prided myself on my ability to concentrate for inhuman amounts of time, but after hours in front of the screen, my focus wavered. My eyelids felt weighted down, tiny anchors tugging with each blink. Battling against overwhelming fatigue, I questioned my next move. Why were we doing this alone? We were just kids. Should I call Uncle Stosh or my mom?

Shaking off the cobwebs of exhaustion, I plowed on, poring over folder after folder. The murmurs of Val and Georgia, huddled together on my bed, were an irritating buzz in the background. But I had to stay focused. So much information, yet so little of it seemed useful. I cranked up the music in my headphones to drown them out.

The drafts yielded nothing but hollow echoes of the final articles. Interviews offered nothing new, and the research was a jumble of technical jargon. Natalia must have kept most of her important notes old-school, pen-and-paper style.

What we needed were names—corrupt insiders within the government or sources within the Staten Island crime family. Someone who could verify her claims.

In the restroom, I doused my face with water, struggling to quell the rising tide of bile in my throat. Dawn's early light spilled through the window, casting a pale glow on the mirror. I locked eyes with my own reflection, steeling myself with whispered words of encouragement. *Think straight, pull it together.* With a sharp, deliberate motion, I slapped my cheeks—a raw, desperate attempt to ground myself.

I returned to my bedroom with nothing more than a series of obvious points. "Without Natalia's notes, we don't have a smoking gun. No names, no hard evidence."

"She wrote an article about Dante and then disappeared," Val said. "Isn't that enough of a smoking gun?"

I pointed to the screen. "The article says he's bribed half the city, including the one-two-oh and FBI. Who would we even go to with this?"

"The Crisco Don," Val said. "If we can't trust the feds, who can we trust?"

That left one person. My gaze drifted to the window, to my neighbor's house. "What about her?"

Val stroked his chin. "That article says cops are on the take, including at the one-two-oh. We can't take that risk."

"I trust Booch."

"Why?" Georgia asked. "What has she done to earn that trust?"

"She's not the corrupt type," I reassured. "Trust me. And she's one of us. No Travis person would sell us out like that."

"You did," Georgia offered. A quiet, emotionless stab.

"Hey, hey now," Val cut in. As he spoke, his finger traced a path across his eyebrow, a sure sign that a lie was coming. "Raj didn't sell anyone out. He didn't know what Dante was up to."

Deep down, I did know. I may not have known Dante sold out Travis with the Fresh Kills scheme, but I knew he was a murderer and a thug, and I took his dirty money anyway. I could tell Georgia wanted to press this point, but she held back, maybe seeing in my eyes that I was already painfully aware of my complicity.

I sat at the edge of the bed and took a deep breath. "Listen. I can't undo what I've done. All I can do is what's right today. And I think that means going to Booch with this."

Val looked to Georgia, whose face was twisted in thought. "What do you think?" he asked.

"Granny has a saying: 'It's never the wrong time to do the right thing.'"

Never the wrong time to do the right thing. I mouthed the words to myself.

Georgia continued. "Heck, I don't know Booch. If you trust her, I guess I trust her."

Val turned his attention to the window facing Booch's house. "I wish there was a way for us to check if she is on the take. Wouldn't Dante keep books on that sort of thing?"

I joined him at the window. "I've never seen those books if they exist. He keeps all of the most sensitive stuff on the second floor of The Linoleum. Only he and Renzo are allowed to go up there. But maybe I go about this a different way. What if I find a way to mention Booch's name to Dante and Ugo?"

"Then what? They'd admit to bribing her?"

"Not necessarily, but I know these guys. I'd be able to tell if they know her in some way."

Val looked to Georgia. "What do you think?"

She shrugged. "Ain't much of a choice, is there?"

Suddenly, a light seemed to flicker in Val's eyes, a spark of realization. "I actually may have a guy."

"What do you mean 'a guy'?" I asked, skeptical.

"Someone who may be able to give us some insight into Booch. Someone who knows the force like the back of his hand."

"Why didn't you mention that before? That sounds perfect."

"Well," Val paused, considering his words. "He's a bit unpredictable."

I racked my brain, trying to guess who he was hinting at. "It's not—"

Val's confirming nod cut me off midsentence.

—

A few hours later, we pulled up to the parking lot of Pizza D'oro at the corner of Richmond Avenue and Victory.

"You sure he'll be here on a Saturday?" I asked.

"He's always working," Val said. "And let me do the talking. He's a weird guy."

We made our way to a nondescript door behind the pizzeria, marked only by a faded sign: Ivanicki Investigations. Val pressed the doorbell, and a gruff voice crackled through the intercom. "Yes?"

"It's Val."

After a moment's pause, the door buzzed open. We climbed the creaky stairs to a private-eye office that seemed frozen in time, cluttered with decades-old gadgets and electronics. To say the furniture was secondhand would be generous: dusty steel file cabinets, a roll-top desk, burgundy leather nailhead tufted couch.

Yuri Ivanicki was a striking presence with an ugly charisma. He was in his late sixties, burly with a unibrow that served as a membrane separating his big brown eyes and massive forehead. An impressive layer of body hair rose above his arms and chest like a force field. He was Val's late dad's younger brother.

Yuri was studying photos, talking on a landline phone. "What is he doing here?" Yuri asked into the phone. "Is he? Is that his wife?"

Val and I settled into chairs across from him while Georgia wandered the room examining the array of vintage gadgets.

Yuri peered closer at the photo, then pulled out a magnifying glass. "What's he doing there? With his wife? Jesus, you fucking idiot," he barked into the receiver. "We can't use this. You can't photograph someone inside their house."

He sifted through more photos, then looked up briefly to acknowledge us, continuing his call. "Lazy fuck claims he can't teach kids math because of his back. And here he is sliding into home plate."

Yuri chuckled. Val and I returned forced smiles.

"Maybe we can slip in the photos of him going down on his neighbor. Just for fun." Yuri winked at Val and continued. "Great. I'll give you two hundred bucks for each of the baseball ones and cover your gas. I'm gonna need receipts, though." The voice at the other end of the phone protested. "Sorry, Igor. I've got another customer here. Duty calls. Bye."

He hung up and ambled around his desk with a slight limp. His hands landed heavily on Val's shoulders. "Handsome boy, just like your pop."

"Thanks," Val muttered.

Yuri turned to me. "Who's your muscle?"

"This is Raj," Val said.

I'd met Yuri at least a dozen times.

"Raj," Yuri said, studying me. "What kind of name is that?"

"Indian," I said. "Actually, we've met—"

"—You don't look Indian."

"Um, thanks."

"I didn't mean that as a compliment."

"I know. I don't know why I said thanks."

Yuri shook his head. "What's wrong with this boy?"

"He's just nervous," Val said. "You have that effect on people."

"Only those who have something to hide," Yuri said with a

penetrating look at Georgia, who was fiddling with a radio receiver. "Young lady, this isn't a petting zoo."

"Sorry." Georgia returned the gadget and took a seat alongside us.

Yuri held out his hand, missing an index finger. "I believe you have something of mine."

Georgia hesitated, then pulled a pen from her pocket and placed it in his hands.

Val and I exchanged exasperated looks.

Holding the pen aloft, Yuri revealed, "A microphone, an old Sennheiser MD 421, a classic from the late eighties."

He returned to his chair, the leather creaking under his weight. "Now tell me, Valery, what this is about? Why you bring a thief in here?"

"We need your help."

"Tell me."

"Would you be able to tell if a cop is clean or not?"

"Clean how?"

"Meaning not corrupt. No Mafia connections."

"I can't prove a negative. But I can do my best, depending on the precinct."

"The one-two-oh," I said.

Yuri raised an eyebrow. "Why are you asking me this? What kind of shit are you in?"

"It's best you know as little as possible," Val said. "Bottom line is we have information we want to bring to a cop there, but we want to make sure she isn't on the take."

"Name?"

"Detective Barbara Bucciero," Val said.

"Booch?"

"Yes," I said. "I live next door from her. Is she clean?"

"I knew her a bit when I was on the force. Kept to herself; had a stick up her ass, like she was above it all. Seemed clean, but I'd have to ask around to make sure."

"That would be helpful," Val said. "How long do you need?"

"This will take some time. What's your deadline?"

"As soon as possible," Val said.

Yuri stood. "I'll see what I can do."

"Thank you," Val said as we rose to leave.

Yuri escorted us to the door, his hand resting on Val's shoulder. "Listen, Valery. I don't know what you've gotten yourselves into, but it doesn't sound good. My advice is to tell your mom, and then we can all go down to the precinct together to sort it out."

"That's not an option," Val said.

"Why not?" Yuri asked.

"Yuri, you're going to have to trust us," Val said. "If we go to the cops, we'll put ourselves and others in danger."

Yuri sighed, a hint of concern in his eyes. "Whatever you're dealing with, be careful. The one-two-oh is a hall of mirrors—even the most honest cop can find themselves lost, struggling to discern the true from the false."

CHAPTER 19

THE RUSSIAN CONNECTION

Travis usually stirred to life slowly on Saturdays, but on that morning, it erupted like a shaken kaleidoscope. The catalyst was an unseasonably cool breeze—a gracious offering from the tidal straits—which coaxed my neighbors out as it swept through the streets.

By nine, Phene's was buzzing. The weekend local crowd now joined the plant and dump workers. The line for sandwiches snaked out the door, winding its way toward the back of the building.

Val surveyed the scene. "Damn, this could take an hour."

I fixated on The Linoleum across the street, scanning for any sign of activity. Nothing yet.

Georgia was restless in the backseat. "Maybe we should try our luck elsewhere?"

Val killed the engine. "Where else we gotta be?"

We took our place behind a pair of sanitation workers at the back of the line. Georgia, never one to endure idle time, pecked Val on the cheek and headed home. That left me and Val to catch up.

"How's *that* going?" I asked.

Val pinned me with a glare. "Do you really want to know?"

"Why wouldn't I?" I asked, though of course, I didn't want to know. I was picking at a painful, irresistible scab.

"Her granny's not well," Val confessed, a crease of worry carving itself across his forehead. "Has been in the hospital for weeks."

"I'm sorry. Georgia mentioned something about that; I didn't realize it was that bad."

"That's why she's been staying with me," he said, as if he needed to explain why his girlfriend spent the night. "She wouldn't admit it, but she doesn't like to be home alone."

It hit me then that Val knew Georgia better than I ever would. The realization stirred a dark undercurrent of jealousy within me.

"How's she handling it?" I managed to ask, shaking off my whiny inner voice.

"It's hard. She doesn't say much about it."

I nodded. "I bet. Not exactly an oversharer."

Georgia was a deep lake. She was seemingly calm, but it was anyone's guess what happened below the surface.

"She makes me look chatty," Val said with a brief twinkle in his eyes.

In that moment, I was reminded of something Granny said the last time I saw her—that day when Georgia arrived with the desktop. Something about Georgia "getting out." I stored the thought away.

"There's no other relative to come take care of her?" I asked.

"Every time I bring it up, she changes the subject," Val admitted, a trace of frustration in his voice.

"Well, at least she's talking to you." I couldn't mask the bitterness in my voice.

"The beef between you two has been hard on her, though she would never admit it."

"It wasn't a beef. She just stopped talking to me."

"Kind of like you did to me?"

"We never stopped talking," I said, looking away, knowing full well this was, at best, a half-truth.

"Don't bullshit me, Raj."

"There's no sense in revisiting that. Water under the bridge."

My words, empty and unconvincing, seemed to evaporate before they reached Val. Something had changed in the past year. We'd always been on divergent paths, but the gap had begun to widen. Standing there surrounded by sanitation workers, Val looked like a man among his peers. Yet I was still a boy, playing mobster with Dante and his crew. Val was taking care of Georgia and Granny while building his tree business. A legit business. Everything in his life was real, rooted in honesty and hard work—everything that was authentically Val. My life was a dangerous charade, a haphazard construction of lies that seemed to grow by the day.

The chatter of the sanitation workers in front of us interrupted my internal pity party.

"I can't wait until we don't have to come to this shithole town anymore," one of them grumbled.

"Stop talking nonsense. We ain't going nowhere," came the gruff reply from his colleague. They were both thick-necked men with weathered faces and hands gnarled like tree roots. Men who'd earned the right the be cynical.

"Jimmy's convinced we'll all be moved to the barges by August."

Val and I were both silent, eavesdropping as best we could.

"Jimmy doesn't know fuck all. I heard the opposite. My wife's sister Carol works at city hall. Says this thing ain't closing."

"Bullshit."

"I'm just telling you what she heard."

Conflicting news had trickled in all year about the city's plans for the dump. Every time the council was set to vote to set a closure date, something would happen to delay matters. It was all playing out precisely as Natalia's reporting had suggested it would. The island's politicians were noticeably silent on the issue, which was odd given how many of them had campaigned to close the dump.

With a shrug, they moved on to a conversation about the Yankees. I was tempted to tap one of the men on the shoulder to ask for more background, but before I could, Ugo walked out the front door of The Linoleum and lit up a cigarette.

"Shit," I said, pressing myself against the brick wall of Phene's, trying to become invisible.

"What's wrong?" Val asked.

"It's Ugo," I said.

Val craned his neck, scouting. "Raj, you can't avoid them. You gotta act normal until Yuri gets back to us."

"But you heard Yuri; that could take a while."

"We don't have much of a choice, do we?"

I pondered that for a moment. He was right. I stepped out into plain sight.

Ugo's eagle eye quickly spotted me. He sauntered over, his high-pitched voice laced with mockery. "Hey there, lover boy."

"Just act normal," Val whispered.

I mustered an eye roll for Ugo. "What brings you in so early?"

Ugo surveyed the long line. "Gotta handle a few things for the boss," he said. He held out his massive hand to Val. "Ugo."

"Val."

Their handshake was a firm, silent battle of wills, like Arnold Schwarzenegger and Carl Weathers in *Predator*.

"Strong grip you've got there, boy." Ugo squinted at Val. "Have we met before?"

Val and I briefly exchanged glances. *The dump. Last summer. Natalia.*

"Probably from around town," Val said. "I come here every day."

Ugo grunted and pulled out a twenty for me. "Can you get me a bacon, egg, and cheese and a coffee regular?"

"Actually, we were just gonna give up on this line. It'll be time for dinner when we get to the front."

Val shot me a puzzled glance.

Ugo pocketed the twenty. "You know that old scarecrow," he said, referring to Chickie. "He won't let you cut to the front?"

The sanitation workers ahead turned at the mention of cutting but snapped their heads back forward at the sight of Ugo.

"We're not exactly cool right now," I said. Even if Chickie and I were on good terms, he wasn't the type to give special favors.

Ugo chuckled. "Your life's a soap opera, kid."

"Funny, I was drama-free until I met you."

Ugo ignored the barb. "You know, in most neighborhoods, people treat us with proper respect. We don't wait in line, and we don't pay."

"Then go to those neighborhoods," Val shot back.

Ugo's jaw clenched into a half-scowl, half-smile.

"We're going to bounce," I said, ushering Val away. "Do you guys need me to come in today?"

"Doubt it," Ugo said, remaining in place in line.

"You staying?" I asked.

"What other choice do I have? There's only one damn deli in this hick town."

—

When we pulled up to my house, Booch was next door working her hedges in a gray tank. Her sculpted arms flashed in the sun like polished steel.

Val eyed her through the windshield. "Does she remind you a bit of Sarah Connor?"

"From *T2*?"

"Scary woman."

"She's been even icier than usual lately," I said.

"Don't get paranoid on me," Val cautioned. "Remember: not a word to her until Yuri gives the green light."

"I know."

I pushed open the door only to be halted by Val's grip. "Been good to hang again, huh?"

"Wish it was under better circumstances," I managed, glancing at Booch, whose gaze was sharper than the shears in her hands.

"She doesn't know nothing," Val assured.

"I hope you're right."

"Schmul tonight? Like old times?"

"What time?" I asked. I didn't have anything else going on. I'd been spending most nights at The Linoleum, but Ugo told me not to come in that night. And given my extracurricular work, I wasn't looking for an excuse to see Dante.

"We'll get there around nine."

"Maybe I'll see you there," I said, slamming the door shut.

As I walked through my front gate, I tried to keep my head down, avoiding any eye contact with Booch, but I could feel her eyes on the side of my skull.

At the door, I fumbled my keys, my nerves jangling.

"Morning, Mr. Patel," she greeted with a cool tone.

"Uh, good morning, Booch," I offered, still avoiding eye contact.

It was an open secret that I now worked for Dante. Booch never broached the subject with me, but any day I expected her to pull me aside for interrogation.

Thankfully, Uncle Stosh came through the door sporting a guitar bag over his shoulder. "Hey, bud," he said, a spark igniting at the sight of Booch.

She gave him a brief, stiff nod.

Stosh fished a ticket from his back pocket. "I'm playing Roseland tonight. Opening for Men at Work. Got backstage passes for you."

"I have dinner plans," she said with a snip of her hedges.

"Oh, we don't go on until ten," Stosh said. "You have plenty of time."

"I'll let you two be," I said, pushing open the front door, taking my opportunity to escape Booch's scrutiny. "You two love birds have fun tonight."

The mail slot was nearly empty. No past-due notices and no letters from Dad. We hadn't heard from him since the letter Sal's crew stole from me. I pulled a stack that included a few coupon books and what looked like a credit card pitch. Mom, ever the easy target for those schemes, had been caught up in their high-interest traps before. Inside, she was at the kitchen table, lost in the ritual of painting her nails, with INXS playing on the radio. I leaned in, kissed her head, and snagged a Coca-Cola from the fridge.

"Some girl called," she said, giving me *that* look.

"Oh yeah?" I tried to sound nonchalant, leaning against the fridge. "Which one?"

We were both taking some time to adjust to my newfound popularity.

"Listen to you—*which one*," she scoffed. "Her name is Antonella. I left a note on your desk with her number."

"Thanks, Ma. What are you up to today?"

She'd recently stopped working weekends thanks to a pay raise. My mom didn't know it, but Ugo had "persuaded" her boss to discover his latent generosity.

"Actually, I have a date," she said, barely containing her excitement.

"Really!" I said, sliding into a chair opposite her. "Who?" The only thing more shocking than me having a date was my mom having one.

"Dr. Agarwal," she said. "Cute young Indian doctor who just started doing rounds at the home."

"Didn't you learn your lesson the last time?" I joked.

"My mistake wasn't that I married an Indian; it was that I married a lazy Indian."

That was about all the romance talk I could endure with my mom. "I'm gonna head upstairs. Mind if I use the internet?"

"Go for it."

Upstairs, I booted up the dial-up modem and loaded AOL Instant Messenger. Antonella was online, but before I could message her, Ornela popped on my screen.

> AlbanianPrincess82: U n ur boyfriend Val back 2gthr?

> Shaolindian: Thawing out

> AlbanianPrincess82: U finally got over the redneck chick?

> Shaolindian: Nothing to get over

> AlbanianPrincess82: Right . . . . Heard bout ur new crush tho.

> Shaolindian: I don't have any crushes.

> XOAntonellaXO has joined the chat

Ornela had invited Antonella to our chat. Now she could see what I said about having no crush.

XOAntonellaXO: Hi :)

Shaolindian: Hi

AlbanianPrincess82: Jesus u 2 r so lame.

A new chat window appeared on my screen.

WhereverUgo: Raj, u there?

A few of Dante's crew, under Ugo's urging, used AOL under the flawed theory that cops were less likely to tap a computer than a phone.

Shaolindian: I'm here

WhereverUgo: Need u at the bar l8r

Shaolindian: Thought I was off today?

WhereverUgo: Boss asked 4 u

Shit. Could he be on to me? Did he know I stole his computer? I took a breath and turned my attention back to my chat with Ornela and Antonella.

XOAntonellaXO: Plans 2night?

AlbanianPrincess82: I was supposed 2 go 2 the movies with Anthony, but I think I'm going to bail

Shaolindian: You two should come to Schmul Park. A bunch of us will be drinking there.

I flipped back to Ugo.

WhereverUgo: 6 p.m., k?

Shaolindian: Dante say why?

WhereverUgo: Just be there

Back to Antonella and Ornella.

Shaolindian: Gotta run. But meet us at 9

AlbanianPrincess82: K, Mr. Popular

XOAntonellaXO: Bye <3

My evening schedule was becoming precariously tight. I was nearly double-booked.

I called Val to discuss Ugo's message. He reassured me it was probably nothing. Still, we set up a plan: If I wasn't at Schmul by nine, he'd go to Booch. If I was just running late, I'd text him "112233."

—

The Linoleum was as packed as I'd ever seen it. In the weeks ahead, many of Dante's men would make an exodus to the Jersey Shore, transforming the bar into a quiet corporate headquarters. But on that night, it functioned more like a social club, with self-organized groups dotting the room. The older men like Neri played dominos at their usual table by the window. The youngbloods were engrossed in various poker games in the middle of the room. The bar counter was reserved for the big shots like Dante, who was flanked by Ugo and Renzo. That night, there was a fourth posse, who sat at the opposite end of the bar from Dante. I'd never seen them in The Linoleum, and they kept to themselves. No card games and none of the shouting and backslapping that came from the other tables. Their shiny tracksuits, stocky build, and tattoos gave them away as Russians.

When Dante noticed me, he paused his conversation and gestured for me to come over with a flick of his finger.

My throat tightened, and I hid my trembling hands in my pockets to control my nerves. Pushing through a thick cloud of smoke and a cluster of mobsters, I reached the bar.

"Take my seat," Dante said.

I did as told, depositing myself between Ugo and Renzo. Dante made his way around the bar, displacing Lente with a nudge. "We'll be fine here; you just take care of them." Dante gestured to the mystery Soviets at the end of the bar.

Ugo's eyes remained fixed forward, unreadable. Renzo, however, twisted his mouth into an unsettling sneer.

Dante leaned in, his eyes like shards of Arctic ice, piercing straight through my veneer of composure. Instinctively, I averted my gaze and scanned the room, now blanketed in a tense hush, every pair of eyes locked onto me. This was it; I was caught. There was no way I could slip out unnoticed without being tackled by a dozen of Dante's men.

"Do you have something to share with us?" Dante's voice boomed throughout the bar.

I looked at Ugo, who still wouldn't look in my direction.

"He's not going to help you," Dante said, his voice perfectly uninflected, which made him all the more terrifying.

Dante pulled out four glasses and filled them with ice and some unidentifiable brown liquid. As he poured, he continued. "I'm waiting."

I racked my brain for an explanation. What did they already know? About the missing computer? My visit to see Yuri?

"I didn't want to bother you about the invoices," I stammered.

"Wrong," Dante interrupted, a brief flicker of annoyance crossing his face as he glanced at Renzo. "But we can discuss that another time."

He arranged the glasses in front of us before raising his own in the air. "Ugo filled me in on last night," he said.

I glanced back at Ugo, whose face had hardened into stone.

Dante continued. "I heard you popped your cherry last night. Heard you had your tongue down some broad's throat."

Ugo let out a thunderous, wheezing laugh. And then the entire bar seemed to erupt.

Dante passed me a glass and offered a toast. "To young Casanova here."

Suddenly, everyone was toasting to me and my supposed conquest. Caught up in the moment, I downed the whiskey they handed me without hesitation, causing tears to sting my eyes from the strong taste.

"Whoa." Ugo patted me on the back. "Slow down there, big shot. That's for sipping."

Dante refilled my glass as the rest of the groups went back to their chatter and games. "Tell us about her," Dante said. "Ugo says she's a real looker."

I proceeded to describe Antonella the best I could. There was something a bit creepy about grown men obsessing over a teenage girl, but

I was in no position to be anything but grateful for the conversation's turn. Every now and then, members of Dante's crew stopped by to buy me a drink. Within an hour, I was fully hammered and locked in a disorienting personal conversation. Even Renzo was being nice to me. I told them about my pathetic track record with girls, my parents' rocky marriage, and the Victory Boys. Dante was particularly interested in my various business schemes.

"Why did you stop selling the CDs?" he asked.

"It takes a lot of time," I said, trying hard to control my slurred speech. "Once I started working here, it became impossible to keep up with."

"So you just gave up the business?" Renzo asked.

"No, I had a buddy take it over for me."

"You just gave it to him?" Dante asked, incredulous.

"Not exactly. I keep half the profits."

"Wow!" Dante said. "A fifty percent tribute! I should give him your crew, Renzo."

Renzo forced a grimace of a smile.

Maybe it was the alcohol, but at that moment, I began to second-guess my plan. These guys had been good to me. They respected me, paid me well, and even took care of my mom. How bad was the dump conspiracy anyway? Corrupt city officials had kept it open for decades without pressure from Dante. At least now Staten Islanders would at least profit from the burden. With Dante's presence in Travis, there was a chance our town could reap the rewards of his operation. It would make a huge difference if I could convince him to hire more Travis residents like me.

I glanced at the clock. It was just past seven. That meant two hours before I was to meet Val and Antonella at nine. I was starting to feel sick. I had to stop drinking if I had any hope of making it.

"Guys, I'm not feeling so great," I said. "I'm gonna go put my head down." The room spun as I walked into the back office, plopped down in my chair, and rested my head on my desk.

Sometime later, I awoke to the sound of a conversation. It was Dante and a voice I didn't recognize. Through my arms, I peeked out to see the neck tattoo of one of the Russian men at the end of the bar.

"What's the latest?" Dante asked.

"The timing couldn't be better," the man said with a deep accent. He handed Dante a folder. "This is the final legislation."

Dante reviewed the document. "When is this going up for a vote?"

"July second. Heading into the holiday weekend. Most won't be paying attention."

"This only says a two-year extension," Dante said. "That's not what we agreed to."

The man pointed to something in the document. "Here. Read this."

Dante took a moment. "I see. That's genius. In plain sight."

"Exactly," the Russian man said.

"Can I keep this copy?" Dante asked.

"Of course."

The Russian man left, and with the file in hand, Dante ascended the stairs to his personal office. It was the one space in The Linoleum that was off-limits. Only Dante and Renzo ever went up there.

I checked my beeper. It was now eight thirty p.m. I had to get going soon to Schmul to prevent Val from going to Booch. But I wanted to see what was on that paper. I put my head down, pretending to still be passed out, and waited until Dante returned from the second floor and walked back into the barroom.

Alone, I made a beeline for Dante's upstairs office. The door to the staircase, a flimsy, hollow-core panel, was guarded by a basic pin tumbler lock. I'd seen Uncle Stosh pick a similar mechanism with a screwdriver. My liquid courage convinced me I could do the same. I rummaged through the closet, finding a small flathead. Kneeling, I inserted the tool into the keyhole, my fingers slick with sweat as they twisted and prodded. Eventually, the metal clicked, but before I could turn the handle, a voice thundered from behind me.

"What the fuck are you doing?"

CHAPTER 20

TRUTH OR DARE

Renzo radiated a triumphant, self-satisfied smirk as he stood at the center of the room. "I've got you now, you little fuck."

In that moment, a surge of panic catapulted my stomach into my throat. I had to think fast, to *move* fast. I slid the screwdriver into the depths of my back pocket. Pretending to be more drunk than I was, I stumbled across the room. Narrowly avoiding a collision with the golden toilet, I then tumbled back into my chair.

Renzo was on me in an instant. He yanked me up by my shirt. His stench was a toxic blend of Brut cologne, sweat, and booze. "Why are you snooping in the boss's office?" he demanded.

Laying on the drunken act thick, I slurred, "Just need last year's invoices."

Renzo pushed me against the wall, snarling. "Bullshit."

His formidable bulk loomed over me, two chins cascading over a stained collar, stubble scattered across his jowly face. Strands of his hair, slick with grease, clung to his scalp. The combination of his grimy presence and pungent odor was nauseating. No need for pretense now, a wave of genuine sickness washed over me. A deep, unsettling churn rose from the pit of my stomach, gaining momentum. And then, with a suddenness that caught even me by surprise, I unleashed a torrent, coating Renzo in an unanticipated shower of my vomit.

Renzo reeled backward, his once pristine shirt now marred with the streaks of bile and brown hues of half-digested whiskey. His eyes were ablaze with a raw, untamed anger.

In that critical moment, Ugo appeared with lifesaving timing. "What in the hell?" he asked with an amused sparkle in his eyes.

Renzo, flustered, let go of my shirt. "The little shit was trying to break into the boss's office."

I affected an even heavier slur. "Jus' lookin' for the books from last year."

Ugo laughed. "Renzo, this kid's so lost, he wouldn't know the boss's office from the bathroom."

"The fuck he doesn't. He knows to steer clear of that office," Renzo said. "Everyone does."

"We gave him enough whiskey to sedate a horse," Ugo said. "Lucky if he remembers his own name."

"I'm getting the boss," Renzo said.

Ugo took an aggressive step toward Renzo and cautioned, "Don't you bother him with this shit. He's got bigger things to concern himself with."

"I'll talk to my cousin about whatever the fuck I want."

Ugo gestured to the door. "It's your world. It's just that if I were you, I'm not sure I'd want to have a conversation with Dante about invoices. From what I understand, Raj saved your ass with this year's books. I bet that's what he was trying to finish."

I gave a weak nod in agreement.

Renzo paused, then begrudgingly made his way to the restroom. "Fine. We'll talk about this tomorrow, Raj, when you're sober."

"You can have whatever conversations with him you want," Ugo said with a protective edge, nudging me to the door. "Just don't lay a hand on him. He's as good as made around here."

As good as made? That's the first time I heard that. Made men can't be killed without the decision of higher-ups.

"Let's not get carried away," Renzo yelled from the sink.

Ugo walked over to the door to the second floor and secured the lock. His eyes narrowed on me, hinting at a dawning suspicion, but he masked it quickly. "Raj, let's go," he said. "I'm driving you home."

—

We made our exit through the side entrance, steering clear of the bar crowd. Ugo meticulously laid towels over the passenger seat of his Cadillac, a precaution against my earlier bout of nausea. As he revved up the engine, the clock on the dash glowed 9:14 p.m.

My heart raced with panic. I'd told Val I'd be at Schmul by nine or he'd go to Booch.

Reaching for Ugo's car phone, I asked, "Do you mind if I send a quick message?"

"Who?"

A moment of hesitation gripped me, my thoughts tangled in a web of stress and alcohol.

"Oh, the girl. You dog. The old tipsy ring, eh? You may want to sit the rest of this night out, champ."

"Tipsy ring? What are you, a hundred?"

"What do you call it?"

"Drunk dial."

"Whatever. Same thing."

"I'm just going to beep her and see what happens." I dialed Val's pager, leaving our agreed-upon code: 112233.

As we approached my house, it became clear Val hadn't received my page. His car was out front, and he was absorbed in conversation with Booch on the porch. They both looked our way as we arrived, but Ugo didn't pay them any attention.

The facade I'd upheld for a year seemed on the verge of collapse. My relationship with Ugo, Dante, and the rest of the crew could be over in a second. And if Booch proved to be crooked, the consequences for Val, Georgia, and me could be even worse.

I had to get between Val and Booch as quickly as possible. "Thanks for the ride," I said before pulling the handle.

"Hold up," Ugo said, gripping my elbow like a clamp. "You can't fuck up like that around Renzo. He's looking for any reason to muddy your rep with Dante."

"I know," I said, trying once again to leave the car. Any hope of derailing Val's confession to Booch was disappearing by the second.

Ugo held tighter. "I had your back there, but Renzo is Dante's cousin. There's only so much I can do to hold him off."

"Why does he hate me so much? It can't be just because of last summer. You were there, and you've moved on."

"You guys embarrassed him. Whispers of him getting beat up by a girl. And now you're closer to his cousin and more important to the business than he is."

"More important? He runs his own crew. I just manage a few books."

"Don't kid yourself, Raj."

Ugo's grip finally eased, and I bolted from the car. "Thanks for the ride and the advice," I threw over my shoulder.

In the heat of our conversation, I hadn't noticed that Val had left Booch's yard and was now seated on my front steps.

"You stood me up," he deadpanned. "Yet, you're still alive."

I started to explain my absence, but Val recoiled. "What the fuck, Raj. You reek."

I eased myself down beside him on the steps, resting my head against the railing. "Dante may be trying to kill me one whiskey at a time."

I let my eyelids fall, and almost instantly, a soothing numbness crept over me. The buzz of alcohol transformed Val's voice into a distant hum, easing me into a fleeting, dreamlike stupor.

Val stood over me, gently smacking my cheeks. "Raj, get up."

I came to and was immediately seized by worry. "Booch? What did you tell her?"

"Relax. You're lucky I saw your page just as Booch was coming to the door."

"What did you two talk about, then?"

"Don't worry about that," he said. "Go shower and brush your teeth. Your girl is at Schmul waiting for you. And I can't let you show up like this."

"She's not my girl."

—

Val and I reached Schmul Park to find a lively scene on the outfield grass of the baseball diamond. The crowd, a mix of our familiar faces, had formed a tight circle, all eyes fixed on Cheetah, who was holding court with an Olde English forty in his grip. Among the onlookers were Ornela, Antonella, Deadbolt, Mercedes, and Declan, all hanging on Cheetah's every word. They were so engrossed that our arrival went unnoticed.

Cheetah was midstory. "It was during the blackout last summer. My mom was away, so I invited a girl over."

"Name?" Deadbolt demanded.

"Let's keep it classy," Cheetah said with a sly grin.

The group erupted. "Nooooo," they chimed in unison.

Deadbolt added, "Rules are rules, yo," as he passed a blunt to Mercedes.

"Fine, fine," Cheetah said. "It was Jessica Trancucci."

A collective "Ooooo" rippled through the crowd.

"Quite a catch," Mercedes said.

"Well, because the AC was out, I, uh, had some performance issues. No matter how hard I tried, I couldn't get it up. She was a sport and did everything you could to help, but it just wasn't my night."

Ornela covered her mouth, half-amused, half-mortified. "Cheetah!"

"I appreciate the story," Deadbolt added. "But this was supposed to be about the time you lost your virginity, not the time you almost lost it."

"Patience," Cheetah cautioned. "I'm getting there. The next weekend, we tried again, and I didn't have any issues that time."

"We need to work on your storytelling skills," Ornela said, patting him on the back. "Your turn to pick someone."

"Deadbolt," Cheetah said without hesitation. The group began a rhythmic thigh-clapping, ushering Deadbolt into the limelight. He acknowledged them with a bow.

Spotting me and Val at the edge of the circle, Deadbolt called out, "Look who decided to show up!"

Antonella eyed me from across the circle, a playful smile tugging at the corner of her lips.

"Don't you stall now," Val yelled. "Get on with it."

"Truth or dare," Ornela commanded.

"Truth, of course," Deadbolt said.

The last time he got a dare, he had to run down Victory in his tighty-whities.

"What do you want to know?" he challenged. "I'm an open book."

"I have a question," Antonella said. "How did you get that scar?" I could feel the energy get sucked out of the crew. I traded glances with Cheetah and Val. This was a story we knew—and it wasn't one Deadbolt should be forced to tell.

"Let's not get into that," Val said.

"No, no," Deadbolt said, his face beet red. "It's all right."

He traced the scar that ran from his mouth's corner down to his chin and plunged into his story.

"One night, I woke up to this crazy yelling, right? It's blasting from the kitchen. So I book it downstairs and see my old man, hands wrapped tight around Ma's neck." Deadbolt demonstrated, his hands outstretched, mimicking the scene. "I didn't think twice, just leaped onto his back and held the fuck on as long as I could. But the guy's a beast, flings me like I'm nothing. Grabs a beer bottle and smashes it right across my face. He's wailing on me nonstop. Then blackness. Next thing I know, I'm blinking awake in a fucking ambulance."

He took a gulp of his forty as the group fell silent. I could see from the horrified look on Antonella's face that she regretted asking about this.

Mercedes mercifully broke the tension. "Next up," she offered, nudging Antonella forward.

Antonella jammed her hands into her pockets, bracing herself.

"Truth or dare," Mercedes challenged.

"Dare," Antonella said without hesitation.

The group erupted into hoots.

"I've got one," Val said has he flashed a smile at me. I swallowed hard. "Antonella should pick someone to make out with."

Antonella instantly looked my way. "Raj, come here."

More cheers from the crowd.

Sweat began to pour down my armpits, tickling my stomach. It was terrifying enough to make out with her alone. Now, I had an audience of my closest friends.

"Wait," Ornela said. "They've already made out. We need to bring this up a notch."

Heads turned in my direction. "Raj made out with a girl?" Deadbolt asked, incredulous.

Cheetah jabbed him in the stomach. "Don't say it like that, bro."

"What are you thinking?" Val asked.

"I need second base at least," Ornela said.

That got another round of hoots from the group.

My heart leaped into my throat. I couldn't remember what second base was, but I'd just gotten to first a few days ago.

In that moment, in the briefest of exchanges, my eyes met Georgia's. Her gaze held a cryptic shimmer that disappeared as soon as I caught it, like a shadow that dances away when you turn to look directly at it.

"Not here," Antonella urged, tugging me by the hand toward the woods behind the dugout. I threw one last look over my shoulder to see Georgia, who was now casually embracing Val, leaving me to wonder if the silent message in her eyes was a product of my imagination.

The whiskey coursing through me did little to steady my nerves. My hands shook as Antonella led me under a sagging oak, its branches hanging heavy around us. She tucked a few stray curls behind her ears, revealing her large brown eyes, high cheekbones, and olive tone. She was stunning, a fact that only deepened my guilt over my fixation with Georgia.

She gently guided my trembling hands just above the line of her jeans. Her lips, tinted with a subtle gloss, parted softly as she whispered, "Relax."

"Sorry, I'm just . . . nervous."

"We don't have to listen to them. You can tell them we got to whatever base you want if you kiss me again."

She gently placed her hand on my cheek, drawing me closer to her lips. The kiss, perhaps softened by the whiskey, melded our lips with a harmony that lacked the awkwardness from the night before, replaced now by a smooth, almost intuitive rhythm.

Eventually, we found ourselves seated on an old log. Antonella produced a joint. "You smoke?"

"Sometimes," I said. Though in reality, I didn't. I'd smoked once with Val, never felt anything, and hadn't tried since.

She took a few expert drags, cloaking us in a haze. When the joint came to me, my inexperience was evident. I inhaled too deeply, too quickly, and soon I was engulfed in a fit of coughing, tears stinging my eyes.

"Easy," she soothed, patting my back. "Small hits." She demonstrated with a practiced ease. "Like this."

We spent the next few minutes in a lazy rhythm of passing the joint and stealing kisses. Each time our lips met, I found myself relaxing more into her presence. But as the night wore on, a dizzying blend of alcohol and weed started to skew my perception. The edges of the evening blurred, details smudging into the haze of a potent, disorienting blend. At some point, I blacked out.

—

I woke up alone in a fetal position under the dugout bench next to a dried puddle of vomit. Dawn's final rays painted the trees in a soft, golden light, casting intricate shadows on the dew-soaked baseball field. The ground was strewn with leftovers from the previous night's party— empty beer bottles shimmering in the morning sun. I began to gather the scattered remnants, throwing them into a nearby trash can.

I found Georgia and Val at the swings. Georgia was soaring high, her legs kicking energetically against the sky, while Val idly swung, his feet dragging along the pavement.

"You're alive," Val observed.

I claimed the adjacent swing. "Barely."

"You and Antonella were going at it last night."

"You saw that?" My memory was a blur; I remembered our first few kisses in the woods but not much else.

Val let out a dry laugh. "Are you kidding? You two were rolling around in the grass."

I blinked in disbelief. It was easier to imagine myself dunking a basketball. "Where is she?" I asked.

"Rode home with Ornela."

Rubbing my temples, I squinted against the brightening day. "I've never been so out of it."

"Go home, get some rest. I'll drive you."

The idea of sleep was inviting, but a sobering memory halted me. "Look, we have a problem. I overheard something last night at The Linoleum."

Georgia slowed to a stop, tuning in.

I continued. "Dante is working with Russians. They've got some kind of bill to extend the contract on the dump."

"For how long?" Val asked.

"Permanently."

Val twisted his face in confusion. "How could that be possible? I know the city is corrupt, but the debate in the papers seems to be a few years versus no extension."

"They're planning to make it seem like a short extension, but there's some loophole."

"What's the loophole?" Georgia asked.

"I don't know for sure. I didn't read the draft. I just heard them talking about it. He locked the document in his office, and Renzo caught me trying to break in and read it."

"Oh shit," Val said.

"I pretended I was hammered, and Ugo walked in at the perfect time to vouch for me and take me home."

Val smirked. "Given what I saw of you last night, it shouldn't have taken much pretending."

I punched his shoulder. "Fuck you."

"Are you worried Dante will find out?" Georgia asked.

"A little. But I'm more concerned we're running out of time. They're planning to pass the extension on July second. The Friday before the long weekend. This Friday."

"They're trying to bury it?"

"Right."

July 4th was the biggest holiday of the year in Travis. We held a huge parade that attracted people from all over the city. Most politicians, including the governor and mayor, came to pay their respects.

Georgia leaped from her swing and faced us. "Maybe it's time we take our chances with Booch. July second is five days away. We can't waste any more time."

"I agree with her," I said. "We don't have many options left."

We were interrupted by the sound of Val's pager. "Who the hell would be beeping me now?" The color drained from his face as he scanned the screen. He cast a fraught look at Georgia. "It's Granny."

—

We arrived at St. Vincent's minutes before they declared Granny dead. For a while, Georgia's grief was raw and unfiltered, her sobs wrenching and deep. She buried her face in her hands, emerging eventually with the familiar, stoic demeanor we knew—as if she had locked away her emotions.

Then, as if releasing a dam of unspoken words, Georgia began to share. Her voice was laced with a vulnerability neither Val nor I had witnessed before.

"I met Granny while I was at Saint Anne's."

Val and I shared a puzzled look. *Met?*

"It was a boarding school, a horrible place for kids who got in trouble at regular schools. Granny would volunteer there on weekends, leading

Bible study groups. I wasn't into religion, but anything to get away from the staff. They were evil; the things they would make us do, the things they would do to us . . . ," she said, her eyes drifting away.

"We have a place like that called juvie," Val said. "Deadbolt spent a few weeks there. Said it was the worst place he's ever seen."

"Granny and I got close. I started to tell her about the staff. After I told her one really bad story, she decided to help get me out."

"What was the story?" I don't know why I asked. I didn't really want to know.

"There was this girl who slept in the bunk next to me. Arlyn. She was all kinds of nervous. Had a problem wetting her bed. Couldn't stop. The staff finally made her sleep inside a cabinet as punishment. It was so small that she would have to pull her knees to her chest to get in there. After a few days of that, she was like a zombie. Barely able to walk, so tired. One day, she was pulled out of class after she dozed off. Later that day, she fell out a window and died."

Val listened, stunned. I could see tears welling up in his eyes. I don't think I'd ever seen him cry before.

"How does someone fall out a window?" I asked.

"Right?" Georgia said. "People got into 'accidents' all the time. After I told Granny about Arlyn, that was enough for her. The next weekend, she got me out of the school in the trunk of her car."

"That's why you moved here?" Travis was as good a place to disappear as any, I guess.

"Right," Georgia said.

Val, tears streaming, realized aloud, "She wasn't actually your grandmother."

"At Saint Anne's, everyone called her Granny."

"Where are your actual parents?" I asked.

"Prison, last time I checked."

I winced before asking the inevitable. "What now?"

She crossed her arms. "I ain't going back to that place."

I turned to Val, aware of the implications. "Once the police dig in here, they are gonna figure out who Granny is and who Georgia is."

Val crouched in front of Georgia. "Listen, do you want to say good-bye to Granny before they move her body? You won't be able to see her again after this."

She wouldn't even be able to attend the funeral.

We walked Georgia over to Granny's room, where a group of order-lies began to prepare the body for transport. Georgia tenderly kissed her grandma's forehead and spoke in her ear.

As I lingered in the doorway, I noticed two suited women speaking with the nurses, their gestures directed toward us.

"Georgia, you need to leave now," I urged in a whisper.

"What?" she asked, confused.

I tugged her arm, pulling her from the room. "They're here for you."

She cast a final, longing glance at Granny before quickly heading down a stairwell.

The women in suits hovered over me and Val. "Is one of you the child in the custody of Florence Hood?"

"No," I said. "We just knew her from church."

"Who's the girl who was with you?" one of the women asked.

"I don't know," Val said. "But said she was heading down to the cafeteria."

As the officers made their way to the elevator, Val and I paid our respects with a sign of the cross. She wasn't Catholic, and neither Val nor I were devout, but we figured she'd appreciate the effort.

We then took the same stairwell Georgia did and made our way to the parking lot through a crowd of hospital workers on a cigarette break.

"What now?" I asked.

"I have to find Georgia. She needs to hide until this blows over."

"The cops will come to our houses," I said. "Can't risk having her stay with either of us."

In front of the emergency room entrance, we passed Sam the Wanderer seated on a bench. He had a bandage wrapped around his head and was reading the *Sunday Advance*.

"What happened to him?" I asked Val.

"We have enough to worry about right now," Val said as we kept walking. We also knew better than to interrupt Sam while he was reading. He was very particular about his routines.

Val continued. "Well, we need to find Georgia. Before the police do."

Entering the parking lot, I spotted the silhouette of someone leaning against the Monte.

"Look," I pointed out to Val.

Val squinted. "Is that . . . ?"

"Booch," I said. Though it was Sunday, she was dressed in a pantsuit like it was any other workday.

"Good morning, boys," she said as we approached. "We need to talk."

CHAPTER 21

A BROKEN MAN

Booch slapped the hood of the Monte. "Follow me down to the one-two-oh."

Val, feigning indifference, turned his key in the driver's door. "What for?"

"I have a few questions for you."

"Are we under arrest?" I asked.

Booch raised her eyebrows. "Why would you think that?"

"You tell us," Val said, leaning against the car doorframe.

Booch offered Val a Marlboro, but he waved her off and pulled out his own. She squinted at us like a chess player, considering her opening move. I should have been afraid, but I wasn't. Until that moment, Booch had largely been able to scare us into compliance. But something between us had changed. Though I was no longer afraid of her, a part of me wanted an excuse to rip the Band-Aid off and tell her everything that'd happened since last summer. To put an end to it all.

Instead, I played it safe. "What are you doing here?"

"I was going to ask you the same question," Booch said.

"A friend died," Val said, blowing smoke in her direction.

"Which friend?"

"Why is that your business?" Val challenged.

Val was needlessly antagonizing Booch. She could easily learn who we'd visited, so there was no sense in stonewalling. "Florence Hood," I said.

Booch pulled out her notepad and took notes. "And how do you know this woman?"

"Knew," Val corrected. "She's dead, though you already know that."

"She lives on Canon Avenue," I said. It was the truth, just not the whole truth.

"Let's cut to the chase, boys," Booch said. "Where's the girl?"

"Which girl?" Val asked.

"I see." Booch pushed her notepad back into her pocket. "Off the record. Just us."

Before Val could open his mouth, I opted for candor. "We don't know everything that's going on—and we don't know where the girl is." There was no sense in delaying the inevitable. Booch knew we hung around with Georgia. The neighborhood was small.

"Don't lie to me, Raj."

I held my hand to my heart. "I swear on my mother." I technically didn't know where Georgia was at that moment.

"Okay, tell me what you do know."

I continued. "We know enough to say Georgia is scared. She lost the one person in the world who looked after her. She doesn't know you and doesn't trust the police."

"She can trust me."

"It's not just about you, Booch," I said. "You can't vouch for what happens to her once she goes back into the system."

Booch took a moment to consider her words. "I don't get to make the decisions for child welfare or the courts. I only enforce the laws, and she and Florence broke a whole lot of them. Serious ones. Do you have any idea what you're dealing with here? How much do you even know about them?"

Her question stirred an unsettling intuition within me. Did Booch know something we didn't?

"We're not playing this game," Val shot back. "Someone just died, one of our neighbors. Can we have a second to grieve before you come harassing us?"

"Right," Booch said, unmoved by Val's emotion. "I want you both to acknowledge for me, on the record, that I've advised you that any aiding and abetting of Georgia Bazemore is a felony."

"We aren't aiding and abetting—" Val interjected.

Booch cut him off. "Do you understand what I just said?"

"We understand," I offered.

"Mr. Ivanicki?"

"I understand," he mumbled.

—

We now had to avoid the cops when we needed them most. And we somehow had to bring down Dante on our own by Friday.

Val and I spent the rest of the morning scouring the neighborhood for Georgia. We weren't the only ones searching. We spotted two separate pairs of uniformed officers also making the rounds, knocking on doors, and questioning passersby.

Exhausted and desperate, we stopped at Phene's for a break. The moment we entered, we became the center of silent scrutiny. Chickie gave me a subtle gesture from the counter toward a man in khakis and a polo shirt at the register. An undercover.

When Deadbolt spotted us, he motioned us to the yard behind the kitchen.

When we found Deadbolt in the back, he was visibly on edge, taking frequent, anxious drags from his cigarette. "What the hell is going on?" he burst out.

"Keep your voice down," Val ordered.

Deadbolt lowered his voice to a whisper. "There've been cops here all morning. Asking about Georgia."

"Her granny died," I said.

"Oh shit," Deadbolt said, putting a hand on Val's shoulder. "I'm sorry."

"It's all right," Val said. "She suffered for a long time."

Deadbolt's eyes flicked from Val to me, a wrinkle forming between his brows. "Why do the cops care about Granny dying, though? Or Georgia?"

"It's a long story," I said. "Just page us nine-one-one if you see her or hear anything about where she'd be."

"But guys—"

Val cut him off. "We don't have time to talk. Just do it."

As we walked out onto the sidewalk, I caught a glimpse of Chickie at the screen window. Had he been eavesdropping on our entire conversation?

———

Val twisted his keys in the ignition. "We've gotta split duties here."

"Split them how?"

"Georgia has to be my top priority right now," Val said, steering onto Victory.

"She's a priority for both of us," I argued.

"We can't let Dante push that bill through Friday. Besides, how much does it really help to have you ride shotgun while I drive around?"

We stopped half a block up from Georgia's house, where there was a squad car parked in front.

I leaned forward, squinting through the windshield to get a better look. "She wouldn't go back there, would she?"

"I wouldn't put it past her," Val said. "All of her stuff is there. Including that damned peacock. She loves that thing."

He was right. Georgia wasn't the type to be deterred by a few cops.

"When they see what she's got in that garage . . . ," I began.

"She can always claim that was all Granny's."

"Yes, but would she? I can't see Georgia pinning the blame on anyone, especially the woman who broke her out of juvie."

"I don't know . . . ," Val trailed off. His mind seemed elsewhere. "Let me worry about this. You go figure out Dante."

"Figure out Dante? What do you expect me to do on my own?"

"Go see my uncle. Tell him everything."

"Everything?"

"We can trust him."

"He's a former cop."

"He's an Ivanicki."

Reluctant, I agreed. "Fine, but if he turns me in, you're visiting me in prison every month."

"If he turns you in, I'll be in the cell right next to you."

———

"Let me see if I've got this straight," Yuri began, fiddling with a paperweight while reclining in his chair. "You fled the scene of a murder, failed to report it, broke into the victim's house to steal her property, and then gave that property to Dante Malaparte before going to work for him."

"Yes," I replied, sinking farther into the chair across from him. "But the victim did tell us to go into her house."

"Did she tell you to give the computer to Dante?"

"No," I admitted, staring at the floor.

"Son, you have me looking into Detective Bucciero. She won't look past all of this, even if she had the authority. Which she doesn't. She won't be your savior."

I chewed the side of my mouth. "There's a little more."

The color drained from Yuri's face. "More?"

"Yes, well, not anything I did. Georgia has been living with a woman in Travis. We call her Granny."

"Okay . . ."

"Granny died this morning."

"My condolences."

"Thank you. You see, Georgia had been at some kind of a state home. Like juvenile hall. Granny broke her out of that place and took her here to Travis."

"Broke her out?"

"Yes"

"Of prison?"

"I don't think it was technically a prison."

"If she wasn't allowed to leave, it was a prison in my book," he said, standing up. He began pacing. "Is my nephew playing some kind of joke on me? You're kids. How could you possibly get into so much shit?"

I shook my head. "I wish it were a joke, sir. When Granny died, the police and child services started to look for Georgia. Booch was at the hospital earlier asking us questions."

"She what?" he asked, stopping in his tracks.

"We told her we didn't know where Georgia is, which is the truth."

Yuri stroked the stubble on his chin. "Tell me, what's your goal here? Your ideal outcome?"

"Well, first, I want to keep Georgia safe, but Val is handling that. He wants us to take care of the rest."

"Good, a division of labor," Yuri nodded approvingly. "Go on."

"I want to take down Dante while ideally not getting arrested or killed."

"What do you mean 'take down Dante,' and why would you want to do that?"

"Well, there's one more thing."

"You just said that."

"I promise this is the last."

"I don't believe you."

I explained to him the article Natalia wrote, how city officials buried evidence of cancer rates from Fresh Kills, and how Dante was working with Russians to extend the lease on the dump indefinitely. As I spoke, he'd gone adrift, a moth to the yellowed ghosts on the wall.

He eventually beckoned me, and I found him before a faded snapshot.

"Recognize him?" Yuri rasped. He jabbed a calloused finger at the man, blond with steel-rod muscled arms draped around a woman.

Squinting, I recognized the features. "Val's dad?" He was a stark contrast from the hairless, chemo-thin ghost I knew.

"Jack," Yuri breathed, sorrow turning his voice to gravel. "My only sibling. My best friend."

My attention shifted to the woman. "And her?" I asked.

"Zofia," he managed, voice catching. "My wife. Gone, two years before Jack. Breast cancer, they said. Just . . . just when we were starting." He choked back a cough. "A family, you see. That's what we wanted."

All I could muster was, "I'm sorry."

Yuri's gaze lingered on the photo. "We were all dump rats."

"Zofia was from Travis, too?"

"We'd been friends since I was a kid." His voice cracked. "Like you and Val. She, Jack, and I used to go swimming in the streams off Meredith Avenue. It's crazy the city hasn't fenced all of that off, even to this day. We were swimming in toxic waste."

As I listened to Yuri, my skin began to crawl. I'd swam in that stream many times with Val and the rest of my buddies. That discomfort, a cold, wriggling sensation on my skin, began to twist and turn, transforming into a fiery anger. How could the city have allowed this, let us swim in poison? Now, in the sepia tones of that photo, I saw not just loss but a gauntlet thrown. A challenge etched in faded smiles and stolen futures. I vowed to myself not to let the dump bury our town.

Yuri continued. "I quit the force after I lost them. I didn't have the motivation for that work anymore. To protect people that turned their backs on us."

"You knew their cancer was from the dump even then?"

"We suspected it. Who really knows what it was from? I know you don't have much to compare it to, kid, but other places don't have as much illness as we do. This place is cursed."

"Why not leave?"

"And go where?" Yuri sank back into his chair. "This is the only place I've ever lived in. Where I met the love of my life and buried her. I'd rather waste away into a pile of tumors in Travis than live to one hundred in Florida."

"Why is that our choice? Florida or cancer?"

"It shouldn't be." Yuri turned contemplatively toward the window. "We can't take this to Booch," he decided.

"Then who?" I asked.

He thought for a moment. "Someone outside the usual channels. No police or the FBI."

"A politician? The DA?"

He shook his head. "Too risky. We don't know who Dante has in his pocket."

Then an idea occurred to me. Someone who'd lost his future to Dante—and who, if armed with the facts, could do something about it. "What about another reporter?"

"Reporters can be just as crooked as cops."

"Not this one."

—

The next morning, I watched as dawn bled into the *Staten Island Advance* parking lot, turning the asphalt the color of weak coffee. I was in the passenger seat of Yuri's Buick, watching for any sign of Connor Davin.

We'd tried Connor at home the evening before, but every prior listed address for him turned out to be a dead end. He must have taken precautions since the murder of his fiancée, Natalia.

Yuri, no doubt a veteran of countless stakeouts, seemed fully in his element. "You sure you'd recognize him?" he asked as he peered through binoculars.

"Positive." Connor had for months been a nightly visitor in my dreams. In the latest version, he kidnapped me and forced me at gunpoint to unearth Natalia's grave under a moonless sky.

Natalia. If she hadn't been killed, she'd be there, in that lot, no doubt taking on the day with gusto along with the stream of eager reporters who made their way from their cars to the entrance.

The tinted windows were beginning to fog from the humidity, making it hard to see. I reached to clear the mist, but Yuri smacked my hand away.

"Leaves smears," he grumbled, firing up the old car's AC.

Minutes later, with the windows still clouded, I cracked mine open. "That defeats the purpose of the tints," Yuri complained.

"Who exactly are we hiding from?"

"*We* aren't hiding from anyone. You are hiding."

Yuri's plan was to talk to Connor without me. Given what had happened to Natalia, Yuri wanted to protect me in case Connor was smoked out by Dante's crew and forced to spill his sources. Of course, that left Yuri vulnerable.

Just then a taxi pulled up to the front of the building. I pointed as a man emerged from the back seat, clutching a bundle of papers under one arm with a messenger bag slung over his shoulder. "It's him."

"Are you sure?" Yuri nudged open the door. "You stay here," he ordered as he exited the car, clutching the folder with Natalia's reporting.

The Connor Davin who stepped out was a far cry from the David Caruso look-alike who had been a fixture on TV last summer when he delivered impassioned pleas for justice for Natalia. He'd since grown rounder in the middle, his skin pale and blotchy like recycled paper.

Yuri caught up with him a few feet from the entrance. The longer they talked, the more Connor fidgeted, adjusting his glasses and running his hands through his thinning red hair.

After a while, the two walked away from the *Staten Island Advance* building, their silhouettes disappearing in the distance.

Thirty minutes had passed when my pager, silent until then, came to life with a jolt. Val's number blinked back at me. I ignored it, but ten minutes later, the pager buzzed again, flashing "911"—a clear signal of urgency.

Ignoring Yuri's strict directive to remain in the car, I headed to a pay phone within the *Advance* building. "Did you find her?" I asked Val the moment the line connected.

"Not over this line," came Val's terse reply. "Remember where you told Georgia to meet post-computer retrieval?"

"Yes," I said.

"Be there."

"I'm with Yuri; we're close to a breakthrough. I can't leave yet."

"No rush," Val said, then the line went dead. This statement was reassuring.

On my way out of the building, I passed Connor, who nervously checked over his shoulder as he arrived for work.

I hurried to the Buick, where Yuri sat with the window down and a scowl on his face.

"I told you to stay put."

"Sorry, had to call Val."

"He find the girl?"

"Unclear."

"You didn't ask him?"

"Wouldn't talk over the phone."

Yuri nodded, acknowledging Val's prudence.

"Do you know Sicilian Swirls on Richmond?" I asked.

"The Albanian place with the watery soft serve?"

"That's the one. Val is there."

As we drove, Yuri debriefed me. He and Connor had walked the neighborhood, sharing only what was necessary: Natalia's story, Dante's upcoming move, and the untrustworthy police. Yuri had omitted details about me and the murder.

"I left out anything about you or Natalia's murder," Yuri said as he maneuvered through the rush hour traffic.

"He didn't have questions about how she died? Or how you came across this information?"

"Sure he did. I told him I received the tip from a longtime source and that I had no specific knowledge about how she died other than an educated guess as to who was behind it."

"How did he handle that?"

Yuri took a sip of coffee from his thermos as we waited at a red light. "Surprisingly well. As you can imagine, he's keen to avenge her death."

"So he's going to publish the story?"

"No. He said he needs more."

"More than what Natalia had? Her reporting seemed thorough to me."

"He said he can't corroborate her sources by Friday. Without the names of her off-the-record sources, his paper would never go for it."

"We've given him everything we have. What would 'more' look like?"

"We either get that draft legislation. Or Dante, on the record, talking about the scheme. Preferably both."

I didn't like the sound of that. "And how are we going to get that?"

"Only one way." Yuri's gaze flickered to the rearview mirror, then settled back on the road. "Are you ready to be the hero?"

—

As our car crunched onto the gravel of Sicilian Swirls' lot, we were greeted by a peculiar assembly. Ice cream truck drivers, each sporting a look more eccentric than the last, were huddled in discussion, with Klo at the helm. Among them stood a man with a Got Milk? tank top, his stomach adorned with a popsicle-shaped belly button ring, and another with a blue mullet and pink spandex pants.

"I can't believe parents trust these creeps around their kids," Yuri muttered.

In the far corner of the lot, we spotted Val and Georgia perched on the bed of a pickup truck littered with spare parts for ice cream machines. Georgia still wore the same ripped jeans and yellow tank top from her hospital dash and the previous night at Schmul.

She clearly hadn't been home in days. Klo had discovered her sleeping in the shed earlier that morning and tipped off Val.

"This will be our home base until further notice," Val said.

I eyed the gaggle of drivers. "Aren't we worried about Klo's dad or one of the workers tipping off the cops?"

"There hasn't been a news report that we've seen mentioning Georgia. They've just posted a few leaflets around Travis and sent in a few uniforms. They'll finish up by the end of the day. They have bigger priorities. We just need to wait them out."

Yuri, with the careful maneuvers of a man battling a bad back and aching joints, lowered himself onto the truck bed next to Val. "Detective Bucciero won't give up. She's dogged," he warned.

As much as I hated to admit it, Yuri was right. Something about Booch's demeanor, her urgency, told me Georgia was more of a priority than Val assumed. But I kept that thought to myself.

"We'll avoid her," Val said. "That's why we're here. She wouldn't know to look here."

Yuri patted Val's knee, a gesture of camaraderie tinged with concern. "She's still a minor. You can't outrun this forever."

"One year and eleven months," Georgia said.

"What's that?" Yuri asked. "How long you've been off your meds?" His attempt at humor fell flat.

"It's how long 'til I turn eighteen. Then I'll be free."

"This is Staten Island, not whatever bumblefuck town you're from. It's like trying to hide in a fishbowl. You'd be lucky if you last a week."

"That'd be one less week I'd have to spend in hell," she said.

Val and I exchanged a look of weary resignation.

I redirected. "Can we discuss Dante?"

I paced, filling them in on our plan with Connor.

"We have two options," I concluded. "We can either get Dante on tape admitting to the scheme, or we can get ahold of that draft bill to extend the dump."

"Preferably both," Yuri said. He was now laid out flat on the truck bed, resting his back. "The draft bill buys us time, but it's not the silver bullet."

"Why not?" Val asked.

Yuri explained, "The bill alone doesn't prove corruption. It's just a piece of the puzzle."

Georgia looked up from the disassembled carburetor she was fiddling with on the ground. "So we need the bill and the tape. Got it."

Val gave a tight nod. "Tape seems like our best shot."

"That's my thinking," Yuri agreed.

All eyes settled on me. I was the linchpin—the only one among us who could get Dante on record. Recalling my recent close call, I said, "Last time I tried breaking into Dante's place, I barely escaped."

Val arm fell around me. "Raj, you don't have to do this. We all want Dante, but this is risky."

Georgia, her hand warm on my arm, reassured me. "You've done enough."

I stared into her eyes, which seemed to reflect back the clear midday sky. "You didn't speak to me for a year," I choked out, the words sandpaper on my throat. "I have plenty to prove."

"You got the computer back. That was more than enough."

My vision began to blur with unshed tears. "It's not enough. I abandoned her, and then I broke my promise to her." The river broke free, cascading down my cheeks.

"Dante threatened your ma," Val patted me on the back. "You had no choice."

"I have a choice now," I said, wiping the tears from my face. I managed a forced smile. "What was your granny's saying? 'Never the wrong time to do the right thing?'"

She nodded.

"Well, now's the time."

CHAPTER 22

BANDITS AND CROOKS

I n the cramped confines of a sweltering U-Haul van, I stood shirtless while Yuri strapped a microphone to my chest.

Val, assuming the role of Yuri's assistant, tried to lighten the mood. "Look at those pecs, bro," he joked, ripping a piece of electrical tape. "You've been hitting the bench?"

"Fuck you," I shot back. Though I knew he was just trying to distract me from the terrifying mission ahead of me.

Yuri struggled with the adhesive. "You sweat like a politician in a confessional," he grumbled.

"You couldn't have paid the extra twenty bucks for a van with working air conditioning?" I asked.

"When you start paying me for my services, you can start making demands. Until then, shut up and be thankful."

Georgia sat in a corner, spinning a tire iron in her hands. "What are we gonna do if he's caught?"

"One thing at a time, princess," Yuri said as he wrapped electrical tape around my back. He directed Val, who carefully positioned the bulky transmitter on my back, securing it with more tape—a makeshift rigging of wires and adhesive.

I pulled down my shirt. "How does this look?"

Val checked my chest with a quick pat. "Front's all right," he concluded, then shifted to inspect my back. "But that transmitter's too obvious," he observed, his eyes meeting Yuri's, sharing a silent moment of concern.

"Can we put it somewhere else?" I asked.

Yuri rummaged through a box, extracting a weathered Sony cassette player. He clipped it onto my shorts. "I installed a transmitter in here a few years ago for another job. Is this better?"

"I don't know," I said. "What kids still listen to cassettes? The guys know my Discman." Music was my way of small talk, so there was a good chance I'd have to explain my new equipment.

"Your call, kid. It's either this or the regular way."

Val tilted his head, examining the device. "Can you fit actual cassettes in there?"

"What do I look like? A magician?" Yuri said. "It took every IQ point I had to get the components in there."

"What about the pen microphone?" Georgia asked. "Ain't that smaller?"

"Range is too short," Yuri said. "The upside to this one," he added, pulling out headphones, "is you can use these instead of the regular microphone. Just throw them over your neck and let them hang."

That meant an exposed microphone. "What do you think?" I asked Georgia.

She eyed my back. "At least you won't look like you're hiding a textbook back there."

"I just hope they don't ask about the cassette player," I said, deciding to go with the less conspicuous option.

Yuri yanked the tape off my back and chest, removing what little hair I had, along with a bit of skin. "That'll wake you up," he cackled. "Consider it a perk—a free waxing."

The sting was like a Band-Aid ripped off a sunburn. As if I needed to be woken up. I don't think I'd ever been more alert in my life. "Let's get this over with," I said.

Yuri pointed to a gray box on the floor adorned with dials and protruding antennae. "We'll be parked outside, in front of Phene's. We can't get more than a thousand feet away, or we'll lose the signal."

"Remember"—Val pressed his hands firmly on my shoulders—"don't force the conversation. We've got a few days."

"Got it." I attempted to mirror his resolve.

"We'll be all ears the whole time, so we'll know if you get into shit," Yuri said. "But we'll need a code word in case it's not obvious."

"A code word?"

"Yes, something you wouldn't accidentally say in normal conversation but not so off the wall that it'd be obvious."

I had to think about that. "How about the Yankees?"

"That works."

Georgia's eyes narrowed in confusion. "So what, Raj is gonna drop 'Yankees' while he's got a gun pointed at his head?"

"Basically," Yuri said.

"Then what?" she asked.

Val pulled a baseball bat from under a blanket. "Then it's our cue to move in."

—

I stepped into The Linoleum just after three. Lente polished the bar while, in the corner, a few lower-tier members of Dante's crew watched horse racing on the TV. The midafternoon lull draped the place in a veil of quiet, ideal for picking up loose threads of conversation that might otherwise go unnoticed.

I offered Lente a halfhearted wave and slipped into the restroom. Under the glare of fluorescent lights, I splashed cold water on my face, then patted my cheeks dry while whispering a quick pep talk. *Just. Act. Normal.*

With a steadying breath, I emerged and headed for the back office. Dante was there, immersed in the *Daily News* while Renzo counted cash and filled envelopes.

"Look who decided to show up to work," Dane said.

Normal. I forced a chuckle. "I'm still hungover from Saturday night," I joked back.

Renzo shot Dante a glance that seemed to carry an unspoken message. Had he told Dante he'd caught me trying to break into the upstairs office? I steadied my thoughts. Don't overthink a mere look. *Normal.*

"You've got a fresh stack of invoices on your desk," Renzo said.

"Thank you," I mumbled and retreated to my workspace.

The afternoon trudged on without any easy opportunities for useful information.

Dante was deeply involved in apparent negotiations, marked by periodic arrivals of men whispering urgent messages. Whenever a new face appeared, Dante and Renzo would slip upstairs, cutting off my access to information. Dante's newfound guardedness, particularly in my presence, didn't escape my notice. Something was up.

By seven p.m., The Linoleum's barroom began to buzz with the evening crowd. Dante and Renzo claimed their usual spots at the bar. My stack of invoices dwindled, leaving little excuse to hang around. We had at least three more days to accomplish our mission. I couldn't force it.

I was about to call it a day when Ugo burst through the door with beads of sweat glistening across his bald scalp and concern etched across his forehead. "Raj, can you help me move a few things in the basement?"

"You need *my* help to move something?" I asked. Ugo could outlift me ten times over.

He grimaced and rubbed the small of his spine. "Tweaked my back."

Alarm bells rang in my head. Ugo didn't work the bar, and I'd never seen him go into the basement. I didn't have much of a choice, though—and hoped the wire would transmit in the basement if I got into any trouble. But even if it did, I'd probably be finished before anyone could save me.

When we reached the top of the stairs, Ugo gestured for me to lead the way. My steps were hesitant, like I was sneaking home past curfew. I kept glancing back at Ugo, half expecting some abrupt, hostile move. His towering frame was a looming shadow in front of me, his head bowed to avoid the low ceiling. The air was musty, thick with the scent of old liquor and damp concrete. We navigated through the maze of boxes and shelves to the far end, where bottles were stacked in disarray—the very place where I'd found the computer only days before. Could that be what this was all about?

Ugo gestured toward a lone crate in the clutter. "Sit."

I complied, feeling a cold knot of fear metastasize in my stomach.

Ugo looked as nervous as I felt. "Has the boss been a little off today?"

"Not really." I matched his whisper.

Ugo shifted uncomfortably, his gaze darting around the room. "Are you sure?"

"What are you getting at?"

"I don't know exactly. Dante seems paranoid about something. Have you heard him say or do anything strange?"

"You're asking me to report on the boss?"

Ugo's large frame leaned against a shelf, causing a few bottles to wobble. "No, not report on him. You've been here all day. Just tell me how he's been."

"I mean, he and Renzo keep going upstairs to talk. They barely said anything in front of me. What makes you think Dante is paranoid?"

Ugo's voice lowered even further. "He had the place swept for bugs earlier, something we haven't done in over a year."

At the mention of bugs, I reflexively glanced at the headphones around my neck, a sudden flutter of anxiety in my chest. "That doesn't sound weird," I said. "It's smart, actually. You all should do that more often."

"That's not all. He asked me to find the computer from last year."

I feigned ignorance. "Which computer?"

"The one you stole from the reporter."

"I didn't steal it. She asked me to get it before . . ."

Ugo looked down, his fingers nervously scratching the back of his neck. "Yeah, we kept it. Right here." He pointed to a spot at the bottom of a liquor shelf. The exact place where I had discovered it days earlier. "Now it's gone. Dante wants it, and I can't find it."

"Why would you keep it?"

"Blackmail. In case any of our collaborators tried to take us down, we'd have evidence to bring everyone down with us. Mutually assured destruction."

Finally, I was getting something useful on tape. I led Ugo on. "Did you guys ever search the computer to find what was on it?"

"We did," Ugo said. "I should have made a damn copy."

"Was it worth killing an innocent woman over?" I asked, going for the full confession.

Ugo's voice took a hard edge. "Not everyone's as innocent as you think." At that moment, I was reminded of the monster who lurked inside of the happy giant I'd grown to call a friend.

"What is that supposed to mean?"

"You ever wonder what would happen if she published that story?"

"Educate me."

"Everyone around here would be worse off, and all of the fat cats who've been running this city forever would continue to shit on places like this town."

Not exactly a confession, but close to it. I needed a clear admission. "You're saying this woman Natalia worked for your enemies? That she deserved to die?" I was careful to repeat her name to make it clear to anyone listening to the tape who we were talking about.

Ugo's face clouded over. "I don't know who she worked for. What I do know is that she was getting information from the true gangsters. The old guard. The crooks who look down on us bandits."

I'd heard this bandits versus crooks bullshit from Dante before. It was the core of his justification for all of the terrible things he did. According to their Robin Hood logic, bandits stole from the rich. The crooks enabled the rich. The problem with this bandit fairy tale was that, unlike the famed outlaw, Dante's crew preyed on the innocent as much as the guilty. Innocent businessmen wound up buried in Fresh Kills because they refused to pay tribute. And people like Natalia, who stood against them, became tragic footnotes in their ruthless story.

I tried to steer him back. "But how does that justify killing Natalia?"

He changed the subject. "I've torn apart this basement, and the computer's gone. Lente must have accidentally thrown it out."

"Sounds like something he'd do," I said, relieved he didn't suspect me. "Have you asked him about it?"

"The old fart doesn't even remember ever seeing it."

"Why would you keep it down here anyway? And not upstairs?"

"Last summer was a clusterfuck, as you know. I left it here and meant to come back for it. And just forgot."

"Why are you telling me all of this?"

"When you guys took the computer, did you make a copy of the hard drive?"

"Of course not," I said. "We're not crazy."

Ugo slumped over, leaning against the wall. "I'm fucked."

"Just tell Dante the truth," I said, eyeing the staircase. I needed to get out of that basement before I said the wrong thing or someone overheard us. But Ugo kept getting close to the line of divulging incriminating information.

"Dante is not the kind to forgive mistakes like this."

"Why does he need that computer now, after a year?"

"He's trying to close the deal on Fresh Kills. I guess he needs to remind someone to stay in line."

"Wouldn't you be the one doing the reminding?"

"He's got other muscle. Maybe he trusts Renzo more with this one?"

Something about the timing of this all didn't add up. The sweep for bugs, Dante's guarded behavior, the sudden interest in a year-old computer.

"Do you trust Renzo?" I asked, delving into dangerous territory. But I felt on firm ground, given Ugo had already divulged enough for mutually assured destruction with Dante.

"He's Dante's cousin," Ugo said. "Of course, I trust him. Do you?"

"He doesn't trust me. Which means I'd be crazy to trust him."

"Renzo's a lot of things, but he's no rat. He's just threatened by you."

"People who are threatened by Renzo don't seem to last."

"Dante would never let him touch you."

Until Dante finds out I'm the rat.

Ugo's true reason for pulling me down into the basement finally surfaced. "That girl you hang with, the one Renzo chased. She had the computer first, right?"

I didn't like where this was going. "She did, but not for long."

"Is there a chance she copied it?"

"Not really. She wouldn't have had the time."

"Can you just check? For me."

"Ugo," I replied, rubbing the bridge of my nose in fatigue. "My friends barely talk to me anymore because of last summer. If I go reminding them about what happened up in the dump—"

"—I've had your back, Raj," he said. "Many times. Including when Renzo was ready to feed you to Dante Saturday night. When your mom needed help."

Ugo's words hit hard. He wasn't lying; he'd pulled me out of the fire more times than I cared to admit. My mind wrestled with a flood of conflicting emotions—a tug-of-war between my indebtedness to Ugo and my revulsion for his actions, especially against Natalia and his complicity in the poisoning of my community. Desperate to break free from the claustrophobia of the moment, I caved. "All right, I'll ask her. But you've got to promise me something."

Ugo's face relaxed into an agreeable nod. "Anything."

"Actually, two things. First, no matter what my friend has, you leave her out of this after I come back to you with an answer."

"Easy."

"Second, Dante never knows we had this conversation. No matter what kind of shit you get into."

"Even if he put a gun to my head, your name will never come out of my mouth."

Something told me this wasn't just a figure of speech.

CHAPTER 23

THE A&P SUMMIT

The Sicilian Swirls neon bled pink through the downpour, staining the raindrops crimson as they spattered on the windshield of the U-Haul. I flung open the rusted gate and waved the van through. It skidded to a stop, the side door flinging open with a clang.

Yuri's voice boomed from within, "That recorder better not be wet."

Georgia tossed me a towel. "Are you okay?"

I glared at Yuri. "I'm glad someone cares about my well-being."

"You want me to take out my violin?" Yuri groaned, yanking the Walkman from my jeans like a fisherman reeling in a reluctant trout.

Suddenly, the rush of adrenaline left me, and I crumpled to the van floor, the world tilting sideways like a funhouse mirror. When I blinked back to focus, Val and Georgia were peering down, faces etched with concern.

"Dude, we were ready to barge in there," Val said.

I sat up. "Is any of that usable?"

"The audio was clear enough," Yuri said. "I'll share it with Davin, but I already know he'll tell us we need more. Something clear and definitive."

"I guess that means we try again tomorrow?" I asked, though the thought was less than appealing.

Val and Georgia exchanged a swift, knowing glance. "About that . . . ," Val began.

Georgia jumped in. "We have an idea."

"Let's hear it," I said, eager to entertain any alternative to going back in with a wire.

They laid out their plan. We would pretend that Georgia kept a copy of the hard drive. I would use the exchange with Ugo to get him to open up about the killing of Natalia and the conspiracy around Fresh Kills.

I wasn't sold. "Couldn't I just get him to talk the same without claiming to have a copy of the documents?"

Yuri jumped in. "The key is you're going to tell him you read the contents."

"That way, you can ask Ugo specific questions about it all," Val added.

I abruptly rose to my feet, eager to make my point, only to be met with a sharp thud as my head slammed against the van's roof. Wincing, I quickly crouched back down and shook off the constellation of stars that assembled behind my eyeballs. "You heard him today, didn't you? He's really good at stopping short of saying anything incriminating."

Yuri, with a note of certainty, said, "I know how these gangsters work. This guy wants to talk. He's getting desperate."

Val chimed in with his usual bravado. "You'll have him by the balls. He'll be so happy you saved his ass that you'll have an opening."

I immediately saw the flaws in their plan. "If we fail, we'd be helping them. We'd be handing back documents they can use to blackmail people to push the bill through."

"It's a risk we feel is worth it," Georgia said.

"I'm glad the Board of Directors had a chance to hash this out."

"Feel free to overrule us," Val said. "You're the only vote that counts, the one in the line of fire."

What I couldn't say was that I wanted to spare Ugo from our plan. Ideally, I'd get Dante on audio. I didn't want the three of them to think I had divided loyalties. Because in a way, I'd been divided. But now I had to make a choice, and in truth, it wasn't a hard one.

"Okay," I let out a deep breath. "I'll do it."

—

The next morning, I was once again in the back of the U-Haul with the three musketeers. It was now Tuesday—one day closer to Friday's city council hearing.

Dressed casually in cargo shorts and an Old Navy Fourth of July T-shirt, I carefully hid the portable cassette player under the loose fabric.

Yuri, ever the tactician, offered a last-minute briefing. "Remember to ask specific questions about the files. We need an admission from him about the conspiracy. And we need him to implicate Dante, too. Bonus if you can get something about Natalia."

"Understood," I said as I stepped out into the light of day.

The rendezvous point was the A&P Supermarket parking lot on Forest Avenue, a spot discreet enough for our purposes, nestled between a Puerto Rican and a Mexican neighborhood. I stood there, observing the early morning crowd—a mix of eager elderly bargain hunters and weary night-shift workers. This was not somewhere Dante's crew was likely to stumble upon at any time of day, especially in the morning.

An elderly Mexican woman struggled next to me, her cart overflowing. As she wobbled under the weight of a milk gallon, I stepped in to assist. "That's quite a load for one person," I remarked, eyeing her Dunkaroos.

"It's for my grandkids," she said with an affectionate roll of her eyes.

I helped her deposit a series of bags in her back seat. When I spun around to grab the last few bags, I nearly walked face-first into Ugo's chest.

"Let me get this," he said.

"My lord," the woman said. "Look at that, two strong men to my rescue."

She went to pull cash from her purse, but Ugo waved her off.

As she drove off, Ugo turned to me. "Back to cassettes?"

I glanced down, realizing my shirt had ridden up, exposing the player. "Um, yes. I borrowed it from my Uncle Stosh," I said, feeling a nervous sweat start to form under my arms.

"If you need any good tapes, I've got loads."

"Might take you up on that." I pulled a disc from my pocket. "This is everything on that computer. Before I give this to you, remind me of the two conditions."

"I didn't get this from you," he grumbled with the tone of a child mindlessly repeating a parent's instructions.

"And?"

"Keep the girl out of it."

I handed over the disc.

"Thanks, Raj," he said, patting my shoulder. "I owe you."

Now, I needed to get him to open up. "Can I ask you something?"

He nodded.

"I read those files," I began.

"Raj, that's not smart—"

"Let me finish," I interrupted. "Natalia claims you guys knew the dump was making us all sick. You not only buried the evidence but kept it going."

Ugo shifted, uncomfortable. "I'm just muscle, Raj. I don't get involved in the big picture. You know that."

No clear admission yet.

"Do you have any idea how many people I've lost to cancer?" My voice broke the script, cracking with a raw edge of emotion that I hadn't intended to reveal. The controlled facade I'd been maintaining slipped as a tide of anger and grief surged within me.

"How many?" Ugo asked, his voice low.

"Too many to count," I said, my voice shaky. "It's like a never-ending nightmare, you know? Going from one hospital room to another, seeing people who once were full of life just . . . deteriorating. To see grown men I've looked up to shit themselves, unable to even stand to shake my hand. Those rooms, with their beeping machines and that antiseptic smell, they're like these chambers where hope and life slowly drain away."

I continued, my voice rising, "Just walk across from The Linoleum and visit the graveyard at St. Anthony's. Almost every other headstone is someone I know. A life cut short, kids without a parent or grandparent. Those ain't just graves, Ugo; Ugo, they're lines on your resume."

Ugo looked away. "Dante says Natalia was exaggerating all that stuff."

"Oh, that's what Dante says? Does he know more than the City Department of Health? They said the cancer rates were more than five times the city average."

"I don't know, Raj. This is above my pay grade."

"Well, tell me this. Dr. Miriam Rosenberg. The doctor who wrote the report. Were you involved in convincing her to take an early retirement? Did you pay her a visit?"

Ugo was silent.

"Answer me," I demanded, my voice escalating, drawing the attention of nearby shoppers.

He glanced around nervously. "Keep it down, Raj."

I couldn't help but push further. "I don't seem to remember Robin Hood poisoning the people of Sherwood Forest. How does this square with your bandit code?"

Ugo shot back, a challenging edge to his voice. "If this is so appalling to you, why work for us? The people poisoning your neighbors."

"Well, I hadn't read this until now," I lied. Though his question cut through. I was a hypocrite. I'd ignored what I knew for a year. I was not much better than Ugo. Which is perhaps why I still held out hope that he'd do the right thing.

"What will you do now?" he asked. "Dante doesn't let people walk away."

"I honestly don't know, Ugo," I said. I needed to get us back on track—to get Ugo to say something we could bring to Connor. "Be honest with me. I need to know. Did you kill Natalia?"

After a heavy pause, Ugo nodded.

"Did Dante order you to do it?"

He nodded again.

The audio wouldn't capture these silent admissions.

"I want to hear you say it," I pressed, but aware I was pushing him into a corner.

"We're done talking," Ugo declared abruptly, shutting down the conversation. "I've already said too much."

I wasn't ready to give up. I followed him to his Cadillac, persistent. "This isn't over, Ugo."

"Raj," he warned, a note of caution in his voice, "don't let Dante see you like this. He won't be as understanding as I am."

But I needed more, a clear confession. I blocked his car door, desperate. "You're just going to hand that disc over and pretend everything's normal? The dump keeps operating, and this all goes away?"

Ugo pulled open the door, forcing me to step back. "Whether it's Dante or someone else, the dump's not closing. You know how this works."

He climbed into his car and drove off, disappearing along with any hope of bringing down Dante.

CHAPTER 24

OUT ON A LEDGE

Yuri slammed the phone down with a sigh, sending dust motes dancing into a sunbeam from the window. "Connor won't budge. Says we need proof."

My meeting with Ugo was essentially a bust, leaving us no closer than we were before.

"Why not play the clips for him and let him decide for himself?" Georgia asked. She was leaning against a corkboard littered with photos of targets of Yuri's various insurance-fraud investigations.

Yuri closed his eyes, pinching the bridge of his nose. "We've been through this before. We can't risk Raj's safety until we know what we have is usable."

"Ugo practically confessed," Georgia argued.

"*Practically* doesn't win the Pulitzer, does it, love? *Practically* won't make it past an editor. It'd be like Colonel Jessup ending his testimony before his code red speech."

Georgia shot him a blank stare.

I cut in. "As much as I hate to admit it, Yuri is right. It's really my fault for getting too emotional."

Val, sprawled on the vinyl couch, finally spoke. "You were right to be upset. They don't give a fuck about us."

Yuri slumped back in his chair. "Right or wrong. It's immaterial. We're at a dead end. Connor said we have until the end of the day tomorrow to send him anything."

"Tomorrow?" I said, my hands instinctively clenching. "Tomorrow's Wednesday. I thought we had until Friday?"

"He needs a full day to spin the yarn. Minimum. He's up against a Thursday night deadline for Friday's paper. And let's be honest, unless we get something juicy, that may not even be enough to stop the bill."

I swallowed hard, thinking about going back into The Linoleum with a wire. "What if we just went on record and told Connor everything we saw last summer?"

"Don't be crazy," Yuri dismissed. "You'd all be accessories to murder, never mind the stolen property and the year Raj spent doing god knows what for Dante."

"We're kids. What can they really do to us?" Georgia asked.

Yuri's gaze shifted to Val, then back to Georgia, the shadows under his eyes deepening. "Val's eighteen, love. They'd treat him as an adult. And you, princess. You may be able to hide now, but once this goes out, they'll find you. And they'll send you to a place that will make you miss whatever group home you escaped from."

"It wasn't a group home," she shot back.

"And Raj, they won't just throw you in juvie. They'd start scrutinizing your mom. If any of that dirty money got to her, then they'd seize her assets."

Panic crawled up my skin like an army of ants. My mom was doing so well lately; we couldn't get her mixed up in this.

"Okay, enough," Val interjected, sitting up. "We get it."

At that moment, a bell chimed. Yuri swiveled around and flicked on an old TV precariously balanced on a shelf behind his desk. The grainy image of the CCTV from the stairwell door flickered on the screen.

"What in the world . . . ," Yuri muttered, squinting at the TV.

"Who is it?" I asked, leaning forward.

"Take a look." Yuri beckoned me. Val and Georgia crowded around as I crouched in front of the set. It was Booch, her eyes fixed on the camera.

"Why would she come here?" I asked.

"You're asking me?" Yuri replied. "I haven't seen her since I was on the force."

Val and I exchanged glances, clueless. Yuri herded us toward a window that opened onto the roof of the adjoining pizzeria. "Go," he commanded.

We clambered up and out, finding ourselves atop the building. As Yuri secured the window, I approached the ledge and peered down—the distance to the ground was at least fifteen feet. Georgia sat on the edge, legs swinging, ready to leap.

"Not here," Val said, pointing to a dumpster at the alley's end. Georgia was the first to drop, landing with a loud clang. Val followed, dropping feet-first into a pile of black trash bags.

I stood motionless, the overwhelming fear of heights anchoring me in place as if invisible chains bound me to the rooftop.

"Come on, Raj!" Val called up.

"I can't," I said, my gaze locked on the daunting drop.

"It's not that bad," Georgia encouraged from below.

But I couldn't move. "Go on without me," I managed to say. "I'll take the bus."

Val's voice was laced with frustration. "Don't be such a pussy, Raj."

Georgia's elbow connected with Val's side. "That's not helping."

I didn't linger to argue. I waved them off and retreated to the opposite end of the roof, finding solace against a brick chimney. From there, I could see Booch's car. I waited, biding my time until she left, then knocked on Yuri's window.

The window swung open, a stream of curses flowing out. I climbed back through to find Yuri seated behind his desk. "Where are the other two stooges?"

I stood over him. "They left."

"Why aren't you with them?"

"Because I wanted to know what Booch was after," I replied, conveniently leaving out my fear of heights.

Yuri rubbed his temples, a look of weary resignation on his face. "You've gotten me into some shit, kid."

"Tell me."

"She'd heard I'd been asking around about her at the one-two-oh. Wanted to know what I was after."

I'd almost forgotten we'd originally gone to Yuri to check out Booch's background. That felt like ages ago. "What did you tell her?"

"I told her the truth: that a client wanted to know who they could trust at the precinct and that she checked out."

"What do you mean she 'checked out'?"

"A friend I know in internal affairs said Booch had fingered a half dozen crooked cops a few years ago and has been a pariah ever since."

"Why is this the first I'm hearing of this?"

"Because I only found out yesterday, boss," he said with an emphasis that made clear he didn't like my tone. "It doesn't matter how clean Booch is now. You can't go to her, as we've already established."

He was right, of course. Though Yuri had a knack for presenting the truth in the most unpalatable way possible.

"Booch didn't ask who the client was?"

"Sure she did, but she knows I'm a pro. I told her I'd fill her in when it made sense for my client."

"Does it bother you that your friend in IA ratted you out?"

He stood up and walked me to the door. "Kid, why don't you worry about yourself right now."

"I've never had a problem worrying about myself," I said. "Speaking of, what's our plan for tomorrow?"

"I need to think it over," he said. "It's been a long morning. I need a nap."

"We don't have much time—"

With that, he shut the door in my face.

—

When I think back to the prior summer, everything came down to a series of coincidences on one Friday. Val's run-in with Sal's brother, my encounter with the New Springville crew in the hallway, the bowling alley brawl, scaling the fence, and wandering into the wrong spot at the wrong time. I had little hand in my fate. I was a leaf caught in a current, on the receiving end of a cascade of ever-increasing threats. Because of that, I'd convinced myself that I was a victim.

The summer of 1999 was shaping up to be different. I decided to reclaim that computer and take on Dante. Things were no longer happening to me; I was happening to them. Though I was in no less danger than a year ago, I felt something I hadn't in a while: control. It felt good.

Unfortunately, that feeling was an illusion, one that began to unravel that Tuesday afternoon.

After I left Yuri's, I decided, once again, to take matters into my own hands. I caught a bus to the *Staten Island Advance* offices, determined to confront Connor Davin myself. I told the woman at the front desk I was a paper delivery boy coming to collect my paycheck. She ushered me through to the payroll office. Once through, I snuck over to the newsroom.

The newsroom was alive with a palpable sense of urgency. It buzzed as a room full of mostly men engaged in hushed conversations punctuated by the incessant ringing of phones. A sleep-deprived reporter stood by the fax machine, his red-rimmed eyes tracking each emerging document with the eagerness of a child awaiting Santa. The room's rhythm changed abruptly when an editor in suspenders climbed onto a chair, announcing a grim discovery at the Stapleton Homes housing project.

Amid the organized chaos, I found Connor Davin. He was hunched over at his desk, running a red pen over a document, stealing bites from a half-eaten sandwich.

I tapped him on the shoulder. "Excuse me, sir."

"I'm on deadline. Come back later," he said without looking up from his document.

I persisted. "Sir, I need to talk to you about Natalia."

He shot upright in his chair and spun around to face me. "Who sent you here?" I could smell the liquor on his breath from a few feet away.

"I'm Yuri's source," I whispered. "Is there somewhere we can speak in private?"

Connor's reaction to my presence was less than welcoming, more of an irritation than an interest. His annoyance hung in the air as he led me into a windowless room, his steps slightly unsteady. He reached for pen and paper, but I stopped him.

"Don't write anything down," I said. "I can't have my name attached to any of this."

A slight smirk spread across his face, not quite reaching his lifeless eyes. "That's called 'off the record,'" he replied, setting his pen aside. "I'm fine with that. For now."

"You promise you won't use any of this?"

He nodded.

I started from the beginning. When I mentioned leaving Natalia to die, he burst into tears. The rawness of his emotion was a sharp contrast to the indifferent exterior he had maintained until that moment.

"I'm sorry" was all I could manage.

"It's not your fault," he managed, his voice breaking. "You're just a kid."

"Do you need me to give you a few minutes?" I asked, taking in his red, tear-streaked face.

"No." He wiped away tears with the back of his sleeve. "Keep going."

I recounted the daring computer heist and Dante's threats against my mom. Swallowing the lump in my throat, I admitted to joining Dante's crew. This is when I expected to lose Connor's sympathy and understanding.

Yet, Connor didn't seem angry. His demeanor shifted to something detached, almost mechanical, as he probed for details but avoided questioning my motives.

At a certain point, my curiosity got the best of me. "Don't you want to ask why I broke my promise to Natalia?"

He shot me a sad look. "Kid, every powerful person on this island has bent to that man's will. What chance did you have? Frankly, I'm impressed you're here at all. Most adults I know wouldn't have this courage."

"What good will it do, though, if you don't publish?" I asked. It came across as a challenge, which is sort of how I meant it.

"Are you willing to go on the record with what you just told me?"

"I can't," I said. "At least not yet. I'd be putting my family at risk."

"And yourself," he added. "I get it. I lost the love of my life to those thugs. If you were older, perhaps I'd try to pressure you."

It was hard to reconcile this diminished figure with the man who might have once captivated someone as beautiful and strong as Natalia. I imagine he was a different person then. The past year had worn him down, stripping away layers of whatever charm and vitality he might have possessed, leaving behind this husk of a man.

If I was going to get a story out of Connor, I'd have to chew his food for him. "What evidence do you need? We have the draft article, and Ugo said some damaging things earlier today on that tape."

"Yuri filled me in already," Connor said. "It's not enough. Maybe if I had longer, I could persuade my editors. Not on such short notice. What we need must be airtight."

"Like a full-on confession? Those guys are too careful for that."

Connor retrieved a flask from his coat and took a quick, steadying swig. "Paperwork is always helpful, too. Anything that spells out what's going on. I told Yuri this, but the draft bill would give me enough to write something. It would no doubt give Dante some headaches."

"Headaches aren't enough. We need to stop the project."

His laugh carried a bitter edge. "Kid, if that's your goal, then you should give up now. What are you, fourteen? You're going to take down the mob?"

"Sixteen," I shot back. I couldn't believe what I was hearing. This guy was completely defeated and cynical. I wondered whether that's why Yuri hadn't let me meet him. Perhaps it was less about keeping me safe and more about preserving my hope.

Connor let out another laugh that transformed into a coughing fit. "Excuse me," he said. "Listen, I have to get back to work. I'm on deadline." He slid his business card across the table, an almost resigned gesture. "Call me if you find that smoking gun."

Then he left, the door shutting with a final, echoing click. The second adult that day to abandon me when I needed them most.

CHAPTER 25

THE RECKONING

I left the *Advance* with a nagging doubt. Even if we somehow obtained the right evidence, we had no way to get it to the public. The adults we needed, it seemed, were either compromised or useless. Ugo was hesitant, Connor was broken, and half the police and political establishment were on the take. Even Yuri seemed tapped out. Our only choice was to forge our own path.

By three p.m., I was back in Travis, greeted by the frenetic preparations for July 4. Victory Boulevard had transformed, adorned with flags and banners, a level of patriotic display more suited for a presidential inauguration than a local parade. The festive atmosphere only intensified my sense of urgency, a reminder of our ticking clock.

I avoided The Linoleum and made a beeline for home, my pager buzzing with missed messages from Val and Yuri. A surreal scene unfolded in front of Georgia's house. Animal control officials were wheeling out her peacock in a cage while a police officer dozed in a nearby squad car.

Thankfully, Booch was nowhere to be seen as I made my way through my front gate. I pushed open my door, expecting no one home, only to find Georgia sprawled at my kitchen table, devouring a bowl of Coco Puffs like a starving raccoon.

"What the hell are you doing here?" I asked.

"Well, hello to you too," she said.

"Booch is literally my next-door neighbor," I said, my hands flailing like a substitute teacher who'd lost control of a rowdy classroom. "And what if my mom saw you here? Or Uncle Stosh? The whole neighborhood is looking for you."

"Everyone's at work," she said. "Calm down."

"Uncle Stosh could be back any minute," I said. Though he was the adult I worried about the least. He'd never turn Georgia in, especially if he knew what she'd been running away from.

"I was sick of staying in the damn shed at Sicilian Swirls," she said. "Plus, I wanted to talk to you."

Famished, I grabbed a bowl and joined her. "Where's Val?" I asked, between spoonfuls.

"He's out on a tree job," she said. "Said he's swing by here after."

I filled her in on my disappointing meetup with Connor.

"Folks mourn in different ways," she said.

"How are you dealing with it?" I said.

"Dealing with what?"

"Granny."

"Oh." She let out a soft sigh and dropped her spoon in her bowl. "She's the last person I knew from home."

"You miss it?"

"I ain't got much else to compare it to, but yeah, I loved it there. At least before they sent me to Saint Anne's."

"You can compare it to Travis. You can stay here."

"I don't mind it here. This place sorta reminds me of home. Y'all are just as crazy as the folks I came up with." She smiled. "But it ain't the same. Everything is so dirty up here. Back home, the sky . . . it's unreal.

Every night, it's like a crazy color show, and it's all natural. No smog. The night sounds are like a song—frogs, crickets, owls, all doing their thing. And the air." She paused.

"I bet it smells better," I joked.

"Sure does. It's heavy and humid too, but in a different way. Granny used to say the air was holding onto stories from the past."

"Do you think you'll ever go back?" I tried to envision her situation in reverse. What if I had fled Staten Island for Mississippi, only to lose my mom, stranded among strangers? I doubted I would handle it well.

"Of course. I'm going to bury her there. That's what she would have wanted. She said the soil of the Delta was blessed. Already have the spot picked out. Gonna head down there once we solve this mess."

I wasn't sure which of our messes she was referring to, but even if we solved the Dante situation, she still had a warrant out for her arrest. The city wasn't about to hand over Granny's remains to a fugitive.

"Tell me about this spot. Maybe I can do it for you."

"I don't need anyone to do it for me." Her gaze drifted uneasily to the window, and her body tensed with a palpable restlessness.

"It's okay to be scared."

A quick flicker of vulnerability crossed her eyes—fear, sadness, maybe both—but she masked it almost immediately. "Ain't no use in being scared," she said. "We need a new plan."

"I wish we had more time," I said. "We basically have one more day. And whatever we get must be extra solid because Connor doesn't exactly seem like he's got a lot of pull around the newsroom. Maybe Val will have an idea when he's done climbing trees."

"About those trees," she said with a sudden burst of energy.

"What about them?"

"I've been thinking." She hopped onto the counter. "The documents we need are on the second floor of The Linoleum, right?"

"Yes," I said, not sure where she was going with this.

"It's in the back, right?"

"It is. Why?"

"I walked past The Linoleum this morning," she started.

"You really shouldn't be walking around the neighborhood," I cautioned. "Dante also has had men guarding that building 24/7 because he's paranoid of a tap."

"They didn't see me," she said. "Trust me. Anyway, I noticed they have a tree that's rubbing up against the side of the building."

"Yeah, Dante has been bitching about that lately. Says it's doing permanent damage."

She popped off the counter and shook me. "Good thing we know the best tree surgeon in Staten Island."

—

Val, Yuri, Georgia, and I hatched the plan that night. We'd make our move in the morning, just as Lente took over from the night guards. Dante was slated to be in Manhattan all day wrangling politicians to get his bill finished. That gave us about a two-hour window before other members of his crew arrived at The Linoleum. A window in which old Lente would be the only one around to keep an eye on us.

I pushed open the bar door at ten fifteen a.m. The wired Walkman clipped to my waist served as a direct line to the others, ready to signal them at the right moment or alert them to any complications.

Lente was perched behind the bar like an ancient owl. "You're here early," he said, casting his droopy eyes my way.

"Got a date tonight," I said, easing down chairs from the tops of tables from the overnight cleanup.

"Oh, to be young again." Lente chuckled, a wistful look in his eyes. "Just make sure to wear a rubber," he added, killing any sentimentality.

"We're not quite at that point yet," I clarified. "By the way, I've got someone coming today to take care of that old tree in the backyard. They'll trim a few branches, so they aren't damaging the siding anymore."

"You read my mind," he said. "Dante has been on me for a while about that."

"You can tell him you arranged it."

"Bless you."

I slipped into the back room and found the door leading upstairs not only locked but fortified with a new deadbolt. *Renzo.*

I whispered into the Walkman, "Fort Knox is secure. The Yankees are in the playoffs," our coded message for a locked door and green light for our plan.

Moments later, Val's bucket truck arrived in the back lot. Yuri emerged from the driver's side, with Georgia and Val following. They wore matching Out on a Limb Tree Care uniforms.

Yuri looked uncomfortable, tugging at his khaki shorts. "These uniforms are ridiculous. I feel like I'm about to lead a fucking troop of scouts."

"Stay in character," Val barked at him.

"Yes, boss," Yuri said with a forced smile.

Our collective gaze shifted to the imposing oak tree, its ancient branches clawing at the side of The Linoleum.

"Back us up to about here," Val ordered Yuri, standing in a spot in the middle of the lot. "If you have trouble with the controls, let me know."

I watched as they initiated the choreographed steps we'd worked out the night before. Georgia and Val climbed into the bucket while Yuri deposited himself into the driver's seat, where he worked the controls to guide them up right next to the window. Val proceeded to cut down one branch at a time using a pair of oversized sheers while Georgia pretended to assist him.

Georgia's mission was twofold. First, she'd enter the second-floor window and steal the draft legislation to extend the dump, along with any other incriminating documents. However, given my disappointing run-in with Connor, we didn't want to stop there. We couldn't be sure he'd put those documents to good use. So Georgia would also install a bug in that room. This was Yuri's idea. He'd followed the government's takedown of John Gotti years earlier. The famed mob boss was obsessive about bugs in his Ravenite Social Club—his version of The Linoleum—and would often take sensitive meetings in the second-floor apartment above the club. But he failed to sweep that upstairs quarters for bugs, which is how the feds got him. We counted on Dante to make a similar error.

With the mission solidly underway, I retreated into the bar to play the role of the dutiful employee. I settled at my desk and pretended to proofread paperwork. Soon, the front door swung open, and Ugo's voice carried through the bar. My heart breakdanced on my ribs. He usually didn't show up to the bar until after lunch. We were only a few minutes into our operation, and we'd already veered off course.

Yuri's words echoed in my head: calm, natural. Easy for him to say. I flicked the blinds shut, concealing the arboreal chaos unfolding outside. I then raced back to my desk and put my head down, game face on.

"You're early," Ugo observed as he entered the office.

"Only in this place is ten thirty early. Normal people have been at work for hours by now."

"I've been working," Ugo boasted, collapsing into a folding chair with the air of a man who'd just completed a marathon. "Been all over the city today."

"Oh? Doing what?"

A sheepish look crossed his face. "Driving the boss," he mumbled.

Dante. That explained why Ugo parked in front. "I thought he was busy all morning." I said, glancing toward the blinded window.

"He wanted to get moving early," Ugo said. "Tie up some loose ends."

"Makes sense." I swallowed the knot in my throat, and the muscles in my stomach clenched. "Where is he now?"

"He and Renzo went across to Phene's to grab the paper and a sandwich. That control freak won't even let me order him food anymore because I forgot to ask them to add tomato last time."

The line at Phene's wouldn't be long this time of day. That gave us a maximum of a few minutes to get Georgia and Val down.

"The Yankees lost," I blurted out, my code word for Yuri to abort the plan. A signal that probably wasn't even necessary, given Yuri could hear the entire conversation.

"What?" Ugo said.

"I mean Dante may be a bit irritated because of the game."

"I'm sure he's got other things to worry about," Ugo said, confused. "You okay, Raj?"

Before I could answer, Dante came through the door, followed by Renzo and his son Enzo, who was sporting a black leather trench coat despite the ninety-degree heat. Enzo, a somehow less refined echo of his father, dropped into a chair beside me, nonchalantly demolishing his sandwich over my desk, using the paperwork beneath as a placemat.

Dante was in business mode. "We've got twenty minutes. Then let's head to Bay Ridge." He then disappeared into the restroom.

Renzo, casually seated next to the golden toilet seat, munched on his breakfast. "What are you doing here? The accounts are already squared."

"I wanted to double-check," I replied. "Besides, it's never too early to start organizing for the next fiscal year."

Mid-conversation, a branch brushed against the window. Renzo briefly glanced up, then returned to his meal, unbothered. Ugo gave me a questioning look and headed toward the side door.

"Where are you going?" I asked.

"Just checking something," he said with a skeptical squint.

I needed to get outside somehow to warn them. "The Yankees lost," I repeated into the ear of the headphones dangling from my neck.

Renzo, holding up the *New York Post*, corrected me. "No, they didn't. 'Yanks Cruise Past Mariners'—right here."

"Must've misheard," I fumbled, anxiously eyeing the window.

Dante exited the bathroom and tapped Renzo on the shoulder, gesturing for him to join him upstairs. I couldn't be sure if Georgia was up there or not, but I had to stop them.

"Guys," I stood. "I need to talk to you about something."

Renzo and Dante spun around. "Later," Renzo barked. "We're busy."

"It's important," I insisted. "You're going to want to hear it."

"Love this kid," Dante said with a smile. "Always urgent." He shot a look at Enzo. "You could learn something from him."

Enzo grunted through a mouthful of sandwich.

Dante continued. "Raj, we've gotta take care of something, but I promise we'll be with you later."

I blocked the entrance to the second floor. "Guys, I really need to talk now."

"You got a head injury or something?" Renzo said. That got a chuckle from Enzo. "Get out of our way."

Our standoff was interrupted by a thunderous crash that split the air from above, followed by the sound of metal scraping against the building. In that frozen instant, Dante and Renzo swapped bewildered glances before shoving past me and racing upstairs. I could have just sprinted out of the bar just then, but my concern for my friends sent me up those stairs, too, with Enzo right behind me.

Bursting through the doorway, my worst fear was confirmed. Renzo had a gun drawn on Georgia, who was pinned flat against the wall, her arms held high in surrender. The open window and filing cabinet left little room for spin.

Through the window, Val's silhouette was unmistakable in the bucket truck—trapped like Georgia's peacock.

Dante, framed by the window, surveyed the scene. When his attention finally settled on me, the bottomless sea of deep-blue calm in his eyes transformed into a monsoon of fury and disappointment.

He approached the closet with a measured pace, extracting a revolver with an air of ritual. As he loaded it, each click of the bullets felt like a preview.

"You two," he directed Renzo and Enzo, "handle her friends downstairs." The ambiguity of the word *handle* sapped me of my capacity to pull air into my lungs. I found myself gasping, nearly hyperventilating. I squeezed my eyes shut, focusing on the rhythm of my breathing, forcing air in and out in a controlled manner.

Then a curt command: "Sit." I sank into a folding chair and caught my head in my hands as panic distorted the room into a dizzying whirl.

With his gun still trained on Georgia, Dante knelt. He began rifling through the files on the floor. "The runaway," he remarked, eyeing Georgia. "You're quite the local celebrity." He flipped through more files. "What are you after?"

"Nothing really," Georgia replied, her tone not quite convincing.

"That question was for him," Dante said with a piercing glare in my direction. "I know something has been off with you. I should have listened to Renzo."

He looked at me as if waiting for me to respond. In that moment, I was more relieved than afraid. There was no negotiation, no quick lie, no distraction that would get me out of this bind. All that was left was the truth.

"You know what we want," I said, the defiance surprising even me.

Dante's face curled into a smirk. Absurd as it seems, he looked as if he was . . . impressed. "Who are you working for?" he asked.

I laughed. "You really have no clue, do you? We don't work for anyone."

"I see." Dante stroked his chin. "Life rarely gives you second chances. I never give them. Yet, somehow you got one, and this is how you treat me?"

"You're right. I do have a second chance, a second chance to do what's right."

"Wow, how corny." Dante let out a booming, scratchy laugh. "Tell me, Encyclopedia Brown, what were you going to do with these files when you got them?"

"Give them to the cops," I said, trying to protect Connor. Georgia shot me a confused look.

"Which cops?" he asked, eyes narrowing. "You must know we have friends everywhere."

"We hadn't thought that far ahead yet."

Enzo barged in, panting. "Got the others downstairs."

Dante and Enzo led us downstairs to the first floor. In the back office, Val and Yuri were on their knees, reduced to their boxers. Their hands were bound, mouths sealed with tape while Renzo trained two guns in their direction.

Yuri's chest bore a tattoo of a topless mermaid, a detail that in any normal circumstance I'd find more amusing.

Renzo gestured toward the receiver on the table, next to the golden toilet seat. "Found this in their truck. Bugged."

Dante scrutinized the technology while Enzo pushed Georgia and me forward.

"Search them," Dante directed.

Renzo ordered us to face the wall and empty our pockets. My pile contained a wallet, beeper, keys, and the disguised Walkman. Georgia's pile was empty.

"You got nothing?" Renzo asked.

"Feel free to check," Georgia retorted.

Renzo's attention shifted to my Walkman. After fumbling with it unsuccessfully, his frustration peaked, and he smashed it on the floor. Among the wreckage, he held up a small, rectangular device with exposed wires and a tiny green circuit board.

Dante knelt in front of Yuri. "Is this your handiwork?"

Yuri's eyes twinkled with pride as he nodded in confirmation.

Without hesitation, Dante's fist connected with Yuri's face, sending a spurt of blood from his nose. Yuri doubled over, then sat back up, a muffled chuckle vibrating behind his taped mouth.

"Clean this mess," Dante commanded Renzo, then turned toward the stairs. "I need to make some calls."

"Wait!" my voice cut through the tense air, drawing every eye in the room. Enzo stepped toward me, fist raised, but Dante halted him with a gesture.

"What's your plan here?" I asked.

"Wouldn't you like to know." His tone disorientingly light.

"Seriously," I said. "You'll kill three kids and a former cop? I know you're the Crisco Don and all, but this would be hard to bury, so to speak, even for you."

Dante slowly walked back over to the middle table and took a seat beside the golden toilet seat, in the exact same spot I'd first met him in last summer. When he gave me the speech about John Brown, his father, and the deadline to return the commuter. "My boys need to hear this anyway, so let's think it through together, shall we? This girl, how much do you know about her?"

"What does that matter?"

"Do you even know her name?"

"Of course I do," I said.

"Raj—" Georgia cut in.

My eyes bounced from her to an amused Dante. *What's going on here?*

Dante's laughter filled the room with a sinister echo, and Renzo and Enzo joined in, mimicking him like puppets. He then sauntered over to Georgia, placing a hand on her cheek. "Georgia Bazemore, right?"

She swatted his hand away but said nothing.

"Or should I say Paisley Kingston?"

Georgia stared at the floor. I shot Val a look, and he appeared as confused as I was.

Dante relished our stunned silence, leisurely lighting a cigarette, each movement no doubt calculated to prolong the moment. "The girl you know as Georgia Bazemore is, in fact, Paisley Kingston. When she was ten years old, she stabbed her father to death while he was watching the evening news. Apparently, when the paramedics arrived, poor Mr. Kingston was so unrecognizable that they had to use dental records to confirm his identity. Over thirty stab wounds, including in the face. The face! We don't even do that, do we?"

"That's savage," Enzo said.

"This girl is an animal," Dante said, almost with reverence. "Honestly, makes Renzo here look like less of a pussy for getting knocked out by her last summer."

Renzo's face turned red.

"Ms. Kingston, feel free to correct me if I got any of that wrong?" Dante asked.

She wouldn't look up. Tears were streaming down her face.

Dante continued. "Now, here's where it gets interesting. I don't consider myself a lucky man. I try to make my own luck. But it's hard not to think someone's looking out for me." He looked up to the ceiling and did a quick sign of the cross. "My boys down at the one-two-oh know everything I just said. They're the ones who told me, in fact. I'd just thought it was a bit of fun gossip, but I'm glad I indulged them."

"Why do all of the posters around the neighborhood still stay Georgia Bazemore then?" I asked, still grasping at some hope he was making this up.

"My guess is they don't want to freak out the island by telling them there's a stone-cold psycho on the loose."

Booch's vague warnings and the heightened police attention suddenly made perfect sense. It wasn't just a simple case of a runaway girl.

"Need I spell the rest out for you?" Dante asked. "The most logical explanation will be that Paisley here turned on her friends like she turned on her father. Once a killer, always a killer."

That didn't explain what they'd do with Yuri, though I didn't want to know.

"Story time is over," Dante said, walking back to the steps. "Renzo, get them ready for their field trip to the dump. Come see me before you go." With those final words, he ascended, disappearing from view.

Renzo waved his gun at me and Georgia. "Strip."

Val's muffled protest was a raw, guttural sound of fury and despair, his eyes burning with a fiery hatred toward Renzo. But he was helpless with his mouth taped and hands bound.

"Look, I have no problem getting naked, but she's a girl," I said. "That wouldn't be appropriate, would it?"

"You heard Dante," Renzo said. "She's not a girl, she's a fucking beast. Now take your fucking clothes off before Enzo here does it for you."

Georgia and I did as told. I was down to my plaid Old Navy boxers and black ankle socks. Georgia was wearing a white bra, floral underwear, and dirty tube socks with conspicuous holes at her big toes.

"What?" she shrugged. "Laundry ain't exactly been at the top of my list."

Renzo stuffed our clothes into a black bag with grim efficiency. Enzo methodically restrained our hands behind us and gagged us with tape—just as they had with Yuri and Val. I should have been more panicked, but the revelation about Georgia numbed me, my mind struggling to keep pace with reality.

The door to the front room swung open, and in entered Ugo. His expression shifted from surprise to concern as he saw us stripped down and bound on the floor. His eyes searched the room, trying to piece together the scene.

"Where have you been?" Renzo barked.

"None of your business," Ugo countered, his focus still on us, his features knitting in confusion. "What the fuck is going on here?"

"We caught Raj and his friends here trying to steal documents from upstairs. Raj was wearing a wire." He pointed to the mangled Walkman on the floor. "He's a rat."

Ugo locked his gaze on me. "No way," he said, his voice barely above a whisper.

"Yes way," Renzo mocked. "And if you hadn't stepped in the other night, we'd have caught him earlier."

Ugo fell silent, his face unreadable.

"Get your car to the side door, open the trunk," Renzo instructed. "We're heading to the dump."

Time then seemed to fragment into disjointed snapshots. Enzo and Renzo had us lie on the floor as they wrapped us in tablecloths. I felt hands hoist me up and then the jarring thump of being dropped into a car trunk. Another body landed beside me, the weight pressing down through the fabric. My breaths came shallow and labored, stifled by the heat, tape, and cloth. Then we started to move.

As we drove, I thought of Natalia—how this must have been the same ride she took. That night, I'd peeled the duct tape off her face. Now, here I was, heading for the same fate, except without anyone coming to save me. My thoughts then wandered to my mom. She'd be devastated if I disappeared, never mind if I turned up mutilated. I imagined her sitting at the kitchen table, going through her elaborate morning routine alone.

The car's jerky movements signaled our arrival at the landfill. The trunk sprung open, flooding my eyes with harsh, disorienting light. I staggered out, my feet unsteady on the rough terrain. As my eyes adjusted, I saw Georgia standing ahead, clad only in her underwear, her gaze fixed on something distant.

Renzo and Enzo emerged from the trunk with shovels in their hands, leaving no doubt about their intentions. A desolate section of Fresh Kills landfill loomed around us, eerily reminiscent of where we found Natalia. In this secluded place, any cry for help would dissolve into the void.

Yuri, a pathetic figure smeared with dirt and sweat, collapsed under his own weight. Enzo tried to yank him off the ground, but he refused. Val crouched beside him, helpless with his hands bound.

"Just shoot him," Renzo said.

"I ain't carrying his dead weight all that way," Enzo protested.

Renzo drew his gun, cocking it with an air of finality, and aimed it at Yuri. "You're strong. You'll manage," he said, a chilling calm in his voice.

But before Renzo could pull the trigger, Ugo intervened, seizing his wrist and pointing the gun skyward.

"Are you out of your mind?" Ugo demanded, his eyes blazing.

Renzo struggled against Ugo's grip. "Get your fucking hands off me," he spat.

Enzo aimed his weapon at Ugo's back. "Everyone just cool it," he said, his voice cracking. "Don't make me shoot you, Ugo."

Ugo, undeterred, wrestled the gun from Renzo's grasp and inspected it. "Put a silencer on this," he commanded, then turned to Enzo. "You too."

As Renzo and Enzo reluctantly complied, Ugo bent down and murmured something to Yuri. Whatever he said galvanized Yuri into action. He stood up and began walking.

"See," Ugo declared triumphantly as Renzo and Enzo rejoined us. "Easy enough."

Enzo looked like he was ready to embark on a guerrilla war—with a machete in one hand, a pistol in the other, and a backpack laden with shovels.

We walked single file along a dirt path up an incline toward the top of the mound. This one had been closed and capped years ago, so there were weeds and grass all around us, past my head. A perfect place to hide a body.

Enzo, leading with his machete, sliced through the overgrown grass, each cut adding a menacing rhythm to our procession. At one point, he flashed a creepy smile and said, "Practice."

I kept trying to make eye contact with Ugo, but he avoided me. Yuri, despite the dire conditions, climbed without a complaint.

At the summit, I took in the perfectly blue sky and the billowing stacks from New Jersey. I briefly looked back and caught a glimpse of Travis and the Manhattan skyline behind it. Yet, the grim realization that we were only alive to dig our own graves made it hard to truly savor our temporary reprieve. This was likely the last time I'd ever see my home.

We didn't rest at the top for long. After a few minutes, we descended to the other side and came to a stop in a valley at the bottom. It was an isolated clearing flanked by the two abandoned trash mounds. No one would find us here.

Enzo dropped the two shovels on the ground. "Start digging," he ordered before cutting free my hands and Georgia's.

"You two, sit," Renzo ordered Val and Yuri, pointing a gun at them.

I pulled the tape from my mouth, gulping the foul air. "Why us?"

"We only need two of you. And that one," Renzo said, pointing at Val, "he looks like trouble."

"Don't take your eye off the girl," Renzo ordered his son before pulling a flask from his pocket and taking a swig. Ugo stood some ten feet away, between us and Val and Yuri. Despite my attempts, he continued to avoid eye contact.

Enzo, with a disconcerting nonchalance, unfurled a tablecloth from the trunk and stretched it out on the ground, setting himself up as if for a leisurely afternoon at Clove Lakes Park.

Georgia removed the tape from her mouth, though she didn't seem to be in the mood to talk. Our shovels moved in fits and starts, carving a shallow grave in the dirt. An hour passed, and all we had was a pitifully shallow trench. "This will take forever," I complained.

"Then dig faster," Enzo snapped.

"Why are you in a rush to die?" Georgia whispered, tossing a shovelful over her shoulder.

She was right. We should be slowing this down. "How do we get out of this?" I whispered back.

"We don't," she replied.

"Hey!" Enzo yelled. "No talking."

"What are you gonna do?" Georgia asked. "Kill us?"

"Maybe I will," he said.

Georgia dropped her shovel. "Go on then. You can finish digging. My hands hurt."

Enzo briefly considered it, then sat back down. "Talk all you want. I don't give a fuck. As long as you keep digging."

"Paisley," I said. "Interesting name." If we were going to die, I wanted to know the truth.

"Don't."

"Don't what?" I pressed. "You lied to us."

"I had to."

"That's bullshit. Not to me and Val, after all we went through last summer." She may have had to lie to others, but not us. It all seemed so incomprehensible.

She tossed her shovel to the ground. "What if I'd told y'all? That I killed my dad?"

"I'm sure there's an explanation. Everyone has regrets."

"I stabbed him over and over. And I don't regret it. I didn't black out or anything like that. I remember every single second of it." As she shared this horrible confession, her eyes were empty, like hollowed-out caves. "I dream about it," she continued. "Not like nightmares, but the good kinds of dreams. The ones you don't want to wake up from. You think y'all would've still been my friends after knowing that?"

"Pick that shovel up," Enzo yelled. Georgia reluctantly obliged.

I resumed digging, taking half-shovelfuls, buying us time. "What really happened that night?" I finally managed.

"It doesn't matter," she said. "We're going to die."

"It matters to me, Paisley," I said.

"Don't call me that. Georgia is my name."

"Okay, Georgia. Tell me what happened. Please. Grant a dying man his wish." I managed a smile.

Finally, she relented, her voice low and haunted. "My dad was a creep. He was dangerous. That's all you need to know."

"Did he hurt you?"

Her eyes, finally alive again, focused on some unseen point beyond me. "He drove my mom crazy," she said, not really answering. "She's not in prison. I lied about that. She's in a special hospital. For people with mental problems, you know?"

"When was the last time you saw her?"

"When I was ten," Georgia said. "My uncle used to drive me to see her. But then he got sent to the slammer. After that, my dad, he never bothered to take me."

"What'd your uncle go away for?"

"Bank robbery."

"So, it's kind of a family trade," I said.

Georgia smiled. "Taught me everything I know."

I blinked back tears and swallowed hard. "I'm sorry I put us in the mess."

"Don't be," she said. "You bought us a year."

We kept on digging for another fifteen minutes or so. At one point, she leaned in and whispered. "I need you to promise me something."

"A promise?" I whispered back. "I don't think I'll be in a position to honor anything after the next few minutes."

"I get that. Just promise me if you make it out—"

"—I'm not making it out."

"Remember how I told you I want to bury Granny in Mississippi?"

"Of course."

"I want you to promise if you make it out, you'll make sure she gets there."

"I'm not making it out."

"Just promise," she said, holding out her hand.

"Okay, I promise," I said, throwing her a quick shake. "You want her anywhere in Mississippi?"

"At my ma's old house. It's my favorite place in the world. Down a dirt road, right behind Sunflower General Store. And there's this thousand-year-old cypress tree right out front. It's got this trunk, you know, all gnarled like an old man's fingers." She held out her hand in a twisted motion. "This may sound crazy, but Granny reminded me of that old tree."

"I'd love to go there with you," I said, tearing up.

"You'd love it."

Renzo, unsteady on his feet, swaggered over with his gun drawn. Whatever was in that flask must have been strong. "Well, isn't this touching," he slurred, swaying slightly. He turned to Enzo. "I gave you a simple task. Thirty more minutes. If this isn't deep enough by then, you're gonna pick up a shovel."

Georgia looked up, undaunted. "It's gonna take a lot longer than that."

"Shut up," Renzo slurred.

Ignoring him, Georgia kept digging. "To think we're going to die at the hands of these losers," she muttered.

Renzo's face reddened. "What was that?"

But Georgia just kept digging.

Renzo, swaying slightly, had a dangerous glint in his eye.

"I have an idea," Renzo said. "Get up here," he commanded to Georgia.

This couldn't be good. "Georgia, don't—"

"I'm good right where I am," she said.

Then a gunshot rang out. Georgia leaped back. Renzo had fired at the ground near her feet. "What's your problem?" she screamed.

Ugo came storming over. "What the hell are you doing? I told you to use a silencer."

Yuri and Val, still bound, watched helplessly from the sidelines.

"You're not my boss," Renzo stammered. "Up here now," he commanded Georgia. She did as told and climbed out of the trench, standing warily between him and Enzo.

"We don't have time for this bullshit," Ugo pressed.

"Quiet," Renzo yelled, waving his gun wildly in the air, causing Ugo to jump back. "I have a deal for you," he said to Georgia. "I'll give you five seconds' head start. You can run as fast as you can before I start shooting. If you make it free, then you're free."

"Dad—" Enzo said.

"Renzo, this is idiotic," Ugo said.

"Shut up," Renzo said, pointing his gun at Ugo to back away. Ugo took two steps back and held his gun in the air. He made quick eye contact with me and looked genuinely panicked, much like he did in the basement days earlier.

Georgia remained the calmest of us all. "I guess this is better than the one hundred percent chance I have if I don't run."

"That's correct," Renzo said. "When I say go, you have five seconds."

Georgia crouched into a runner's stance and faced a clearing that was about twenty feet away.

Enzo stood behind Renzo and was now in full-blown spectator mode.

"This isn't right—" Ugo tried one more time.

In a burst of desperation, Val, his hands still bound, charged toward us.

As Georgia braced herself to run, Renzo aimed his gun. "Ready, set, go!" he shouted.

Georgia bolted as Renzo counted down. "Five, four." Val's fall, just behind Renzo, briefly halted the count.

Enzo, momentarily distracted, attended to Val.

Renzo's mouth curled into a smirk as he resumed. "Three, two."

The air crackled with the sudden eruption of a bang. In a blur of motion, Renzo crumpled face-first to the dirt, and Ugo had a pistol pointed at him.

Enzo drew his gun, but before he could pull the trigger, Val's leg swept out from beneath him, sending him sprawling. Then Ugo, without hesitation, silenced Enzo permanently with a shot between the eyes.

I used Enzo's machete to free Val's hands. He wasted no time, ripping the tape from his mouth, his lips red and raw. "Did she make it?" he rasped.

"I think so," I replied, scanning the clearing. Georgia was out of sight, Ugo now in pursuit.

We hurried to Yuri, who sat slumped like a forgotten scarecrow; his sunburned face was the color of dried leaves. "You both look like you shit your pants," he said, eyeing our dirt-streaked boxers.

"Don't make me put this tape back on your mouth," Val joked.

"Check to make sure they are dead," Yuri said, gesturing to the motionless bodies of Renzo and Enzo.

"They're dead," I assured. "I'm positive."

Yuri dragged himself over to Renzo's body and fished out a flask from his pocket. He collapsed beside the still body, kicking up a dust cloud that began to cling to his sweat-beaded chest. Then he tilted the flask and began to chug.

Val and I set off toward the spot where Georgia had disappeared. The sun cast long shadows on the grass, making it hard to see clearly. Ugo's silhouette eventually materialized, cradling something—or someone—in his arms. My heart plummeted as he lowered it gently to the ground. It was Georgia.

I fell to my knees beside her, the world blurring through unshed tears. Her face, peaceful in the fading light, seemed like a cruel trick. "Wake up, Georgia," I demanded, my voice cracking. I pressed my ear against her chest. She wasn't breathing.

Val, eyes wild with denial, knelt opposite me. "She's just unconscious, right? There's no blood . . ." His voice trailed off as I gently shifted her, revealing the horrifying truth. A single, dark stain marred the back of her head, her hair matted with crimson.

The faint echo of the gunshot then clicked in my mind. Ugo had a silencer. Renzo must have fired a shot before he was hit.

Ugo confirmed the inevitable. "She's gone. No pulse."

Val's sob escaped as a primal wail, his body convulsing with pain. I sat there, frozen, grief building into a dam threatening to burst.

Minutes blurred into a chaotic dance of activity. I vaguely registered Yuri accepting car keys, Ugo's solemn promise to bury Georgia "properly," Val's choked goodbyes.

Finally, I was alone with her again. Kneeling beside her still form, I unclasped her gold cross necklace. My fingers traced the worn metal, a silent prayer escaping my lips before I slipped it into my pocket. A single tear, warm against my cheek, trickled down and landed on her pale skin. But a perverse pride held me firm. She wouldn't want to see me like this, broken and weak. So I swallowed the sob rising in my throat and walked away, leaving Georgia to be claimed by the muck. It was the last time I ever stepped foot in Fresh Kills.

EPILOGUE

June, 24, 2000

The city council passed Dante's bill that fateful Friday in July of 1999, but his victory was short-lived. Weeks later, a reporter at the *Daily News* broke much of the story Natalia had started, with a special focus on the buried scientific report. The article was peppered with quotes from an anonymous official within the Staten Island Mafia, who I presumed was Ugo.

Around that time, Dante disappeared. I assumed this was also Ugo's handiwork, though I couldn't be sure because I never saw the giant again. Of course, the equation could have gone the other way; Dante could have offed Ugo. Though, I choose to believe the first version of the story.

Without their leadership, the Staten Island Mafia crumbled. Russian factions swooped in, eager to claim Dante's fallen empire. Yet, the political landscape surrounding Fresh Kills had irrevocably changed. Following the *Daily News* exposé, one politician after another made the pilgrimage to Staten Island to deliver populist speeches about the forgotten people of Travis. No doubt, many of these were the same politicians who'd been paid to look the other way for so long.

By year's end, the council reversed course. The garbage would now be shipped off on barges to distant states, marking an end to an era. Half a century after it first opened, Fresh Kills would be shuttered permanently.

—

Val and I didn't speak much of what happened to Georgia. He put his head down and focused on his tree business while I threw myself into my schoolwork. But we had one last mission.

On the morning after the last day of my junior year, the two of us set off south in his Monte. Armed with fake IDs we'd procured from Chinatown, we spent a night in Nashville under the neon glow of Broadway, raising red Solo cups to a Brazilian country band named the Brazilbillies.

Our journey then took us through the forgotten arteries of western Tennessee, snaking through the undulating landscapes of the Hill Country. Under a clear blue afternoon sky, we crossed an invisible threshold. The air began to thicken with the Delta's humid embrace as the road traced a sinuous route through the cotton expanse.

With Val at the wheel, I flipped through a *Lonely Planet* guide, tracing our route to an iconic Delta landmark. "It says it should be right around this bend," I noted.

We pulled up to Po Monkey's, a roadside juke joint hunched low on the asphalt plain like an old toad. Its corrugated iron skin bore the scars of countless storms, and its windows were boarded up like a sealed tomb.

Inside, a blues band anchored by T-Model Ford, a grizzled man with the weathered face of a mud turtle, pulsated in the corner of the smoke-filled room. His fingers danced across a Fender Stratocaster, reviving the spirit of the recently deceased singer Junior Kimbrough, a Po Monkey's regular.

I perched on a barstool, nursing a whiskey while Val danced with a group of British tourists. A stout middle-aged woman, her hair bleached the color of straw, slid onto the stool beside me.

"That ain't Junior's song," she drawled. "He's just butcherin' it."

We fell into conversation, and she recounted how Kimbrough, who'd passed away a few years earlier, had fathered two of her children.

"Junior had more kids than stars in the sky," said the bartender, an older African American man with a beard like Spanish moss.

"Oh, you hush," the woman said. "Don't speak ill of the dead."

My gaze drifted to Val, now lost in the throes of a clumsy two-step with a pretty brunette in a cowboy hat.

"You got a way with the ladies like your friend there?" she purred, her hand creeping onto my thigh.

I recoiled, spilling my whiskey. "Uh, I need to . . . excuse me for a moment," I mumbled awkwardly, standing up in a rush.

I navigated through the lively crowd to Val, who was deeply engrossed in a passionate moment with his new lady friend.

"Val, we need to go," I said, tapping him on the shoulder.

"Just a minute," Val said, barely glancing my way. "Warm up the car. I'll be right out."

We left Po Monkey's behind and drove south for a half hour as the sun dipped in the horizon, turning a bruised orange.

As we passed the weathered Welcome to Sunflower County sign, a sense of solemnity settled over us. We pulled up to a general store with cracked windows and a sagging stoop. Run by a Chinese immigrant couple, their accents were an intriguing blend of Southern drawl and Mandarin tones. The man, wearing a faded Yankees cap and a checkered shirt, greeted us with a nod as he rang Val up for a pack of cigarettes.

"That will be two fifty," he said.

"Two dollars and fifty cents?" Val asked.

"That's what I said."

"For the entire pack?"

"Yes."

"Then I'll take five of them."

In the fading light of the parking lot, Val lit a cigarette, its ember glowing against the encroaching dusk. I eyed the dirt path that ran alongside the store. It was a rugged trail of bumpy earth and scattered rocks.

"You want to drive the Monte down that?" Val eyed the uneven road.

"We don't have many options," I pointed out, watching the sun dip lower, staining the sky with shades of purple. "It's this, or we walk in the dark."

Val opened the trunk to check for a spare tire. "Okay, let's do it," he said, his voice reluctant.

At the end of the road, we squeezed the Monte through a rusted open gate. As we passed through, a large white plantation-style home emerged. Its stately brick facade, dulled by years of weathering, stood proudly at the end of a long yard. The shattered windows and creeping vines told a tale of abandonment. The grand white pillars were chipped and fading.

Val guided us onto the unkempt grass, and his attention was seized immediately by the cypress in the front yard. No doubt the tree Georgia described. He leaped out of the car and rushed to run his hands along its twisted trunk.

"This is gorgeous," he said in wonder, his eyes tracing the tree's branches as they stretched toward the darkening sky.

I rummaged in the car's trunk, pulled out a hammer and nail, and fished Georgia's cross pendant from my pocket. With Val looking on, I affixed the pendant to the rough bark with a few gentle taps. She said she wanted to bury Granny here, but without either of their remains, this was the best we could do. As far as we were concerned, this was their final resting place.

For a long time, we just sat there, staring into the dark caverns of the tree, neither of us ready to move on.

The silence was shattered by a rusty groan from the house, sending a jolt through my ribs. A woman, gaunt and weathered, materialized on the porch, a threadbare bathrobe hanging from her thin frame. The ghost of Georgia shimmered in her blue eyes.

"Can I help you?" her voice rasped.

"Ma'am," Val drawled in a phony Southern accent, "I'm an arborist, just admiring your magnificent tree."

"A what?"

"Tree doctor," Val clarified. "I keep old beauties like this healthy."

"Wow," she said, her tension disappearing, "a doctor for plants. That tree is something, ain't it?"

"It's a marvel," Val agreed, laying it on thick.

"Can I make you boys some tea?" she offered, her gaze drifting toward the darkening horizon.

"We really have to get going," I said.

Val ignored me. "Ma'am, of course we'd love some," he buttered up, already easing onto the creaking porch swing.

She disappeared back into the house, leaving us to watch the shadows lengthen across the overgrown yard.

"What are you doing?" I asked, taking a seat alongside Val.

"Don't be rude. She just wants someone to talk to."

Moments later, she emerged with a tray laden with frosted glasses and a plate of sugar cookies. I took a cautious sip of the tea, nearly choking on the sugary assault.

"Wow, this is good," I said through my watery eyes.

For the next half hour, Val played the charmer, asking questions about the tall magnolias that lined the property, the creeping kudzu that blanketed the fence, and the vibrant bougainvillea clinging to the crumbling porch. As the sun fully disappeared, I rose to my feet. "Ma'am, we'd better get going before it gets too dark."

"Where are you off to next?" she asked, walking us down the steps.

"Memphis," Val said.

As she walked us to our car, I caught a glimpse of a flash of pink behind the bushes. A bicycle.

"You got any kids?" I asked, my voice low, eyes searching hers.

She shook her head, a tremor in her voice. "Just my niece," she muttered, her gaze distant, shadowed. "This was hers."

"Where is she now?" Val asked.

I shot him a warning glare.

Her eyes slammed shut, then cracked open into slits. "Time you boys got moving," she said, her voice cutting through the air like a shard of glass. We didn't linger, leaving her to wrestle with her own shadows.

Val and I shuffled back down to the Monte. "Let's swing by the store again," he suggested. "I need to grab a carton."

We arrived to find the storekeeper hauling a box from his truck.

"What were y'all doing up there?" he asked with a skeptical tilt of his head.

"We wanted to check out the cypress tree up the road," Val said.

The man's face grew serious, the wrinkles deepening around his eyes. "I'd stay away from that house if I were you."

"Why's that?" I asked.

"Place is haunted."

Val laughed. "Haunted by what exactly?"

The man shook his head. "The man who lived there. He was a monster."

"In what way?" I don't know why I asked; I really didn't want to know.

"One day, he turned up dead. His own daughter did him in."

"We've heard a little something about that," Val said.

"I was here that day, followed the cops up to the house. It was a horrible scene."

"He was stabbed multiple times, right?" I asked.

"He was. I ain't talking about that. He deserved what was coming to him."

"Then what did you mean?"

"When the cops searched the house, they found bodies buried in the basement. They dug up four of them. All kids, all missing from across the Delta. Teenagers have been going up there to do satanic rituals and all that garbage. That's what I thought you were here for."

"Is that why his daughter killed him? Because of what he did to the kids?" Val asked.

"Anyone's guess. They sent her away after that. Haven't seen her since."

"You knew her?" I asked.

"Very well," he said, his voice soft, sad. "Used to come in here all the time. Skinny thing, always hungry. Didn't have much of a life. She'd steal candy bars, but I never stopped her. Figured she needed it more than I did."

The shopkeeper's wife called out to him from inside the store. "I've gotta run. Y'all have a safe drive home," he said with a tip of his cap.

—

The drive back to Staten Island unfolded in near silence. Our car's headlights sliced through the darkness, briefly illuminating rest stops along the northern route. My mind was a tumult of thoughts, swirling around Georgia and the twisted path of her life. It seemed every adult had failed her, except for Granny.

We arrived back in Travis the following day. The neighborhood, bathed in the soft light of sunset, felt simultaneously familiar and transformed. I don't think I'd ever been happier to see the place. Though it was no doubt an average summer night, the sounds, the colors, and even the smell felt more real.

Approaching Georgia's house, a long green Bekins moving truck cast a shadow over the familiar structure. We drew up to my home, marking the end of our journey.

Val rolled down the window and stared at the For Sale sign in my front yard. "This wasn't here before, was it?"

"Was only a matter of time," I said. "If we don't sell it, the bank will own it by the end of the summer and kick us out anyway."

After Ugo disappeared, my mom's managers quickly rediscovered their greed—cutting her pay and forcing her back into double shifts.

"Where do you go after that?"

"I'm sure we'll find an apartment somewhere. But for now, I need a job."

"You wanna come work on my crew? We can build some callouses into those hands?"

"Maybe. Let me take a nap and think it over."

"Schmul later?"

"Deal," I said, pushing open the car door. Val drove away, and I started to walk through my gate but hesitated, glancing toward Georgia's house.

I walked over to find the front yard cluttered with moving boxes and furniture. A man stood there, his features distinctly Puerto Rican, offering a friendly hand. "I'm Bobby."

"Raj," I replied, shaking his hand. "Welcome to the neighborhood."

"Thanks," he said with a smile. "Priscilla, come say hi!" he called toward the house.

A girl emerged, her long black hair cascading down her back. She was at least half a foot taller than me.

"Meet Rob," Bobby introduced me.

"Raj," I corrected.

"Raj?" She asked. "What kind of name is that?"

"It's Indian. Half." I extended my hand, meeting hers in a handshake that simultaneously felt like a betrayal and a tribute.

"Your name is half-Indian?"

"No, I mean, well, never mind. It doesn't matter."

As I turned to leave, something caught my eye—a hint of gold under a mound of old furniture. I walked toward the pile to get a closer look. There, partially hidden under a broken chair and a dusty rug, was a canvas. It was just a corner, but enough to pull me in. I crouched and started clearing the heap.

The debris gave way, and my old friend revealed himself. Naked Jesus.

"Mind if I take this?"

Priscilla raised an eyebrow. "You want a naked painting of Jesus?"

A nervous laugh escaped me. "I can pay you for it."

She smiled. "No, keep it. It looks like it could use a good home."

I thanked her and lugged the painting home, keeping my head down to block out the curious glances from neighbors.

Reaching my front stoop, I carefully leaned the painting against the wall and sank down. It was heavier than it looked, and my arms were tired. A tear had ripped across its surface, offering a glimpse of something unexpected. I reached out, a hesitant finger brushing against a crisp corner. Money.

My breath caught in my throat. A surge of emotions washed over me—confusion, disbelief, and finally, a flicker of understanding. Glancing around to ensure I was alone, I flipped the painting around and carefully removed the back frame, revealing stacks of neatly bundled bills pressed against the wood—eight piles in total, easily worth tens of thousands of dollars.

Was this Grannie's savings? The proceeds from Georgia's stolen goods? I would never be able to find out. What I did know was that it was a gift. A silent offering from the past.

I just sat there and felt the weight on my shoulders dissolve and the burden lift from my soul. It turns out we wouldn't need to sell the house. I wouldn't even need a job.

Maybe, just maybe, I could finally have a normal summer.

ACKNOWLEDGMENTS

I am deeply grateful to my family from Staten Island—Mom, Grandma, Natalie, Uncle Ray, Uncle Richie, Aunt Denise, and others—for their unwavering support throughout this journey.

Much love to the Victory Boys: Jeff, Sweeney, Walaid, T-Bone, Danny, Dave, Teddy, BJ, Kenny, Garrett—and to the rest of my wonderfully eclectic neighbors in Travis and Westerleigh, who've inspired many of the characters and scenes from *Garbage Town*.

This book owes much to those who reviewed early drafts over the years: Mary Kay Zuravleff, Sam Ashworth, Jason Kander, Alex Rice, Gena Hong, Jamie Hodari, and the members of the Neil Strauss writing crew. I'm also indebted to everyone who supported this project when it was a script: Andrew Miller, Sam Eliad, Sujeet Rao, Jake Gardener, MC Lader, Whitaker Lader, and Kim Dang. Your insights and encouragement were invaluable.

A special note of gratitude to Supriya Randev, whose love, patience, and optimism propelled me through the final stages of writing. And to Kate Malekoff, for expertly managing everything outside of this book.

To all who have contributed to this work in ways big and small, thank you. Your support has made this book possible.

ABOUT THE AUTHOR

Author photography by The Branch

RAVI GUPTA is a serial social entrepreneur dedicated to reforming civic institutions. He is the cofounder and CEO of The Branch, a media company committed to combating online polarization. At The Branch, Ravi hosts several shows, including *The Lost Debate* and *Majority 54*—two podcasts focused on bridging the political divide—and *Killing Justice*, a collaboration with Crooked Media investigating an alleged political murder in India.

In addition, Ravi serves as the CEO and founder of Squadra Health, a company focused on longevity and wellness. Before these ventures, he cofounded Arena, where he led efforts that helped elect dozens of candidates and launched one of the largest campaign-staffer training academies in political history. Earlier in his career, Ravi founded and served as CEO of RePublic Schools, a network of charter schools in the South, and established Reimagine Prep, Mississippi's first charter school. He also played key roles in Obama's first campaign and first term, serving as an assistant to Chief Strategist David Axelrod and Ambassador Susan Rice.

A native of Staten Island, Ravi graduated from Yale Law School and Binghamton University. He's won numerous awards, including the Truman Scholarship, the Webby Award, and Binghamton's University Medal, along with recognition in *Forbes*'s "30 Under 30" and *Crain*'s "NYC 40 Under 40."